I0668914

The Appalachian Cowboy

A Tarheel Favorite Son Goes Western

Anthony E. Ponder

YAV PUBLICATIONS

ASHEVILLE, NORTH CAROLINA

I dedicate this work to my wife, Glennis.
For always being by my side when I, perhaps too often,
was prone to take a road less traveled; let me say thanks.

You were and will forever be the wind in my sail and the
flame in my heart. For being my rock and comfort,
I can say that I truly have been blessed.
I'll always love you.

Contents

Chapter 1 The Arrival 3

Chapter 2 The Welcoming 17

Chapter 3 The Train Robbery................................... 35

Chapter 4 The Missing Gold.................................... 55

Chapter 5 The Visit to the Crier 73

Chapter 6 Return from the Cattle Drive 87

Chapter 7 Junior goes to the Polls.........................101

Chapter 8 Off to Colorado..................................... 113

Chapter 9 The Search for Lightning.....................131

Chapter 10 The Gunfight...147

Chapter 11 Musing on the Range 171

Chapter 12 The week in Wedgewood......................181

Chapter 13 Oscar Takes a Squaw 209

Chapter 14 Last Days in Los Villas 231

Characters

Junior Justus	*The Appalachian Cowboy*
Josh Justus	*Reporter & Junior Justus's brother*
Oscar Ames	*Cousin & Sidekick of Junior Justus*
James "Whitey" Black	*Los Villas Avalanche Saloon owner*
Roberto Abernathy Black	*James Black's wife*
Roy "Lightning" Loftis	*Mr. Black's foreman*
Rosita "Hurricane" Rodriguez Loftis	*Roy Loftis's wife*
Fanny "Lil" Hutchins	*Saloon singer & Mr. Black's mistress*
Cliff "Peddler" Daniels	*Traveling salesman turned rancher*
G.W. Mabry aka: Harry "Weasel" Warren	*Busybody & Tale carrier*
Bill "Tumbleweed" Adams	*Errand boy*
Robert "Guts" Myers	*James Black's barkeeper*
James "Shortchange" Clancy	*Los Villas merchant*
Uriah "Morty" Ramey	*Los Villas undertaker*
Benjamin "Ivory" Jones	*Mr. Black's saloon piano player*
Julie "Goldie" Rush	*Saloon singer & Mr. Black's mistress*
Alvin "Red" Rowe	*Substitute stagecoach driver*
George "Washtub" Jacobs	*Blacksmith shop owner*
Harlan "Longarm" Brooks	*Los Villas sheriff*
William "Word Twister" Jackson	*Lawyer*
Pedro Gonzolez Rodrigo Estevez, Jr., and Sr.	*aka: Mad Mex, Jr. & Sr.*
Wheeler	*Dromedary*
Gabby	*Parakeet*
Ringer	*Billy goat*

Preface

The Appalachian Cowboy

Into a shack far back, first born was he,
Beloved by his mom and family.
Not much for work or toil did he employ,
Carefree, this Appalachian cowboy.

His father worked so hard in the sawmill.
His mom was there a toiling in those hills.
He wasn't meant to be a turn plowboy;
Became the Appalachian cowboy.

Imbibing his desire to take a drink,
Just minding his own business; free to think.
A chasing dreams or just an odd decoy
Oh, he's an Appalachian cowboy.

You may find him within a brothel suite,
Or, on the range under a tall mesquite.
At home is he with idle scheme or ploy,
That's him, the Appalachian cowboy

To go over the foam was not to be,
He's riding on the range so wide and free.
No, never went to sea or said ahoy,
For he's an Appalachian Cowboy

He owned a good harmonica so dear,
He loved to play for everyone to hear.
He was always his mother's pride and joy;
A special Appalachian cowboy.

Gold coins had wings and slipped through his hands;
He couldn't keep a dime this mountain man.
And yet, his heroes were Gene, John, and Roy;
Beloved by this Appalachian cowboy

They all were asking where he hailed from;
It's not New York, Utah, or Michigan,
Or Zona, Texas, or een Illinois.
He's N. C's Appalachian cowboy.

For Uncle Sam he fought in wars that come.
At Cowpens, Gettysburg, and at San Juan.
Twas at the Bulge, but neer Hanoi;
Brave is the Appalachian cowboy.

The world calls him a motley fool or bum;
Or, at the best a witless simpleton.
He'll be ahead of you my friend, killjoy,
For he's the Appalachian cowboy.

The Appalachian Cowboy

Chapter 1
The Arrival

In the arid West Texas panhandle, a gusty dust devil is often seen swirling across the dry grassy plains. The parching sun and a relentless wind are so uncomfortable and disconcerting to outsiders in summer that a group of visiting British cattle ranch investors once advanced an opinion that the Texas panhandle town of Los Villas was comparable to the opening scene of John Milton's Paradise Lost. This could be why this parched panhandle was the last part of the continental United States to be settled and civilized as we now know it. This early Los Villas settlement appeared to be but a dot on an early Texas map. This cattle town's name in Spanish means "the house."

Los Villas sprang up near the first large house in the panhandle. It was noted for treeless streets that included Main Street and a few short side streets. Both sides of Main Street were lined with crude, wooden, business buildings that stretched a distance of forty rods from end-to-end. An advantage of wooden construction in West Texas is that the buildings last longer in the dry air and arid soil conditions than they do in other more moist parts of the country. It is said by some of the old timers that migrating termites carry their own water in tiny waterproof pouches that they strap across tiny, ivory colored backs. In West Texas rain falls, but usually it falls by accident.

July 6th, 1879 was a typical hot, dry, gusty day. On the eastern side of Los Villas's Main Street, a rough-hewn timber-constructed building named the Avalanche Saloon sat two hundred paces from the mansion for which the town was named. That mansion, once called Virginia House, had become the residence for a few of the ladies who entertained cowboys, fur traders, and miners at Bell's place. Bell's place simply wasn't large enough or roomy enough to accommodate all the ladies who worked there.

Some men in the saloon were sitting in heavy chairs around round, wooden, oak tables where they were drinking, telling tall tales, playing cards, and listening to a petite, female saloon singer. Others were sitting on round barstools drinking and listening to the music. In some respects these men were as tough and rugged as their hostile West Texas environment. It was difficult to discern whether the patrons were more delighted by the singer's cacophonous performance or by its merciful ending. Tepid applause greeted the young, slender singer as she sauntered away from the slightly raised stage.

It was a busy day in the Avalanche Saloon. The proprietor, thirty-three-year-old James "Whitey" Black, sat at one of the fully occupied tables near a bleak, windowless inside wall. His table was near the wide, dark door to his office in the back room of this high-ceilinged saloon. Neatly attired in a tailor-made, black, worsted wool suit with matching wide necktie, and a waist-length vest that he bought in St. Louis, he was sitting with four other poker players. Although he left St. Louis abruptly after being caught with an ace up his white shirt sleeve during a high-stakes poker game, he managed to sneak back there from-time-to-time to reward his good sartorial taste with a visit to Gene Cameron's Tailor Shop. His titillating decorum was admired by the West Texas ladies.

Mr. Black sat comfortably in his sturdy, mahogany chair. He observed the world through a pair of close-set, brown eyes that peered down a long, sharp, cunning nose. His small, delicate hands cradled a self-dealt hand he meticulously protected from view of the other card players. With short, smooth, slender fingers, he discarded one card and then drew another from the deck that lay before him on the round, beverage stained table. After taking a long look at his horrible hand that consisted of an ace of spades, a jack of hearts, a nine of clubs, and a pair of deuces, he elevated his eyes over his cards and cast them in the direction of a casually dressed gentleman on his left.

Mr. Black said, "What are you going to do, Lightning?"

Roy Loftis was the poker player Mr. Black addressed as Lightning. He earned the moniker because his actions were slow and he never got in a hurry. Lightning was simply a nickname used in jest. He was thirty-five years old and stood six foot three inches tall, which was three inches taller than Mr. Black.

Mr. Loftis grew up near San Antonia and his grandfather died while in Sam Houston's Army that fought to free Texas from Mexican control. His father was a Confederate Veteran, and, after that brutal war, he settled near San Antonia where he raised horses and cattle. Mr. Loftis married his childhood sweetheart, Rosita "Hurricane" Miguel Lopez Rodriguez. She was from an old Spanish family that had settled in San Antonia in the shadows of the old Catholic mission that the Spanish had established, better known as the Alamo. They moved to the Texas panhandle when Mr. Loftis found work laying tracks on the Western Railroad. It was one of the many railroads, at that time, laying tracks all across the western United States. When work on the railroad was nearing completion, he found steady work in Mr. Black's employment. He later became Mr. Black's foreman.

Mr. Loftis studied his cards through pensive, gray eyes. He ran his rough fingers through a full head of greasy, thick, dark-brown hair and dropped the left portion of both lips to contort them into a crescent moon shape. He drawled and said, "I bet ten." He folded his cards into his big left hand and placed a large cigar into his mouth with his right. He then pushed his chips into the small pile in the center of the table. Since he had shut his left eye due to smoke pother from the big cigar, he took the stogie from his mouth and knocked some hornet's-nest-like gray ashes onto the dark, wooden floor. He awaited the reaction from the other players.

An observer stood behind Mr. Loftis. It was the saloon's singer, twenty-three-year-old Fanny "Lil" Hutchins. She had black hair, pale blue eyes and occasionally observed Mr. Black as he sat playing poker at his favorite table when she wasn't on stage singing. With a good natured scowl, she addressed Mr. Loftis and said, "You're a nasty one flicking ashes, Lightning. I bet you don't do that at home. If you did, Hurricane would clobber you with a broom. She would then make you clean up your mess. No, sir, she wouldn't tol—"

Before she could finish, Mr. Loftis interrupted her by saying, "Go on, Lil. Git back up there and beller out another ballad. Let me smoke this here cigar and play poker. Besides, these here cowboys need to be punished fer playing cards and drinking whiskey." Mr. Black gave a tacit nod for her to comply with Mr. Loftis's order. As she was making her way back toward the stage to sing another song to those sitting at his table, Mr. Loftis said with a nasal twang, "She's becoming a pain in the butt."

"Yes, I'd like to get rid of her and that pesky sheriff too," said Mr. Black. He shifted his eyes and noticed her motion to the short little piano player who was seated on the saloon's dark piano stool. She began to sing to the piano music of the Stephen Foster song "Nelly Bly."

"It's hard to get rid of one when you're sleeping with her," said Cliff "Peddler" Daniels, who was forty-two years old. "This one has your child." Mr. Daniels held three jacks, a six, and an eight. He was seated on Mr. Black's right and was a former traveling dry goods salesman. He found the woman of his dreams and decided to settle down near Los Villas where he became a successful cattle rancher. He never regretted quitting his sales job after he absconded with a wagon loaded with dry goods and $3,523.31 that he had collected from his employer's customers. Mr. Daniels was never indicted for his calculated indiscretion because his friend Whitey Black exerted his influential political and social connections in North Texas to protect him from prosecution. His Lazy K Ranch lay two miles east of Los Villas.

"You're one to talk Peddler," retorted Mr. Black. "You've got four illegitimates by three different women. You've got one in about every town on your old sales route. It's people like you that give traveling salesmen a bad name. I wonder if Carla knows anything about half the women you've toyed with? Heck, with your reputation you ought to run for public office. You'd make a great governor."

"Yeah, that would give you a shot at screwing everybody in Texas," added Mr. Loftis.

After a pause, Mr. Black looked in the direction of John "Boomer" Mills. He was a T & E Railroad employee who was seated across the table from Mr. Black. Mr. Mills was twenty-four years old, solidly built, stood five foot seven inches tall, had blonde hair, disarming blue eyes, and looked through a pair of gray, metallic spectacles with lens so thick that they could be have been mounted in a small telescope. His moniker was Boomer because he possessed a deep, booming bass voice. According to the locals, Mr. Mills's mother's only regret was that his mind was not nearly as strong as his voice. Her first marriage produced two sons and a daughter. When her husband died unexpectedly in a Mississippi River barge accident, in order to provide security while raising her small family, she had married Boomer's unsophisticated father, Roger Mills, who was a hardworking muleskinner in the Western Kentucky hills. They migrated to the Texas panhandle to lay tracks for the S & O Railroad when a recession hit the timber industry. In a deep voice through curled lips that carried from wall-to-wall in the busy saloon, Mr. Mills said, "I call." He pushed ten chips into the center pile. He held two pair—tens and fours.

Mr. Black shifted his head and eyes to his right. He asked, "How about you, Weasel?" Thirty-six-year-old Harry "Weasel" Warren talked with a syrupy, cloying voice, had a barrel chest, and stood five foot six inches tall. When he walked, he was like a battleship in water; he didn't appear to move. He settled in Los Villas after he left a Cincinnati Bank carrying a $5,500.00 army payroll that never reached its distant Fort Remorse destination. He was born George Washington Mabry in a log cabin near Urbana, Ohio. His parents were devout Quakers and they expected him to further the Quaker faith by becoming a minister of the gospel. One trait in his childhood was the fact that he was always getting his siblings and neighbor children into trouble because he couldn't keep a secret. He not only couldn't keep a secret, he had to broadcast all the details of those secrets to the detriment of everyone concerned. This tale-carrying trait continued when he became an adult. He changed his name because the army wouldn't be inclined to spot a deserter who was living in an out-of-the-way place like Los Villas. In a smooth, velvety voice, Mr. Warren said, "I call." He pushed his chips into the center pile. He held two pair—queens and eights.

"What are you going to do, Peddler?" asked Mr. Black.

"I'm calling," he replied as he pushed his chips into the growing pot.

"Well gentlemen," Mr. Black said confidently, "I call and raise you twenty." He pushed his chips into the pile.

"Well, I'm a calling, and raising you ten," replied Mr. Loftis with his usual vocal asperity. He slid his chips into the center of the table to combine his with all the other wagered chips. Mr. Loftis's bet was enough for the three players on his left to fold.

"Well, I'm calling," said Mr. Black, "and raising you another twenty." He scooted more chips into the orderly piles.

Mr. Loftis fidgeted with his cards for a few short seconds. He looked hard at his hand once more while squirming as though a mischievous mouse was gnawing inside his underwear. As perspiration popped out onto his furrowed brow, he finally leaned toward Mr. Black and with disgust in his voice, he said, "Ah, heck, you've bought another pot Whitey." Onto the table littered with cards and poker chips, he slammed down a losing hand that consisted of three kings and two aces.

"Yeah, and Whitey didn't even have to show his cards," Boomer added.

Mr. Black tossed his unexposed hand onto the now cluttered table. With his two arms and hands enfolding the winnings, he dragged them to the edge of the table where he was sitting.

While Mr. Black was collecting his winnings, a skinny, sandy-haired, hazel eyed, young man rushed inside the swinging doors. This was twenty-two-year-old Bill "Tumbleweed" Adams who had been a tracklayer for the T & L Railroad. His parents were going from Dallas to Salt Lake City when they stopped in Los Villas where he currently performed odd jobs for the town's business owners. Mr. Adams was only a small lad when he awoke one morning and his parents were gone without leaving a forwarding address. He, like thirty-three-year-old Avalanche barkeeper, Robert "Guts"

Myers, became a ward of the girls at Virginia House before competition from Bell's put "The House," as they called it, out of business. He nervously glanced back toward the dusty street and said in a loud, high pitched voice, "There's a fellow out here trying to alight a camel."

"You pulling our leg again, Tumbleweed?" asked barkeeper Robert "Guts" Myers.

Mr. Myers was born on a small farm in southern Indiana. Like so many children in those days, he came from a very large family. He was the youngest child and had five brothers and seven sisters. His parents struggled to survive on their small Indiana farm, so, they decided to move west to find a better opportunity for their livelihood. One day he became separated from the wagon train taking them west to California, and he was found by some big game hunters who deposited the little fellow at Virginia House. He enlisted in the Union Army at an early age. It was said that he deserted Custer's Army because he couldn't abide the sight of blood. Bravery was not his forte, and he had an unenviable reputation with the townspeople to prove it. After his undistinguished army service, he returned to Los Villas where Mr. Black hired him as a barkeeper in his newly opened saloon. Mr. Black's extensive political connections kept the army from testing the strength and quality of the manufactured fibers of a hangman's noose around Mr. Myers's neck. Army desertion was customarily treated as a very serious offense.

"Boys," said Mr. Adams, "I ain't lying. There's a man out here at the hitching post trying to figure out how to get down off a camel. He's the first fellow I ever saw spit so much without a chew of tobacco in his mouth. Heck, see for yourself. Come and look!"

Reluctantly, the curious patrons began to scoot back their heavy chairs. To witness the event, they slowly began to file between the swinging doors an out into the sweltering street. These curious cowboys viewed a background of wooden buildings pasted against an endless, distant mountain range, and, to the right near the saloon's watering trough, they saw a strange-looking, drooping dromedary with flies flitting around his awkward frame. Atop the malodorous beast was a tall, wiry, relaxed, young man who had short, light brown hair and violet blue eyes. He was talking to the balky, old, brown animal as the curious crowd from the saloon began to gather. "Kneel Wheeler, kneel!" said the young rider as the gathering crowd looked on. In balky agitation, the animal only wiggled and writhed nervously at the rider's command. There seemed to be no way he could safely dismount.

Curiosity in seeing a camel in Los Villas slowly abated. While the contemplating crowd mulled as to how to help the young man down, it continued to swell around the marooned rider and uncooperative dromedary. At last, after much discussion and little action, which would have easily passed for legislative deliberation, a husky, red-faced, thirty-seven-year-old Alvin "Red" Rowe observed the man's plight on the obdurate dromedary. He was a substitute Silver Eagle Stagecoach driver who was held in reserve to fill any driver vacancy that might occur on their stagecoach line. Mr. Rowe was born in Mississippi and left his parents' cotton plantation to find his fortune in the west. He hunted wild game for pelts and panned for gold in the Colorado Rockies before settling in Los Villas. Mr. Rowe had a strong odor of whiskey on his breath. From his right hip, he drew his six-shooter out of his leather, handgun holster, and said, "Why, the devil; all you got to do is blow the kneecaps out from under this ugly critter. He'll drop down to where this here feller can git off."

"Now hold on, Red," said thirty-five-year-old George "Washtub" Jacobs. Mr. Jacobs's father was a blacksmith in

Charleston, South Carolina. He too came from a large family and decided to leave home at an early age. Mr. Jacobs came west to search for gold and settled in Los Villas when his vein search for wealth ended in vain. He became a highly sought-after wainwright and also did some blacksmith work. He could spend leisure time in the saloon because he had three trusted employees who carried on the business at Jacobs Blacksmith Shop located on the north end of town. "I can't let you do that," he said. "Next thing you know, you'll be shooting real people to git them out o' their misery. Know that?"

"Ah, heck, Washtub, it's just a darn worthless camel," he replied. He cocked the Colt .45 and took aim at the kneecap of the dromedary's left front leg.

"Fire that pistol, Red, and I'll blow your durn fool-head off," said Mr. Jacobs as he flicked some gnats away from his face with his left hand. He drew his own pistol, pulled back the hammer and added, "I said it was cruelty to animals. Now, put that cannon away!"

"Now, I'm as humane as the next man Washtub. What's more, I'll blow any man's head off that says I ain't. Now, are you threatening me? Mess with me and I'll blast ya to Kingdom Come right here in the street."

Mr. Rowe and Mr. Jacobs were standing in the middle of Main Street. Those around the street side of the dromedary moved to the saloon side for safety and to give the combatants ample room for a shoot-out. They stood facing one another ten paces apart with firearms cocked and pointed at one another. Mr. Jacobs replied, "The dickens you—"

"What's a going on here?" asked a tall man who approached them. This was fifty-eight-year-old, Harlan "Longarm" Brooks—the Los Villas Sheriff who never wore a badge. He was a former Texas Ranger who had retired and became the sheriff of Los Villas. When his wife died of consumption while they resided in Fort Worth, he decided to move to Los Villas in order to bring law and order to this small, lawless panhandle cow town. Longarm was a moniker the locals saddled Mr. Brooks with when he became the town's chief law enforcement officer. This tall, potbellied man had the physiognomy similar to the obdurate dromedary that drew this large crowd gathered around the hitching post. He continued to swagger toward the gathered throng.

Tumbleweed Adams's high-pitched voice rang out above the crowd chatter. He said, "Longarm, they can't get that slender man off the camel. Red and Washtub's cleared leather over it. They're ready to kill each other." When he finished speaking, he was standing on tiptoes and looking up into the sheriff's face.

"Step back, Tumbleweed," said the sheriff. He pushed him aside with a quick writhe of his protruding stomach. "Put them guns up, boys. There'll be no gun-play in my town. Now, what's the problem here?"

"It's like Tumbleweed said," declared twenty-nine-year-old James "Shortchange" Clancy. He was a small, bespectacled man who owned the Los Villas General Store across the street. He came from a small family in Houston where his father had given him enough money to start his own business. Mr. Clancy decided to use the money to buy his uncle's store in Los Villas where he could sell general merchandise to what he considered would soon be a rapidly growing and thriving community. "We can't figure how to get that tall fellow down off that stubborn camel."

"Thank you, Shortchange," said the sheriff. He looked down at the man wearing the round, wire-rimmed glasses that sat firmly on a rounded ruddy-face. He turned his attention from the storekeeper to the two men who were holding pistols that were pointed at one another. In a loud, authoritative voice, he said, "Now, put them guns up; Red, Washtub! Morty's out o' town and there ain't nobody here to bury you boys. Try using yore heads for a change."

"Why didn't you say so, sheriff," replied Red and Washtub almost simultaneously. They slowly replaced their six-guns deep inside their tanned leather holsters.

Sheriff Brooks turned his attention to the casual man atop the brown dromedary. He removed his dirty, sweat-soaked, black Stetson hat, scratched his balding, perspiring brow, looked up at the man and asked, "Do you want down, young man?"

"You need to git him down before Governor Asher comes back to town," said Mr. Rowe. "Don't want the town to be embarrassed by a man stuck on a camel."

"Heck, Red, they better hurry," said Mr. Collins. "Governor Shorty is up here every other week to see Whitey."

"Why, yeah. Shore be nice to touch the ground agin," said the man on the balky dromedary. He spit once more into the street, and added, "Be nice to have a couple o' jugs."

"Now, listen here," said the sheriff. "We'll git you down, don't worry about that; jist leave our women alone!" After a pause, the sheriff held his chin with his left hand and began to look at the mulish animal. He slowly began to waddle around the stock-still dromedary to determine a satisfactory solution for the stranger's dilemma. After making three circles around the beast, he rocked back and forth on his heels before the observant, quiet crowd that was anticipating his reasoned recommendation. He was like a practicing lawyer about to address an impaneled jury when he began to speak to the gathered throng. "Okay," he said. "Somebody untie the rope on both the stranger's ankles that runs under this here camel's belly. I'll need four big bruisers to git behind each leg. Everybody will have to throw their bodies into each leg at the same time. That'll bring him down."

On either side of the camel, Mr. Clancy and Mr. Adams began to untie the stranger's ankles that held him atop the beast.

"That won't work, Longarm," said a soft female voice. Its wispy owner came softly slipping through the dense crowd, approached the sheriff, and peered at him through experienced, knowing eyes. This was young Lil Hutchins who sang for Mr. Black in the saloon. He had found her singing in the Orange Blossom Saloon in St. Louis where he soon became infatuated with and ultimately convinced her to move to Los Villas. Lil was from a large West Virginia coal-mining family of twelve children. She began to sing in a Free Will Baptist church at a young age and to her parents' consternation, she slowly gravitated toward singing in bawdy saloons. She had not seen her family in years.

"Oh, yeah," replied the sheriff. His was a patronizing tone that deeply resented his visionary wisdom being challenged by a mere mortal female. "And I suppose you're a Gypsy that drove camels through the Sahara Desert. That's before you began to torture cowboys by singing in saloons."

"Here, give me the reins," she said. She took the leather straps of the bridled animal and stood facing him. With a rein in each hand, she looked deeply into the limpid pools of the animal's dark, misty eyes. She said, "Alia gazam." With those two strange words that no one in the large crowd understood, like magic and to everyone's astonishment, the beast promptly knelt on all four knees. A saddle-sore Junior Justus slid off and stepped clear of the obedient, kneeling dromedary. The crowd stood by silently in disbelief.

Those words "alia gazam" that Miss Hutchins had uttered were superfluous. She was born with an innate ability to handle the most unwieldy of animals and compel them to comply with her commands. When she looked into the dromedary's droopy eyes, there was a telepathic communication between her and the animal. Alia gazam meant nothing to

Wheeler. It was the tacit communication between the bulky beast and little Lil Hutchins that resulted in the rangy dromedary's kneeling. Hers was a rare gift with animals.

"Well, I'll be darned," said the surprised sheriff. He tugged at his wide-brimmed hat and shook his head. He looked into Mr. Justus's inanimate eyes, and asked, "What brings you to West Texas?"

"Why, this here camel," replied Junior innocently and without a trace of a smile. He spit into the street beside the sheriff's left trouser leg.

"I can see that, darn it!" ejaculated the sheriff in anger. Once more Sheriff Brooks looked into the hawk-nosed stranger's vacuous eyes for a few long-seconds, and added, "Oh heck, forget it." As the crowd began to disperse, he began to sidle back toward the sheriff's office with its wooden porch awning and attached jail.

Chapter 2
The Welcoming

Shortly after Junior Justus's arrival, Mr. Black returned to his private office. It was a small, quiet, frugally furnished office in the back room of the Avalanche Saloon. Two small windows provided daytime lighting and four kerosene lamps provided lighting at night. Mr. Black was seated comfortably in his padded, leather swivel chair behind his mahogany desk and talking with his casually dressed foreman, Roy "Lightning" Loftis. They often discussed business in Mr. Black's private office.

As usual, Mr. Loftis was pacing the hardwood floor. Under discussion was the robbing of an east bound train laden with a Colorado gold shipment. "All you have to do if Boomer is right," said Mr. Black softly, "is block the railroad track at Eagle's Pass. That gold train will be forced to stop. After it stops, lift the gold from the second boxcar, and load it onto the four waiting pack-mules. Take it to our hideout in Buzzard Canyon, and I'll meet you there in three days. Send the rest of the men back. I don't want that nosy sheriff to get suspicious. Yes, sir, I've got a lot of men working for me now. I've got more working for me than I've ever had. We'll use about all of them on this job. Have them to dress as drab as they can, look as nasty as possible and shoot a couple of train employees. The James gang will get the blame. This ought to be an easy job."

17

"Which train employees do ya want shot?"

"Well, let's see . . . there's the fireman."

"Don't want to shoot him. He's like one of us working hands. Heck, some of the boys might git mad if we plugged the fireman."

"There's the engineer."

"Oh, no! They'll need somebody to run the train so they can git back. Besides, engineers make big money and usually have big families by lots o' different women. Jist think of the suffering that would cause."

"Okay, I'll leave it up to your discretion," said Mr. Black. He watched his foreman flick cigar ashes onto the floor.

Ignoring some loud talking that had erupted in the saloon, Mr. Loftis continued: "Don't think we'll have to worry about the boys o' dressing drab or looking nasty. Most of them ain't had a bath in four months. In fact, the only time some of them git washed up is when they git caught out in a bad thunderstorm. Sometimes they git soaked down pretty good when they're out a rustling cattle. It ain't rained now nigh on four months. Boys are smelly and plenty dirty."

"Yes," replied Mr. Black, rising from his brown swivel chair behind his big, dark desk. "It looks like we can pin this one on Jesse and Frank with no problem. Right now, I've got a man coming in to get rid of that pesky sheriff. It won't be long until I'll have this town in the palm of my hand." They walked toward the wide door to enter the saloon. As Mr. Black was opening the door, he said, "I just wish I could figure out how to get rid of Li—"

In the doorway Mr. Black's eagle eyes quickly surveyed his saloon's patrons. He noticed a tall, young stranger tugging at his clothing and getting acquainted with some of the customers, especially Lil. After observing the pair for a split second, he whispered, "An answer to my prayer."

"Answer to yore prayer?" asked Mr. Loftis. "I didn't know you was a praying man. In fact, I've never heard o' you opening a church-house door. Not since I've knowed you."

"That's just a figure of speech, Lightning," said Mr. Black, who was obviously irritated.

"Figure of speech," replied Mr. Loftis, who was obviously baffled. "Is that sort o' like a teacher writing stuff on a blackboard? Shorely it ain't that fuzzy looking stuff they spray on pages o' books and sell fer big prices."

"Never mind, Lightning," said Mr. Black, cutting him short. He approached the stranger and said, "My, my; who do we have here?" He offered his hand to the stranger.

"I'm Junior Justus," said the lanky stranger, taking Mr. Black's proffered hand and crushing it in a vice-like grip. "Please to meet ya."

"I'm pleased to meet you. I'm James Black. Most folks around here just call me Whitey."

He rubbed his right hand to check for broken bones from the painful handshake. "So, your name is Junior Justus. What's your first name?"

"Why, Junior," he replied, drawling from the back part of his mouth that contained white teeth close-set together.

"It's strange that Junior is your first name. It's usually added to the end of a last name. That indicates that you were named after your father. You must have a first name other than Junior. So what's your first name? John, Peter, Tom, George, James, Ron, Richard?"

"Na, shoot. It's none of them. It's jist Junior," he retorted, exposing upper, front teeth where two on the right side were crossed almost into an X.

"Well, what's your father's name?" asked Mr. Black.

"Why, his name was Senior Justus. We buried him a couple o' years back."

"I'm sorry. You have my condolences."

"Ah, heck. Don't want none o' yore money. Don't believe in handouts. I believe in working fer the thangs ya git. Where I come from, we believe ya have to work fer the thangs you git."

"I see," rejoined Mr. Black, looking the stranger over thoroughly and confirming his first impression. "Where are you from?"

"I'm from Jewel Hill in North Ca'lina."

"Jewel Hill; where's that?"

"It's between Warm Springs 'n Lapland. Heck, it's back up in the mountains of the Western part of North Ca'lina. Ain't too many people living around there."

"Let me put it this way. What big town is located near you?"

"Why, Altamont."

"Well, what brings you to West Texas?"

"Why, that camel out there by the watering troft. I didn't git to thank the fellers that he'ped me git off that critter. Shore was a rough ride."

"I see," replied Mr. Black.

"Yeah, his name is Wheeler," interjected Mr. Adams who was standing in the group that was gathered around the two interlocutors.

"Wheeler?" asked Mr. Black as he contorted his face in such a manner as to reflect the fact that he was confused. "That's an unusual name for an animal."

"Yeah, he was name after Vice President Wiliam A. Wheeler. I thank it's because he goes so long between watering holes. That's the way Mr. Wheeler goes so long between elections. Got him down in Oklahoma. He'ped a man for three weeks, and he give him to me."

"Well, you're in West Texas now. If you got here, you must have a reason. Isn't that right boys?

"Yeah, that's right, Whitey," said Mr. Loftis. They all shook their heads in agreement.

"I'm a hunting fer my brother. He went to college at Ca'lina to become a newspaper reporter. His name's Josh Justus. I aw-ways call him Dickens. He aw-ways wanted to be a writer. Calling him Dickens was my way o' teasing him. Supposed to meet my Cousin Oscar Ames here. He's gonna he'p me hunt fer him."

Junior didn't notice a hush that fell over those assembled around him. When he mentioned the name of his brother, Josh Justus, most of the patrons looked knowingly from one to another. Mr. Black continued the conversation and asked, "When is your partner supposed to meet you here?"

"Heck, he ought to be here anytime now."

"Well," said Mr. Black, "we'll keep an eye out for your partner; won't we boys?"

"Yeah, sure, Whitey," said Mr. Loftis. They all nodded their heads in agreement.

"Well, young man, you're in West Texas now. We want you to feel welcome. We always like to make strangers feel welcome. We want to make you our friend. In fact, we want to make you one of us; don't we, boys?"

"Yeah, sure, that's right Whitey," said Mr. Loftis and they all agreed by nodding their heads in avid, positive approval.

"Gosh, that's real nice o' you fellers," replied Mr. Justus, swelling with pride.

"Yes, sir, you'll fit right in. You look like a young man that's going places. We'll help you to find your brother, too; won't we, boys?"

"Yeah, sure we will," said Mr. Loftis. They all nodded in agreement.

"Lightning, would you go into my office and get that special gunbelt hanging on the wall. You know the one. It's the one I hung up there a month ago. Yes sir, since you're in Texas, we're going to make you one of us."

"Gosh, ya fellers oughtn't to. I mean ya really shouldn't."

"Nonsense. We welcome strangers in these parts; don't we, boys?"

"Yeah, sure, that's right, Whitey," said Mr. Adams as he substituted as a lackey for Mr. Loftis. The men that were gathered around Mr. Justus nodded their heads approvingly. There was a short silence as they awaited Mr. Loftis's return.

Mr. Loftis returned from Mr. Black's office and handed him the wide gun-belt. It was a brown, leather belt and in the deep holster was a loaded Colt .45 six-shooter. "Now, since we want you to be one of us, we'll strap on this shooting iron. You can be just like us West Texans; isn't that right, boys?"

"Yeah, sure, that's right Whitey," said Mr. Loftis and they all agreed once more.

"Gosh, I don't know," said Junior with hesitation.

"Come on, stand up straight and hold out your arms," said Mr. Black. He proceeded to reach-around Junior to wrap the large belt around his waist. He finished by buckling it tightly in front. "There." said Mr. Black, stepping back to admire the gun belt strapped around the waist of the recipient of his gift. He added, "You're a real Texan, now; isn't he, boys?"

"Yeah, sure, that's right Whitey," said Mr. Loftis to the agreement of all.

"He needs the bottom holster straps tied around his leg," said Mr. Adams. "That keeps the holster steady."

"Well, tie them, Tumbleweed," replied Mr. Black. With ample nervous energy the slender, little man went anxiously about the task of tying the narrow leather straps around the inside of the stranger's right thigh.

"That make ya happy, Tumbleweed?" asked Mr. Rowe, laughing from the bottom of his high-heeled cowboy boots. He was joined by most of the others who enjoyed a long belly laugh.

"Love these little juicy assignments; don't you, Tumbleweed?" said Mr. Jacobs as the bantering continued.

"What do ya do with this here thang? I mean, it looks purty and all, except it's sort of heavy. Don't know if I can git use to it or not. It's a lot of weight to carry around." said Junior.

"Why, you'll get used to it. It will become a part of you. Just look at these boys standing around here. They would feel undressed without their six-shooters. You use it in self-defense; don't you, boys?"

"Yeah, sure, that's right Whitey," said Mr. Loftis. They all nodded their heads in agreement.

"But, heck, I don't have a problem. I git along good with ever'body anywhere I go."

"Oh, but out here there are lots of bad outlaws and wild Indians. You never know when you'll have to protect yourself. That six-shooter strapped on your side can be a lifesaver, isn't that right, boys?"

"Yeah, sure, that's right Whitey," said Mr. Loftis as they all nodded in total agreement.

"Drinks are on the house, boys. Set 'em up barkeeper," said Mr. Black. He and Mr. Loftis departed for the back room.

"Ya don't meet fellers like that too often," Junior said. He began to make conversation with the big barkeeper as his drink was being poured. "He's shore got a big heart. Boy, he shore is a real feller."

"Yeah, sure is," replied Mr. Myers perfunctorily.

"Hey, here comes one of Diaz's Mexican Demons," shouted Mr. Adams who was standing at the swinging doors of the saloon. "He'll be coming through the swinging doors any minute now."

"Pulling our leg again, Tumbleweed?" asked the big barkeeper.

"Swear on a stack of California raisins if it ain't," he responded in a fit of fidgety agitation.

"Can't pay no attention to Tumbleweed," said Mr. Myers who was standing across from Junior at the bar. "He come east with the Frisco Coolies to lay some railroad tracks. He couldn't cut it with the railroad, so he now does odd jobs around here. Most of the tracks are laid except in a few places. Of course, he grew up here before he went off to California."

"Yeah, he looks like a Chinaman," added Mr. Rowe. They all had a hearty laugh.

"Tracks ain't all he's trying to lay," said Mr. Jacobs to more roistering.

"Yeah, he got rounded up with them Chinamen and got sent east," added Mr. Rowe. His remark reaped more guffaws. "He couldn't cut it working with them Chinamen. Heck, they can work circles around just about anybody."

"Yeah, he must not have any Chinese blood," added Mr. Myers.

Suddenly, there was a lull in the laughter. Quiet reigned like the silence after the Battle of Little Big Horn. A huge, virile, swarthy man, who had two six-shooters buckled around his ample waist and supported by an x shaped bandoleer strapped across his broad-shoulders and chest, stepped quickly inside the swinging doors. "I told you it was Mad Mex, Jr." said Mr. Adams, breaking a deathly silence as he exuded uncontrollable tension. He sneaked behind the huge Mexican and trepidly tripped outside through the Avalanche Saloon's swinging doors. He stationed himself beside one of them and peeped back inside.

Who was this bad man who aroused so much fear? It was Senor Pedro Gonzalez Rodrigo Estevez, Jr. who had the Texas moniker, Mad Mex, Jr. He was the son of Senor Pedro Gonzalez Rodrigo Estevez, Sr. Senor Estevez, Sr. was known in North Texas as Mad Mex, Sr. due to his renowned reputation for extreme violence. He earned his Texas moniker in the most recent Mexican revolution where he robbed banks, waylaid stagecoaches, and held-up trains to finance the cut-throat rebels in the overthrow of an unstable Mexican Federal Government. Some of his brazen banditry took place in southern Texas. He not only used the money to finance the internal revolution; he also used some of the ill-gained proceeds to become extremely wealthy and to make large land purchases as well as to buy influence. His extensive wealth and influence enabled him to become the largest and most powerful landowning hombre in Northern Mexico. He and his three sons had an undisputed reputation for being violent, sadistic, and wealthy. Very few crossed the Estevezs' and lived to tell their story.

Fear gripped the remaining saloon patrons. They made a quick rush to find safety by the nearest route. Many jumped through open windows, others overturned tables for the purpose of hiding behind them for protection while still others dashed through the swinging doors. Barkeeper Myers dropped facedown on to the floor behind the bar.

"Where are you fellers a going?" asked Junior.

"They're all afraid of Diaz's Demon," said Lil who was standing among some overturned tables in the center of the saloon. "He's standing right behind you."

Junior spun around on the barstool. He faced an intimidating pair of eyes staring down at him. "He's a Mexican?" asked Junior. "Looks more lack a green-eye darkie to me. Course, he's got a few more scars on his face than most darkies got."

"Well, this particular green-eyed darkie happens to be Mad Mex, Jr." said Lil in a voice that echoed throughout the disordered and mostly deserted saloon. There was several pair of anxious eyes watching the proceedings from positions of protection at side windows, overturned tables, and beside the swinging doors. These disorganized patrons were extremely curious, cautious, and afraid.

"I'll be durn," said Junior whose eyes were locked onto those of the swarthy Mexican. "Could a swore he was a darkie."

"Gringo calls Mad Mex, Jr. a darkie. Senior Gringo must pay for insult with hees life."

"Now, hold on Mad Mex, Jr." said Lil. "This man doesn't know who you are." She rushed up to Mad Mex, Jr. as he started to draw his pistols.

"Anglo senorita stay out of thees," said Mad Max Jr., shoving her aside as if she were windblown tumbleweed. "Mad Max, Jr. ees going to keel Yankee. Nothing I hate more than a filthy Yankee."

"Hold on!" shouted Junior. "Who in blazes do ya thank yore a calling a Yankee? That's a fighting word!" He jumped off his barstool and prepared to fight the larger adversary.

"I am, senor. Go for your pistola."

"Ya mean this thang," said Junior as he reached for the weapon strapped on his hip. With both hands, he struggled with the weapon but could not jerk it from the holster. It was stuck. He did not realize that a newly arriving tenderfoot in the west is often treated to all sorts of playful pranks and perplexing tricks. He was experiencing the honor of enjoying the glued-to-the-holster six-gun trick. Had all the fearful patrons not left the saloon or been cowering in fear behind tables, they would have enjoyed a jolly belly laugh at Junior's expense. He was animated in his contortions as he attempted to extract his stuck, immovable six-gun.

Junior twisted his body in frustration. He became so agitated and disconcerted that he fired the unwieldy weapon from its position inside the deep holster. Instantly, after firing the shot, he began to hop around the saloon on one foot and to scream at the top of his lungs. He was totally animated and beside himself, as he yelled, "Oh, oh, oh, my foot! My foot! Oooh!"

While Junior was screaming and hop-scotching in circles on one foot, smoke was boiling from his holster. Curious spectators viewed the frantic action from a safe distance. As the Mexican became engulfed in a violent fit of uncontrollable laughter, he removed his hands from the pistols at his side. During his laughing fit, he began to sputter like an out of control, gyrating windmill in a fast moving tornado. Suddenly, he began to gasp for breath.

"You're keelling me, senor. I'm dying, Senor Yankee," he said as he doubled into a laughing fit of hilarious contortions. He laughed so hard that he fell and hit his dark head on an upturned corner an overturned oak table. After precipitously hitting the protruding table corner, he pitched into the hardwood floor and lay there silently while twitching in the throes of an uncontrollable spasm. His laughter ceased; Mad Mex, Jr. was deceased.

Torpidly, Mr. Adams tiptoed back through the swinging doors. He crept toward and then stood over the huge Mexican who was lying facedown in the littered floor. He stood there for a few seconds to make sure that the notorious badman lying there would no longer be a threat for renewed violence. Finally, he took the long fingers of his right hand, wrinkled them through the air twice, and placed them on the fallen man's wrist to feel for a pulse.

Patrons rose from their hiding places like curious rats while Mr. Adams was checking the man's vital sign.

"My lands," exclaimed Mr. Adams in disbelief, "the Greaser is a goner. He's deader than a white Christmas in San Francisco."

"Mexican food will do it every time," said Mr. Myers who had risen from the filthy floor behind the bar. "Darn stuff would kill nigh anybody."

Activity in the saloon soon returned to normal. There was a beehive of activity around the bar that centered on Junior who was in a great deal of pain. "How about this hillbilly," said Mr. Jacobs. "Killing this here Mexican without even drawing his gun? Beats all I've ever seen."

"Shore was the strangest gunfight I ever saw," added Mr. Myers.

Junior finally found enough self-possession to seat himself on the nearby third step of the wooden stairs leading to the rented rooms on the second floor. He removed a malodorous, brown boot to examine his big toe with most of the end blown away by hot lead from his blazing pistol.

Mr. Myers was once again pouring drinks from behind the bar. He peered over a drink he was pouring in a shot glass for Mr. Rowe when he took a look at the gruesome injury. "Well," he said, "you won't have to worry about gout in that big toe." He laughed while missing the small glass with some of the ninety-proof whiskey he was pouring.

"Yeah," added Mr. Jacobs, "Ain't nothing there to hold it in. He shot it off." There was more laughing.

A man entered through the swinging doors. "It's Sheriff Longarm," said Mr. Adams who was standing near the doors.

"We can see that," replied Mr. Myers who was wiping spilled whiskey off the countertop.

"What's going on here?" asked the sheriff as he was looking down at the big Mexican lying in the cluttered floor.

"There's been a shoot-out, sheriff," exclaimed Mr. Adams.

"That ain't what happened," interjected Mr. Jacobs. "This here newcomer tried to draw on this here big Mexican. He couldn't git his gun out o' his holster. Shot his own big toe off and the Mexican died laughing."

"Exactly," added Mr. Myers with certainty. "I saw the whole thing. It happened jist like Washtub said."

"Well, I'll be," exclaimed the sheriff. He looked down at the visitor who was being assisted by Lil. He said, "Tumbleweed, go find Morty. Might as well git this Greaser buried before he starts to stink."

"Too late for that, Longarm," said Mr. Jacobs.

"How come, Washtub?"

"He was a stinking when he walked through them swinging doors. That's why everybody ducked for cover. Heck, his stink is worse than his bullets."

"Thought you said Morty was out o' town, sheriff," said Mr. Rowe.

"That's what I said. Didn't see no need of you and Washtub a plugging each other, Red. Not when it was over, which one o' you boys was the most humane."

"Well, that was a dirty, rotten trick sheriff. I'll never vote fer you agin. You ain't nothing but a deceitful liar."

"Yeah, that's my strong point," said Sheriff Brooks as he turned his attention to the wounded Junior Justice. "Why are you wearing a gun? If you're going to be around here long, you've got to start obeying the law. You're supposed to check your guns when you're in the saloon."

"It's not his fault," said Mr. Black, breaking into the conversation as he emerged from his office. "The boys and I were welcoming him to West Texas. I strapped that gun on him to make him a present of it. Out here a gun is a man's best friend; that and his horse. Isn't that right, boys?"

"Yeah, that's right Whitey," said Mr. Loftis. All the patrons standing around the sheriff agreed.

"You ought to know better, Whitey. I ought to run you in fer disturbing the peace. Just look! A man's toe is shot half off and another man is lying there in the floor," he said, pointing his finger at the big Mexican. "He's deader than a hammer. You're certainly making my job difficult."

"You're right, sheriff. I just wasn't thinking straight."

"Well, you better let Doc Witt take a look at that big toe young man."

A slender man dressed in black entered the saloon. "Hey, here's Morty now," shouted Mr. Adams. A tall, slender man in a baggy, black wool suit that hung loosely on a gangly frame began to take visual measurements of the man lying in the floor. After making his visual observations, Mr. Uriah "Morty" Ramey knelt beside the deceased man to check his vital signs. After checking his pulse, he struggled to roll the victim over. With fingers moving as deftly and precisely as those of a surgeon, he checked all his deep, secret pockets. He found nothing of value.

Mr. Ramey was apprenticed to be a dentist in Memphis, Tennessee. He was the second eldest son of eight children born to a respectable family in Memphis where his father owned and operated a huge cotton warehouse that was near the Mississippi River. His intention of becoming a dentist died when he discovered there was more money to be made by becoming a mortician. His motive for moving out west was strictly volume. In the west there were an excessive number of deaths due to disease, Indian raids, and shootouts. It was a golden opportunity for a man in his profession.

He rose to his feet, pursed his lips and cupped his chin in his left hand. At last, he said, "I can't do it."

"Can't do what?" asked sheriff Brooks.

"I can't bury him," replied Mr. Ramey. He peered through steely, greedy, brown eyes at the sheriff. "He ain't got a dime on him. I don't work for nothing."

"Well, he's got two six-shooters and a horse tied out there at the hitching post. They ought to be worth something," the sheriff informed him.

"Yes, I suppose I could consider that," said the mortician, smacking his long, thin, avaricious lips.

"Yes," added Mr. Black, "You could take the horse, saddle, and guns as a burial fee. Everybody needs a good horse. That Mexican's horse can probably burn the wind. I dare say that Mr. Justus here would trade you his camel for that Mexican's stallion. He would probably give you fifty dollars to boot."

"Shore would if I had it," said Junior, grimacing from pain emanating from his big toe.

"That's no problem, said Mr. Black. I'll advance you the money. You can pay me back at your convenience."

"Gosh, I don't know. I ain't got a job and the way thangs are a go—"

"Don't worry about a thing. You can work for me. Out here we're big hearted and take care of people," said Mr. Black as he watched two men ponder how to lift and carry out the big Mexican.

"Yeah, the hillbilly kin work for Whitey," said Mr. Rowe.

"Well," said the sheriff, "git this Greaser out o' here before he starts to stinking. Don't want him smelling as bad as some o' these here cowboys. Git that six-shooter checked, stranger," he said as he departed through the swinging doors. Two men strained every muscle in their bodies while trying to lift the deceased Mexican to carry him from the saloon. After having little to no success, the two men each grabbed a boot and dragged him across the floor and through the swinging doors.

Mr. Ramey remained a few minutes longer. To Junior in a low, weak voice, he said, "Now, I want you to come and see me." Junior noticed a wild, conspiratorial gleam in the mortician's eyes that matched the greedy twang in his voice. Junior squirmed where he sat on a rough, third tread of the dark stairs.

Mr. Ramey departed the saloon. Junior spit into the floor barely missing Miss Hutchins's right shoe. He said, "'How do ya like the way Morty said, 'Now, I want ya to come and see me.' Gives me the willies jist looking at him. He's creepy."

"Let's have some music and git back to normal," suggested Mr. Jacobs.

"Yeah, Lil; do an assault and battery on another ballad," said Mr. Rowe who began to laugh.

"Can't; haven't got a piano player," she said, pointing in the direction of the black stool near the upright piano. It was empty because her piano player, Benjamin "Ivory" Jones, was lying passed out in the cluttered floor. It was a position quite familiar to him.

Benjamin Jones grew up in Pittsburgh, Pennsylvania. He was the eldest of five children and his father, Joseph Jones, made all types of leather goods in Sam's Leather Shop. He later carried the mail for home deliveries in the greater Pittsburgh area. Benjamin stunned his parents, kin folks, and neighbors alike by playing the piano by the age of three. He could hear a tune and play by ear every note of a song without ever seeing the sheet music. In his teens he worked at Hal's Music Shop as a piano tuner and salesman. Customers would hear him play a piano, and they would insist on having one just like it so their children could play like Benjamin Jones. Mr. Jones was renowned for his piano playing.

One day the Wendell Wallace family from St. Louis came into Hal's. They were there to look at the shop's assortment of new and used pianos. Benjamin was smitten by the Wallace's oldest daughter Wanda. He immediately traveled to St. Louis and began to play the upright piano in Tinky's Saloon where he landed and launched Wanda as the saloon's up-and-coming singer. Soon they were married.

He was devastated, crushed, heart broken, and became a drunkard when Wanda jilted him for a smooth talking New Orleans gambler named Hubert Holloway.

Mr. James Black literally picked Benjamin from a St Louis gutter and settled him in Los Villas so that he could be his saloon's piano player. Drunk or sober, Ivory Jones was the best piano player Mr. Black had ever heard.

"Drunk again," said Mr. Rowe, shaking his head. "Looks like Whitey's going to have to git himself another piano player. That's all I kin say."

"Either that, or close the saloon," added Mr. Jacobs.

"Let me play fer her to sang," said Mr. Justus. He reached inside his Levi's pocket.

"You play a piano?" inquired Mr. Rowe.

"Heck no. I play a harmonica," he replied. He fished out a metallic, silver plated harmonica. He spit into the floor, wet the instrument with his lips and blew a few notes.

"You need Doc Witt to look at that big toe," said Lil. "That wrap I used won't be enough." She gave him an understanding, concerned look

"I'll be aw right," he said. "The fellers want some music." With his right shoe on the second step beside him, he painfully rose to permit his left leg to hold him upright to take most all his body weight. He enthusiastically began to play his small wind instrument. Lil picked up the rhythm of the tune and began to sing "Buffalo Gals." That was pretty good except for the fact that Junior was playing "Oh! Susanna."

Mr. Black had retired to his bleak office in back. To his foreman inside the closed door, he said, "Darn, Mad Mex, Jr. is dead. Send for somebody to get rid of that lousy sheriff and what happens? He kills himself while watching a clumsy hillbilly shoot off his big toe. And it's my fault, darn it. I play the old glue the gun in the holster trick on a dumb tinhorn and it backfires in my face. How am I ever going to get rid of that thorn-in-the-side sheriff? If only I could get rid of that pest, this town would be mine. Mine, all mine, lock stock and barrel Lightning, Mine!"

"Now that Mad Max, Jr. is out o' the picture, you could send fer Philadelphia Phil," suggested Mr. Loftis.

"No, he's not quick enough with a six-gun."

"How about Charlotte Sean?"

"No. He's too eastern, Lightning. I want a man more masculine, more western. I want a man who can take a bull by the horns and brand him in a stampede. Those eastern boys just aren't made of the right stuff."

"How about Carlsbad Blackie or Frisco Frank?"

"No. I need somebody really fast; somebody like 'Walla Walla' Wally. This job calls for somebody tough; somebody with grit that won't back down."

"Yeah. But he wouldn't do fer this part o' the country."

"Why do you say that, Lightning?"

"Nobody around here can say Walla Walla Wally with a straight face. Heck, half the town would look at him and die laughing while saying Walla Walla Wally. He'd shoot them fer laughing at him."

"Nonsense. I'll wire for him today. Walla Walla Wally is one apple that Washington can part with for a few days. Now, according to what Boomer told us, we've got a gold shipment that is just waiting to be taken late next week. I'm going to line up that hillbilly with a missing big toe to ride with you. I want you to break him in by having him to hold the horses. He can hold them while you and the boys relieve that train of its gold. Surely that dumb hillbilly can hold the horses."

"You going to tell him about us a robbing the gold train?"

"Of course not. I'll explain to him that I'm merely taking back some of my possessions that were stolen from me. He's so dumb that he'll never be the wiser. In fact, he's so dumb I believe that I can pawn Lil off on him."

"Gawd, that is dumb!" ejaculated Mr. Loftis. He realized that he had insulted his boss's taste in women because Lil had been Mr. Black's mistress for three years. He cleared his throat, flicked some ashes onto the floor, and made his departure.

Chapter 3
The Train Robbery

Twenty tired riders and four pack mules were traveling across the hot, dry plains. They were approaching a wide, swollen river a mile before them. A beautiful, rugged mountain range covered with tall, glossy pine trees thrust its head above the plains. These large coniferous trees endowed the majestic mountains with the appearance of verdant strands of long, green hair. Mr. Loftis and Junior were in the lead. Mr. Loftis stopped his sorrel mount and turned around in his saddle to face the men following him. He took the cigar from his mouth, and shouted, "Won't be long now. It's jist across that pass there in that mountain over yonder." He turned his face to the river and added, "When we cross the river we're about there."

Junior was riding his spirited, black stallion beside Mr. Loftis. "I shore appreciate you and Whitey letting me ride with ya and the fellers," said Junior. "Shore hope we kin git Mr. Blacks brown bags back. They meant the world to him. Belong to his mama. Ain't life a funny thang, lightning? The only time a woman becomes sacred is when she's called a mama."

"Yeah, them bags meant a lot to her," replied Mr. Loftis. Their conversation stopped when twenty rods in front of them, they spotted a screaming female rider heading straight toward the raging, swollen river. Without hesitation Junior spurred his big, sturdy mount that had belonged to the big Mexican, and rode in the direction of the screaming damsel in distress. "Hey! Where do you think you're going," shouted Mr. Loftis. "That river's too dangerous to mess with."

In what seemed like seconds, Junior was in the swollen, muddy water. It appeared that he and the female rider would be swallowed by the wild, swirling, current of turgid water in the raging river. Junior urged his big black stallion into the raging water where huge boulders, large trees, and assorted debris were bobbling in the flood waters. His odds of survival appeared to be slim indeed.

"Ah, let him go," said Mr. Loftis. "We got pressing business past that gap. That train is due before long." He and his large band of outlaws continued without Mr. Justus along the river in the direction of a safer crossing upstream.

Soon the bandits crossed the turbulent river where it forked. In a safer location, they crossed a smaller, less raging river two miles above where Junior and the endangered damsel were last seen floundering in the muddy, swollen waters. They rode through a narrow, winding staircase gap in the rugged Rockies and marveled at the endless canyons where a pine-scented aroma drifted from the tree-covered serried mountains. After two hours of tortuous riding, they arrived at their destination.

At Eagle's Pass the men dismounted and tied their sweaty, frothy horses. Immediately, Mr. Loftis began to supervise the blocking of the railroad tracks at the most narrow point in the pass. With fervor and bustling energy, the relentless outlaws began blocking the tracks with dead tree trunks, brush, and large boulders. After completing this task, they hid behind rounded rocks of all shapes and sizes to await the train and its precious cargo. Mr. Loftis left no one with the horses tied nearby because he believed that Mr. Black was being overly generous by appointing Mr. Justus for the horse holding task. They relaxed, rested, and waited.

A chugging train's whistle blasted the silence in a Colorado Rockies canyon. From their perch, the bandits heard the choo-choo sound of the approaching train and saw the smokestack's red sparks flying through a thick, black smoke from the loud, front locomotive engine that was pulling twenty-six black boxcars. It would soon arrive.

When the roaring train rounded a sharp curve, the engineer spotted the blocked tracks. He applied screeching brakes to the steel wheels of this ponderous, unwieldy machine that was entrusted to his care. With brakes screaming and the train moving at one quarter of its original speed, it crashed with a thunderous thud into the variegated pile of debris stacked atop the iron tracks. When the train stopped, the area around the engine was engulfed in a pother of engine smoke and boiling dust from the pile of rubble blocking the tracks. All was quiet after the train's sudden stop.

From the boulders, the hiding outlaws made their move. They swarmed like angry wasps as they descended toward the first boxcar of the halted, helpless train. When these masked, armed outlaws clambered aboard the motionless train, one masked man shoved the frightened engineer off the right side of the dark engine car while another slugged the fireman with the butt of his six-gun. A quick acting brakeman jumped off the stationary train on the side opposite the swarming outlaws. These bold bandits soon found the shipment of brown bags filled with yellow gold packed in wooden, oak crates where their inside information reported it to be. Five busy outlaws inside the train handed and pitched the heavy, brown bags into the waiting hands of those on the ground where they quickly stashed them into the leather saddlebags of the four waiting pack mules. Soon the heist was finished and the outlaws prepared to mount their nearby horses to make their escape. Lightning felt that the heist had been too easy.

There was a surprise in store for these bold, brazen bandits. Windows without curtains were unlatched in the boxcars behind the gold shipment. Long rifles were poked forward through the windows in the direction of the scurrying outlaws. Behind the mounted, masked robbers, repeating rifles began to spit fire that began to echo resoundingly around the wide canyon and rustic mouintains beyond. Blue uniformed men cut down the scurrying bandits and rearing horses as they spurred their frenzied mounts to leave the scene. In the confusion, the outlaws yelled, horses nickered and reared in blind terror while rifle smoke obscured most all of the helpless horse and outlaw victims. A stench of rifle smoke and a pall of death hovered over the robbery scene. Lightning Loftis suffered three bullet wounds but managed to escape with the stolen gold on the four pack mules. He was the only outlaw to get away.

In the fifth boxcar, Sergeant Randolph Sanders ordered his uniformed soldiers to cease firing. There was so much smoke that the soldiers were unable to survey the damage they had inflicted on the bold robbers. Amid the malodorous stench of boiling gunsmoke, Sergeant Sanders turned to Captain William Jones who was in charge of the detail that was entrusted with protecting the gold shipment.

Sergeant Sanders asked, "Whose idea was it to come out here in the middle of nowhere without horses?"

"Don't ask me," replied Captain Jones. "I just follow orders."

"Well, if you'll pardon me for saying so sir, I think it was a pretty dumb idea to shoot all the outlaws's horses, too. We could have rounded up some of their horses and give chase. The way things have worked out we may not even find the gold. If we don't, we'll hear about this."

Captain Jones tugged at his blue army hat, and said, "It looks like the smoke is clearing. I believe we've wiped out the James gang."

"Yeah, now let's get down and find the gold they heisted."

Junior caught the runaway horse in mid-river. He was still on his swimming horse when he took the dripping wet leather reins of the woman's small horse. He led her paint pony with its exhausted rider back to the gently sloping river bank on the side where they first splashed into the raging water. They were a half mile downstream from area where they first rode into the dangerous flooded river. "Ya aw right" he asked while firmly holding her mount's reins and leading them onto dry land. He looked back into the young woman's bright, blue eyes and spit beside his horse.

"Am I what?" she asked with a puzzled look.

"Ya could a drown-ded. Are ya hurt?"

"No. I'm all right. You saved my life. I'm so grateful. Is there anything I can do to thank you?" Their horses were now on dry grassland and safely away from the perilous, muddy river.

"Well," he said, in a licentious tone of voice, "We might git off these here horses and step over yonder behind them bushes. We could make music together." While looking her over as if she were a pet rabbit, he spit into some dry weeds between the horses.

"I'm not that grateful," she replied. She gave him a disdainful look after repulsing what she considered to be a crude advance.

"Well, I didn't see no harm in asting," he said in his usual drawl that curled the words in the back portion of his mouth.

"Let me be honest with you, cowboy," she said. "I'm not interested in you. You're not exactly my type. If I were looking for a companion, you would be the last man in the world I would consider. You're just not my type. Sorry."

"Oh, I'm not really a cowboy. In fact, I'm from North Ca'lina . . . the mountains o' North Ca'lina."

"Oh, you're an Appalachian cowboy," she said coldly. "Well, you can keep your cotton picking hands to yourself, and we'll get along fine."

"Don't raise no cotton where I come from," he said, spitting between them once more. "Got a lot o' corn and backer and even raise a little feed cane. We've been knowed to git drunk and raise a little hell." After a pause, he added, "My name's Junior. What's yours?"

"That's not important. What is important is that I get to Los Villas, Texas. That's where I was headed when my horse got spooked by a rattlesnake."

"I was coming from there when I seen ya in trouble. We was going to meet a train. Guess I'm too late fer that now. I might as well head back that way myself. But first we ought to set here a while to rest the horses. They need to be rub down and rest. It might he'p to let them graze fer a while. Don't want to wear them out before we head back to Los Villas. That muddy river took a lot out of them. I hate walking. Heck, Mr. Black give me this here six-shooter. He said it was fer protection agin outlaws and Indians. I been practicing shooting it, too. At first, it was hard to git it out of the holster. Some scalding water took ker of that," he said as he held the reins after dismounting. "Guess I ought to clean it while I got a little time. Right now I'm going over yonder and take my pants off and wrang them out so they'll dry faster. Got to take care o' my big toe, too. Then I'm going to spread my blanket out to dry. Ya can't sleep under a wet blanket."

A few minutes later Junior sat on a rock holding the rope of his grazing, tethered stallion. After passing a few hours, he bridled his horse in preparation to leave for Los Villas. Miss Rush was sitting on a rock opposite him and holding the reins of her paint pony. They were resting comfortably when sixty rods away, he spied four wandering mules laden with the gold stolen from the robbed train. They were winding toward some short, lush grass that spread across the sprawling plains.

"Them looks like Mr. Black's mules," said Junior as he observed them. "Let's ride over yonder and take a look."

They approached the grazing mules. They calmly looked up at Junior and the young lady as the pair unhurriedly approached. He dismounted and began to search a bulging, brown, leather saddlebag. He found a small, brown sack, untied the taut string, and began to shake the yellow contents from the bag into his cupped left hand. "Wonder what this here heavy, yellow stuff is," he asked. He held up some of the heavy contents for the auburn-haired, snub-nosed, lightly freckle-faced, young woman to see. "These bags must be full o' this here stuff," he added.

"It's gold!" she shouted.

She lost all reason as she dismounted so quickly that the ground came rushing up to meet her flush in the face. While spitting out dry grass and damp dirt from her mouth, she rose from the ground and hurried to Junior's side to examine the contents in the weighty bags. "My name is Julie Rush. You're some kind of cowboy. You want to make love to me? With this gold we can see the world, live in a palace, and make all my dreams come true," she said with an excited sigh. She was gazing dreamily into the far, distant vastness of a blue sky as though she were in a disoriented daze. She then turned to look longingly into his eyes and in a breathy, sexy voice, she said, "Oh, you're so handsome."

"Yeah, heck. I knowed that," he replied, kicking Modesty in the shins. "Except, heck, this here gold ain't ours. Belongs to somebody else."

"Don't be a fool, cowboy," she cried. "When does somebody like us get a chance like this to be rich? With this gold, you can have everything you ever dreamed about. Oh, the things we could do and the places we could go. We could have a paradise on earth."

"But this here stuff don't belong to us. Heck, since we're both going to Los Villas, we kin take this stuff to Sheriff Brooks. He'll know what to do with it. Thank these here bags probably belong to Mr. Black. He wanted them back; they was his mama's," he said with finality.

"I suppose he *would* want his precious brown bags back," she said. There was acid in her voice and vinegar in her countenance.

They mounted and began to ride toward Los Villas. They occasionally flushed a covey of birds along a dusty trail that was once a wild buffalo path. They had traveled no more than a mile when before them, Junior began to notice some round, fluffy, gray, smoke rings rising into the sky. To his female companion, he said, "Somebody's smoking a mighty big cigar. Look at them smoke rings they're a blowing."

"They're not cigars. Those are smoke signals. I'd say we're probably surrounded by Indians that want our scalps."

Miss Rush was right. Within seconds Junior spotted forty scantily clad Indians slowly rising and creeping forward in the short prairie grass. They were moving furtively on foot toward them. They approached so closely that Junior stopped his strong mount because he felt that it would be unsafe to continue any further in their direction. He dismounted and removed his harmonica from a pants pocket, placed it to his lips and began to play "Home on the Range." Miss Rush was puzzled.

"Why are you playing that stupid harmonica," asked Miss Rush. She dismounted, and added, "How can you play that thing when our lives are in danger?"

"Well," he said upon removing it from his mouth and expectorating vulgarly. "They say that music tames the savage beast.

We don't have a chance agin them Indians. They've got us out number. We ain't got nothing to lose. This here's our only chance."

"By golly, you may be right," she replied. "Play 'Down in the Valley' and I'll sing."

While holding the reins of their horses, they stood side by side. He played and she sang while facing in the direction of the feathered, hostile Indians smeared with earth tone swatches of war paint. When the egregious notes from the harmonica and the cacophonous sounds of Miss Rush's female voice were wafted into the air, the wide war party halted their stealthy advance. With a pained expression on his face, the chief looked into the sad eyes of his befuddled braves and tacitly pointed to his aching ears as if to say that they could no longer endure this musical bombardment. He took a quick reading of his braves. One third of his war party had queasy stomachs, another third had headaches, and the last third was retching. An odd Indian suffered from all three maladies. Soon the entire war party made a silent retreat and vanished into the endless prairie. Junior and Miss Rush continued their journey.

Late that night Miss Rush and Junior were sleeping. He lay in a warm wool blanket beside the dying campfire opposite her. She was unable to fight the howling coyotes in her ears that woke her from a fretful, restless sleep. By the light of a full, luminous moon, she searched for and found a heavy, dry pine limb that if used properly, would keep a larger nemesis from prematurely waking. She approached a snoring Junior who was having no somnolent problems with the howling sounds that prevailed in a western night. She drew back the heavy club that glistened in the moonlight, and, with the full force of a pair of swinging arms, she brought the club crashing across the unprotected head of the unwary sleeper. A few seconds after the sound of the club crashing against Junior's head, shattered limb parts were strewn all across the hard ground on his side of the campfire. At the sound of the crashing club, even the baying coyotes stopped their never ceasing, incessant howling. All was temporarily quiet.

Junior slept more soundly than before. While he was lying there on the hard, dry ground, multitudes of all size and shape stars, too numerous to count, began to float gently through his battered brain.

In his new state of deeper sleep, he was with his little partner, Cousin Oscar Ames. Oscar was a big hearted, affable man who was short, stocky, and thirty-six years old. He had disarming blue eyes and stood five foot four inches tall. An odd feature about him was that his two upper front teeth had a gap between them that was as wide as the Oklahoma panhandle. Each tooth was large enough for an outdoor sign company to lease for a Texas size billboard. They were strong enough to chew iron nails and spit out sharp tacks as a finished product. They were perfect for removing difficult bottle caps and cracking black walnuts. He was blessed with ideal teeth that perfectly fit the purpose for which he used them: opening alcoholic beverage containers. After uncapping hard to open bottles with them, he could bring the opened container to his lips and permit the free flow of intoxicating beverages between them. This was the Oscar Ames he saw in his dream.

Junior continued to dream. He, Oscar Ames, and Sheriff Brooks, who was wearing his big, black hat that contained a gallon of oil on the brim and in the sweat band, were sitting in the saddles of their resting horses when in the distance almost a mile away, they saw a young rider racing across the endless, rolling plains. His horse was galloping at breakneck speed while he was being pursued by a mounted band of hostile Indian warriors. Arrows filled the sky behind the rapid riding mail carrier who was racing madly for his life. They all watched the unfolding drama before them. "Boy, he's a flying!" said Junior to the pair.

"The mail must go through," said Sheriff Brooks.

"Post office shore takes chances to git the mail through," said Mr. Ames. "Wonder if the post office hires them Indians to chase their mail carriers. That speeds up delivery." A slight breeze tugged at his long, flowing, blonde hair that was under his brown, wide-brimmed hat.

"Shore does," said the sheriff. He watched the racing rider and the chasing Indians disappear behind a grassy mound in the distance. "If anybody can git the mail through, ole "Slim" Long can git it through. Never seen him move so quick. Boy, he likes to fish."

Junior awoke with a throbbing head that felt as big as a galvanized washingtub. It was noon when he groggily got to his unsteady, giddy feet. With legs of India rubber, he stumbled to find his dark, half empty canteen. He splashed some tepid water against his numb face for a quick wakeup. To wash the crust from his throughly matted, blurry eyes, he used a second splash. He wondered how his painful, excruciating head could hurt so badly without being rip-roaring drunk the night before. After a quick inventory of his new situation, he found that his big horse, four pack mules, camping equipment, saddlebags filled with sacks of gold, and Miss Rush were missing. He stumbled from his deserted campsite and began to amble in a southeast direction that he hoped would lead him to Los Villas. A long afternoon lay ahead of him in the unforgiving, blazing sun.

Late that afternoon, Junior stopped beside the narrow trail. As he was sitting on a large boulder rubbing his sore foot with the injured big toe, he spied a big, black stallion cantering toward him. As the horse approached, Junior recognized him as being the one that once belonged to the huge Mexican they called Mad Mex, Jr. "Found me, didn't ya boy?" said Junior. The horse snorted and began to sniff the odor of Junior's dirty, brown shirt. He mounted the sturdy animal and began to travel along the winding trail in the direction from whence the horse came. He was so happy that he jerked out his well-worn harmonica and began to play "Dixie."

It was twenty minutes before dark when Junior rode into an occupied campsite. It was located beside a small stream and belonged to a white bearded, animated, old man by the name of "Cactus" Jack Mitchell. Mr. Mitchell was a seasoned, old miner that didn't seem concerned about Junior's being a total stranger; in fact, he welcomed him into his camp with open arms. After Junior dismounted, Mr. Mitchell noticed that the large stallion was an exceptional animal. Being the horse trader that he was, Mr. Mitchell asked, "How much ya take fer that there horse?"

Junior replied, "He ain't fer sale."

Mr. Mitchell went over and looked into the big black's mouth. "Tell you what," said Mr. Mitchell. "I'll swap my old Sagebrush over there fer yore mount and throw in fifty dollars to boot."

Junior refused the offer.

"Look," he said in exasperation as he swiped several gnats away with his hand, "I'll swap you this fantastic gray fer yore old black, dead even and a fifty dollar gold piece. Not only that; I'll throw in a bottle of the best whiskey west o' the Pecos. That's my final offer."

"Got yoreself a deal," said Junior. He grabbed Mr. Mitchell's hand and crushed it with a handshake. He couldn't resist the miner's final offer.

Junior ate dinner with the old miner. They sat around the campfire that night sharing the bottle and Mr. Mitchell's tall tales until the contents of Junior's whiskey bottle was consumed. At dawn he ate breakfast with Mr. Mitchell and was soon on the circuitous trail toward Los Villas.

Junior was riding along on his jaded horse when his stomach began to feel queasy and unsettled. His new horse's gait made him feel as though he were on a precipitous landscape climbing young mountain saplings and applying his weight to ride them to the ground. His was an uncomfortable ride across the fertile plains.

Later that day Junior spotted a plain, unpainted wagon forty rods away. It was mired in a muddy, dry creek bed. He approached the forty-one-year-old owner, Travis Tillman, whose canvas, covered wagon had its rear spoke wheels mired to the iron axles in sticky, thick mud. Mr. Tillman had broad shoulders, dark hair, brown eyes, and a portly appearance. "Hello, stranger," said Mr. Tillman as Junior approached.

"Howdy," replied Junior. His roving eyes came to rest in the back of the large wagon where seven of the most beautiful, young women that he had ever seen were sitting.

Mr. Tillman coaxed Junior away from the stranded, stuck wagon. "Tell you what, Mr. Justus," said Mr. Tillman. "If you'll help me out of this mudhole, I'll let you sleep tonight with any one of the girls in my wagon. You can take your pick."

"Gosh, I don't know," replied Junior.

"I'll even throw in a fifty-dollar gold piece."

"I really got to git back to Los Villas."

"Tell you what. I've got some of the finest whiskey ever brewed in the back of my wagon. If you'll help me get out of this predicament, I'll add a bottle to the girl and the gold piece."

"Got yoreself a deal," said Junior. He promptly gave Mr. Tillman a vise-like handshake.

They immediately set to work to free the heavy wagon. With an aching right hand, Mr. Tillman urged the wagon's hitched horses forward while from behind, Junior heaved in the deep mire to free it. It wouldn't budge. The younger man toiled for the better part of two hours by shoveling, pushing, heaving, and lifting the overloaded wagon. When they finally decided to scuttle the contents in the wagon to include the girls and supplies, they were able to at last roll it onto solid ground.

Mr. Tillman was grateful and impressed. "I want you to know that I won't forget what you've done, Mr. Justus. Me and these young ladies really appreciate it," said Mr. Tillman as he patted Junior on the shoulder.

"Ah heck, it wasn't nothing. Glad to be o' he'p."

"I'm headed west with these young ladies. I've got lots of business to conduct. Now, you look like a man that I can trust. I'm tired, and I need your help to pitch camp for tonight. If you'll help me, I'll give you another fifty-dollar gold piece and a second bottle of whiskey. I certainly could use a hard-working man like you."

"Got yoreself a deal," said Junior without hesitation.

Mr. Tillman withdrew his hand that Junior reached to shake.

Junior gathered wood and buffalo chips to start a campfire and helped Mr. Tillman and the young women to setup a large, tan tarpaulin tent. After they ate a hearty dinner that the young women prepared, Junior and Mr. Tillman were sitting on a small, pine log forty paces from the fire and sharing a bottle of ninety-proof whiskey. Both were tired and were relaxing.

"You seem like a man that I can level with," said Mr. Tillman. "I work for Mr. Racketguy out of New Jersey. I'm roughing it out here because I'm buying legislatures. That's why I've got these lovely, young ladies with me. They're bait for balky lawmakers. Those we can't buy, we can influence with these adorable girls. We plan to get legislatures to approve our proposals to help with our mineral rights and railroad interests. I'm on important business."

"Let me give ya a clue," whispered Junior. He tugged Mr. Tillman's arm to bring him closer so that he could whisper in his ear. "It don't take as much to buy democrats as it does republicans."

"Is that a fact? How do you know?"

"Why, heck, most folks know democrats are fer the pore working people. Since they are, their expectations ain't high. They are more honest, too. Heck, buy them off and they won't change on ya. They'll stick with ye."

"Is that a fact?" replied Mr. Tillman with pretended interest. "I'll keep that in mind. Well, it's about time to turn in. Which one of my girls do you want?"

"I notice ya got three squaws, the best I kin tell."

"They're to get me through Indian Territory. It seems that everybody likes to take advantage of the Indians. Now, I'm a man of my word; which young lady do you want for a companion tonight?"

"They are all real purty. Kind o' had my eye on that there blond over by the burning far."

"Mona's a doll all right. Tell you what. You've done a dandy job for me and the girls. We appreciate it." Mr. Tillman reached into his coat pocket and drew out two fifty-dollar gold coins and handed them to Junior. He continued, "I'm going over to the wagon and get you a bottle of whiskey I promised. I'll give you the other one in the morning. Now, I want you to enjoy yourself."

It was time to retire for the night. All the young women with the exception of Mona, retired inside the large, heavy tent. Mr. Tillman made his bed in back of the solid, sturdy wagon while Junior and Mona rolled out two warm, thick, wool blankets by the bright, crackling campfire. With Mona by his side, Junior felt that this was his lucky night. He peered into her scantily clad bosom, took a long, lustful look at the soft, tender flesh that glistened in the flickering flames of the briskly, burning fire, and his heart began to race like a runaway freight train. As an expression of his affection, he leaned away from the young woman and spit in the direction opposite her. He wiped his mouth with a dirty shirt sleeve, and, with his dry lips, he gave her a slight peck that passed for a token kiss on her bare right shoulder. He wanted another drink.

He opened the bottle that Mr. Tillman handed to him a few minutes earlier.

"I wouldn't touch that stuff if I were you," said Mona.

"Why not," he asked as he lifted the opened bottle to his lips.

"Because," she said as she watched him guzzle the liquid flowing down his throat in urgent swallows. "That stuff has been doctored to put you out like a campfire in a cloudburst."

"Well, I'll be," he said as he moved his trembling left hand to his swimming head. He dropped the bottle when the world in an eddy went floating across his waning consciousness.

He could offer no resistance to a deep sleep as he sailed off into a prolonged slumber with vivid dreams. He was on foot when he entered a pass in the serried Rockies. He came upon a man fishing in a little gurgling stream flowing down a rugged mountainside. He was sitting on a huge boulder by a steep creek bank. Junior approached the man who appeared to be extremely relaxed in the coolness of the Colorado mountain air. He thought he recognized the slender man when he saw on a nearby rock, two sets of leather saddlebags with the deep impression letters U.S. Mail on the front. His small pony was tethered to a nearby slender birch sapling.

"Hey, ain't you Slim, the mail-rider?" asked Junior as he approached the man.

"Why, yes. How did you know?"

"Heck, it was easy," he replied modestly. "Seen ya in my dream last night. You was out running from a whole passel of wild Indians. They were after yore scalp. You was on a horse and they was a chasing ye."

"By golly that's right," agreed Slim. To get a better look at Junior, he rose while dropping his fishing pole into the small, clear stream.

"Tell me, how do ya git to fish?" asked Junior as he looked into the slender, young man's freckled-face. "Ain't you suppose to be a carrying the mail?"

"Yeah, like they say, the mail must go through eventually. Heck, I don't want to set no bad precedents. You see, our postal service is new. If I was to be a model of efficiency, them coming after me wouldn't have nothing to shoot for. This way, if a man gets his mail, he feels lucky. No matter how late it is, he'll think that the postal system has done a good job. See what I mean?"

"Yeah, that makes sense; I guess," replied Junior.

Junior woke at one o'clock the following day. His head was throbbing when he stumbled to his feet under a blistering sun. He saw two full whiskey bottles with an attached, handwritten note on the edge of his wrinkled blanket. As a kindness to the bottles before opening them, he read a note attached to one of them. In the brightness of full sunlight, his lips began to move as he began to read, "Dear Mr. Justus: I used the whiskey you drank last night to keep you away from Mona. She's my favorite. I'm sorry. You do have your gold pieces and the two bottles of good whiskey I promised. Should we ever meet again, I still consider ourselves to be warm friends. Many thanks for all you've done. Best wishes, Travis Tillman."

Junior had one goal for the day. He would sample the two bottles to make sure that they had not been tampered with and were safe to drink. By late afternoon he was satisfied that he was drinking good, safe whiskey. By the time he was completely satisfied, the bottles were empty, but it didn't matter, he was too intoxicated to care. He came to the conclusion that although he hated him, Mr. Tillman wasn't all bad.

He slept beside the narrow trail that night. His throbbing brain felt as if tom-toms were beating inside it the following morning. To ease the intense throbbing, he felt compelled to find a saloon as quickly as possible. He remembered that the Red Fox Saloon was in Colorado not far from Texas border. He set out south in that direction and arrived at his destination just before sundown. He tied his horse at the saloon's well worn hitching post.

Junior sidled up to the quiet bar. All eyes were on saloon singer "Longhorn" Linda Blevins who was belting out a popular ballad to the piano music being played by Bill "Piano" Williams. He plopped down a fifty-dollar gold piece to pay for a shot of ninety-proof whiskey. With the buzz created by Junior's ringing gold coin slapped on the hard counter, it was obvious to the busy barkeeper that Miss Linda would find him charming, intelligent, and irresistible; not to mention the fact that he must possess several more gold pieces that he most surely had in his possession for the taking—*her* taking. Junior purchased a second drink and found this lovely creature perched on a barstool beside him.

"You thirsty, cowboy?" she asked.

"Why, yeah," he replied. "Would ya like a drank?"

With the young, beautiful, dark-eyed woman with black hair sitting beside him, they enjoyed a few drinks together. With the talking mostly hers and the drinking mostly his, the pair became well acquainted; so well acquainted that he bought a big, brown bottle of whiskey from the tall, wiry barkeeper. They were set to retire to Miss Linda's room over the busy saloon. She steadied a tipsy Junior while he held to the mahogany railing for the jaunt upstairs. He was expecting a pleasure filled night.

It was a typical morning for Junior. He was all alone in an unkempt, empty room and was enjoying his usual morning headache while his stomach was performing double-backflips and endless cartwheels. Downstairs, he was denied a drink because he had no money to pay for it, and Mr. Williams had no idea where to find Longhorn Linda. So, once more he was back on the dusty trail and headed in the direction of Los Villas.

That afternoon he was five miles from his destination when he saw before him, approximately a half mile away, a woman riding a paint pony while she was holding the reins of four pack mules. Seemingly, out of nowhere a lone rider began to chase her.

Gallant as always, Junior spurred his mount. Although his mount lacked the speed to catch the villain chasing the woman in distress, he drew his six-shooter and fired once at the pursuing rider. Junior and his horse could probably have made better time had they switched places. To the bandit's chagrin, his brindle stallion found a round gopher hole that was the perfect size and fit for the fragile ankle of the horse's right, front leg. The bandit turned his lame horse aside from chasing the young woman, and headed straight for a dry river bed one rod away. He was in hopes of finding cover provided by the small trees and thick brush along the river bank. It would provide him with an excellent opportunity to return Junior's gunfire.

With the young woman now safe, Junior chased the bandit.

Too late, the bandit discovered that he was in peril. He was only ten paces into the soft, loose sand of the riverbed when his horse, still with enough speed, split the oozing goo of a large, gray, puddle of quagmire.

A few minutes later Junior rode his slow mount into the sandy riverbed where the outlaw was last seen. He discovered the horse and rider sinking deeper into the large, glistening puddle. From his sinking position in his tan saddle, the outlaw turned to face Junior.

"Uh, uh, throw me a ropa! Rope! Rope! A rope! Make it quick," the man yelled frantically.

Junior accommodated the panic-stricken outlaw in peril. He immediately lifted the wound rope from his brown saddle and pitched it to the man in the mire who was now up to his waist in slick, slivery, slimy mud.

"No, no!" he shouted. "I meant for you to unwind it first and hold one end! Gee whiz! You're dumb!"

"Well," replied Junior, "I may be dumb like ya say, but I ain't mired up to my belly button in a mudhole."

"I can't git this rope unraveled. Get me a long pole and reach it to me. And for heaven's sake, hold the other end so you can pull me out. Find one, quick!"

"Don't see one right off. Oh, yeah, over yonder's one," he said as he went to get it. "Don't ya go nowhere; I'll be right back." He returned with the long pole to the bubbling puddle where the sinking outlaw was in extreme peril. As he held out the pole to him, he asked, "By the way, what's yore name?"

"Walla Walla Wal—"

"Ya got a speech problem?" Junior asked.

There were a few slow ripples emanating from the slimy pool where the man's head was last seen. Floating atop the gooey mire of messy mud was a few rainbow, colored bubbles, a coiled rope, and the outlaw's black Stetson hat. All was quiet in the dry, sandy riverbed.

Chapter 4
The Missing Gold

Late that evening Junior hitched his horse outside the sheriff's office. He also tied the string of four mules to the same wooden rail and ambled inside with a sack of gold. He and the sheriff made several trips to tote the weighty bags of stolen gold into the small office. While Junior and the Sheriff were stashing the gold, Miss Rush sashayed into the Avalanche Saloon across the street but not before noticing the unusual activities of the two men. After the last brown bag of yellow metal was stashed safely inside the sheriff's office, Sheriff Brooks said, "There is two-hundred and fifty thousand dollars worth o' gold here. Jist got word from the telegraph office. There is a thousand dollar reward to git this stuff back. It was stolen in a railroad heist in Colorado. With a thousand dollars you could buy a nice, big ranch."

"I'll be doggone," replied Junior in astonishment. "Them fellers shore was careless after they stold it. A letting them mules walk all over the Colorado countryside. Nobody was a watching out fer them."

"They all got cut down by the army so far as anybody knows. They think it was the James gang. But after the shoot-out, they never found either Jesse or Frank. We'll have yore reward money in a few days."

An out of breath young man came rushing into the office. "What is it, Tumbleweed?" asked sheriff Brooks.

"Bad Ben is boarded up with Big Bertha. They're in the back of the Barton bungalow on Vandeveer Boulevard. Bad Ben's boasting that Big Bertha is barter."

"You shore it ain't on Berry or Broadway Bypass?"

"No, it's Vandeveer. Why do you ask?"

"Well, first of all there ain't no boulevards in Las Villas. Secondly, Vandeveer don't have the letter 'b' in it. That messes up all yore b's."

"Hey, you're right."

"Another thing."

"What's that, Longarm?"

"You shore it is Big Bertha that is a hostage and not Broad Bula? Hate to waste time on a needless trip if I don't have to. When yore enforcing the law, ya have to pick yore spots. Ya don't butt in needlessly. Most of the time things work out jist fine without the law."

"It's Big Bertha sheriff, why?"

"Nobody in their right mind would hold Big Bertha hostage."

"Why's that, Longarm?"

"Well, she's fat, nasty, and stinks. She ain't had a bath since she was baptized when she was ten years old . . . and she's a Methodist. Not only that," he said, smacking his thin lips, "she's just like Lil. She'll talk a man's ears off and reach them to him and say, 'Here, you ain't listening to me.' A man crazy enough to hold her hostage will wind up being *her* hostage." Rising from his chair behind the desk and to no one in particular, he said, "Might as well go rescue Bad Ben." He looked down at the slender, young man who was nervous with excitement and continued, "Tumbleweed, git Popcorn in here. He should be jist outside the door at Bell's. Then run across the street and find Short Fuse and Trigger Happy. Have them to me meet me down on Vandeveer."

"Yes sir," replied Tumbleweed. He departed from the jail in haste.

Ronald "Popcorn" Perkins strolled into the office. "Popcorn," said the sheriff as he scratched his dark hair with dirty fingernails, "I want you to keep an eye on these here brown bags. I've got business down the street." He turned to Junior and asked, "Want to come with me? I'll show you how a real rescue team works here in West Texas."

"Yeah, be glad to," he replied, drawing the words from deep inside his mouth.

After they left the office, Junior had to race to keep up with the rapid striding sheriff. They were approaching the middle of the street when an old, bearded, haggard, wild-eyed miner Harold Loggins approached the sheriff. He had just staggered through the swinging doors of the Golden Clipper Saloon and was out in the middle of the street where he met the sheriff who stopped. He looked the sheriff over thoroughly and stood before him without speaking a word. In an attempt to touch his face with his wiggly, filthy fingers, he reached forward with his hands toward the stationary sheriff. Sheriff Brooks was surprised by the miner's actions and snapped back to avoid contact. Mr. Loggins jerked his hands and arms back to himself as if startled. To the sheriff, he said, "Doggone, I thought Whitey got rid o' that ugly camel."

"I ain't half as ugly as you are, Claim Jumper," replied the angry sheriff. He side-stepped the whiskey in a man container and continued to stroll down the street as his raging temper began to slowly cool. Before them, Junior noticed a sad-faced man dressed in black.

To the sheriff, Junior whispered, "Why has that man got a white collar around his neck?"

"He's a padre."

"Why does he look so sad?"

"He has a reason to look sad. He spends most all his time praying fer drunk, oversexed cowboys. He's praying to pry them into Heaven. Praying for drunk oversexed cowboys would put a sad face on anybody."

They neared their destination. They approached a small, run-down, two room, adobe abode accented by dry yard grass. It was one of a few similar houses on Vandeveer, which was a short, side street with six adobe houses on either side. A short, bald-headed man with a drawn six-shooter rushed up to them. He was nervously pointing it in their direction. He said, "Sheriff, this is the wrong house. Bad Ben's holed up in that little, gray house over there across the street."

"Watch where you're pointing that durn thing, Mirror Head." James "Mirror Head" Cox was a short, local barber who migrated to West Texas from Biloxi, Mississippi. He left town when his barber partner, James Smith, fired a pistol at him as he was leaving through a closed bedroom window. The bedroom window was in the house that belonged to his partner, Mr. Smith.

"Me and the boys got training in this type o' work down in Austin. We know what we're doing. Now git back across the street before the gun-play starts."

Slowly Mr. Cox slinked back toward the Golden Clipper Saloon on Main Street.

Sheriff Brooks began to give orders to his arriving deputies. Jack "Short Fuse" Evans had short, brown hair, brown eyes, and a narrow chest. He had been deputized, when barbed wire fencing, or at least the threat of it, ended cattle drives to an eastern railhead in St. Louis. Short Fuse was a moniker for Mr. Evans because he had a quick temper and tended to go off half-cocked. Sheriff Brooks said, "Short Fuse, I want you on the back side o' the house."

No sooner was the order given when Scott "Trigger Happy" Randall arrived. Mr. Randall had become a deputy when he settled in Los Villas after throwing away the tin plate he had used to pan for gold nuggets in the clear streams of the Colorado Rockies. He earned the moniker "Trigger Happy" because he was easily frightened and quick to fire his six-shooter in the direction of fleeting shadows that he deemed to be a danger to himself. "Trigger Happy, I want you to stand at the side o' this here house where you can see Short Fuse. Don't you dare start shooting until I give the order. Got that, Trigger Happy?" asked the sheriff.

"Yes sir, Longarm," replied Mr. Randall.

Sheriff Brooks watched Mr. Randall take his appointed position. The sheriff was not suspecting anyone to be behind him when a hand tapped the sheriff once on his left shoulder. "Oh! My gawd!" shouted the sheriff at the top of his lungs. "Don't shoot! Don't shoot!"

A frightened, timid, little man stood behind the sheriff, frozen. He was as startled by the sheriff's reaction as the sheriff was by the initial tap on the shoulder. "I didn't mean to sneak up on you sheriff. I want to give myself up. I'm Bad Ben."

Sheriff Brooks turned to face his temporary tormentor. Sheriff Brooks said, "The devil you are! Git your can back in your casa! I know what I'm a doing. There's going to be gun-play. Somebody around here is going to git blasted if they don't watch it. Now git!"

"Yes sir, sheriff," said the man. He retreated as directed and marched toward a little, white house across the street.

Tension mounted outside the little house on Vandeveer. Suddenly, Trigger Happy opened fire whereupon Short Fuse and the sheriff followed suit.

In order to avoid being hit by the flying bullets, Junior made his way back toward the Avalanche Saloon. He was seated on a barstool hoping that his saloon credit was still good. With the promise of payment of the reward money he had coming, he convinced Mr. Myers to keep the drinks flowing into his small shot glass. With each gulp, the outside gun-play became less and less piercing to his ears.

Mr. Black entered the saloon from his office and perched himself on a barstool beside Junior. Both men's shoulders were hunched due to the lack of a firm back support. Mr. Black ordered a drink to be sociable and to pick information from Junior. "Miss Rush tells me you found some loose mules on the trail," he said casually. "She said they were carrying some brown bags."

"Shore did. Brung them into the sheriff's office. They look like the bags you describe as being yore mama's. They shore was heavy."

"I'm sure the bags weren't my mother's. I've decided not to worry anymore about those bags. Looks like whoever took them sold them to some mine owners. Tell me about the outlaw that was chasing Miss Rush."

"Why, he must o' been awful slow. He said words like ropa fer rope and act real dumb."

"What was his name?"

"I ast him that very thang. All I got out of him was Walla Walla Wal . . . Kin you believe that? I would a laughed at him right there if his head hadn't gone under in a mudpuddle. He went under right in the middle of a dried-up stream-bed. That feller was either slow or couldn't talk plain."

"You must have had an exciting time going with Lightning and the boys," said Mr. Black. He felt disappointment in ever muscle and bone in his body as he tried not to let his feelings show. He slid off the barstool to stand in the floor. He glanced at Junior's profile. "Tell me. What happened to that black stallion with the white arrow in his forehead? You know, the one that belonged to that big Mexican."

"Heck, I swap him to a miner in Colorado. Don't remember his name. Got a real deal fer him, too. Don't you worry, Mr. Black, I'll pay ya back that fifty-dollars I owe ye."

"I'm sure you made a good swap," said Mr. Black. It was hard for him to mask the disappointment of a top breeding stallion being swapped for a broken-down jade of a horse. "Don't worry about the fifty-dollars," he continued. "I'll chalk it up to the furthering of my education. A man needs to further his education after his formal schooling is over." Mr. Black returned to his office.

Three minutes later, two strangers took seats on barstools on either side of Junior. These two were the brothers of Mad Mex, Jr.—Miguel and Carlos.

"Well, looks like we've got some Mexican visitors," said Mr. Myers in a friendly tone of voice. "What will you boys have?" he asked. He looked first at the man on his left and turned to face the man on his right.

Junior glanced to his right and then to his left to follow barkeeper Myers's focus. He offered an unsolicited opinion when he said, "They don't look like Mexicans to me. Look more like darkies."

"They're not darkies, Junior," said Mr. Myers. "I assure you they're Mexicans."

"Gringo keeled my brother, Mad Mex, Jr.," said Miguel who was sitting on Junior's left. He gritted his snow white teeth. As his words were spoken, there were sounds and echoes of continuing gunfire from Vandeveer. "Got Gringo, now!" said Carlos who was sitting on Junior's right. On either side of Junior, each man reached for his gun.

Chairs began to scrape and scoot as tables were overturned to protect those who sought cover. Other patrons made a mad dash for any available exit. Mr. Myers dropped facedown in the floor behind the bar.

Junior surmised that he must act quickly. He pressed his left hand against the bar while simultaneously attempting to stand. Having more intoxicants in his system than he realized, his legs gave way when he applied weight to his right leg. He awkwardly fell backward and landed on the messy hardwood floor. That was a split second before the two spiteful, vengeful Mexicans pointed their drawn six-guns and fired in the direction where Junior had been sitting a split second earlier. Instead of shooting Junior, both groaning Mexicans crashed into the floor following their blazing gunfire. A stench of acrid gunpowder smoke filled the air around the bar.

Miss Hutchins rushed from her room above the bar. After hearing the gunfire, she glided down the steps that rose above the saloon floor, and in a flash she was kneeling by Junior's side. She wondered in horror if he might be dying. "Oh! they've killed you," she cried as she held his head against her small bosom.

"What happen?" he asked as he regained his composure.

"Did you see that?" asked Mr. Jacobs as he peeped around the corner of an overturned table. "He erased two o' Diaz's Demons and never even got a scratch."

"Yeah, he done it without even drawing his six-shooter," said Mr. Rowe who was peeping through an open window.

"That Hillbilly is some kind o' gunfighter," said barkeeper Myers. He rose to his feet from the gritty floor behind the bar. "Only man I ever saw to come in second in a gunfight, not git plugged and live to tell about it."

A winded sheriff came puffing into the saloon. "What's happening here, boys?" he asked. He looked first at Miguel and then Carlos. Mr. Adams pointed to Junior who was in a sitting position on the grimy floor. Lil was kneeling by his side.

Mr. Adams said, "Them two Mexicans drew their guns on Junior, and he leveled them both. Shot them deader than four o'clock."

"That ain't right, Longarm," said Mr. Jacobs. "I seen the whole thing. They were sitting on either side o' Junior at the bar. They drawed and fired at Junior as he dropped to the floor. They leveled each other."

"Yeah, it's just like Washtub said," added Mr. Myers. "I saw the whole thing. Junior was sitting between them. They fired just as Junior slipped off the stool and fell onto the floor."

"Well, I'll be," said the sheriff. He scratched his thinning hair and stared straight at Junior. He said, "Ain't checked yore gun yet? Let something like this happen agin, and I'll run you out o' town or hang you. I'll see that you don't get a penny o' that reward money."

"Now sheriff, I ain't drawed this thang yet," Junior replied with a slur.

"Lord help us if you ever do," replied Sheriff Brooks.

The deputy he left in the sheriff's office to guard the gold came rushing into the saloon and up to the sheriff. He turned to face his deputy, who shouted, "The bags are gone! The bags are gone."

"What do ya mean, Popcorn? The bags are gone. I left you at the jail to guard them until I could free Bad Ben. Them was the bags o' gold from that Colorado train robbery."

"I stayed in the jail like you said. Ivory come in and the next thing I knowed, I went outside. Then I got popped from behind. Besides, I'd have guarded them bags better if I'd knowed they was gold."

"What was ya baited with?"

"What do ya mean, Longarm?"

"Was it money or women? I know you don't drink."

"Well, Ivory said there was uh pretty redhead outside. Said that she was too bashful to come in to see me. He said she liked me. Sure enough, I took a peep through the window. The next thing you know, I went outside the jail to see her. I got popped from behind."

"And you wonder why we call ya Popcorn. Where's Ivory?"

"Right here, sheriff," said the little piano player. He was descending the saloon stairs.

"What do you know about Popcorn gitting popped, Ivory?" asked the sheriff gruffly.

"It's like Popcorn said. We went outside the jail, and he started talking with this gorgeous lady. I didn't see any need for me to hang around, so I left them. That's all I know, sheriff."

"I think you know more than you're telling. Search his room, Trigger Happy, Short Fuse. We'll see if he's telling the truth," said the sheriff.

His two deputies who had just returned from locking up Bad Ben, made their way upstairs toward Mr. Jones's room. They soon returned after a short, wall banging and drawer rifling commotion.

"Didn't find a thing except some o' these here girlie books," said Mr. Evans.

"Yeah, uh—uh—they're real uh—girlie stuff uh—uh—all right," said Deputy Randall. He waved a magazine high in the air for all to see.

"Okay, we'll book him fer violating moral decency laws. He'll do more time for that than he would fer stealing the gold." With the sheriff's concluding observation, the officers departed toward the jail with the piano player in tow.

Junior looked up at the barstool he recently occupied. He stared at it as if it were a climb up Mt. Mitchell. Once more he perched himself thereupon and requested another shot of whiskey. Mr. Myers, realized that the reward money might not be forthcoming for Junior. Consequently, he refused to refill his clear shot glass.

"Go git Morty, Tumbleweed," said Mr. Myers. "Don't want these dead Mexicans stinking up the place any more than it already is."

Mr. "Tumbleweed" Adams departed.

"It sure is dull around here," Mr. Myers said, addressing Junior. "Since the town was depleted of manpower last week, this place is dead. But it'll fill back up before long, the way the west is growing. But right now we need some excitement." He pulled a dark cloth off a large, black-barred, bullet-shaped cage to expose a brightly-colored bird.

"Has that cage been there all the time?" Junior asked. He ogled the multi-colored parrot.

"Shore has. Usually we're so busy, we don't need his company. Since we don't have many patrons right now, Gabby provides entertainment. Just listen to him, '*Squawk, squawk,* Shorty's a cuckold. Shorty's a cuckold, *squawk, squawk.* Whitey's a crook, Whitey's a crook, s*quawk, squawk.*'"

"Is that bird a telling the truth?" asked Junior. He squint his eyes first at the barkeeper and then the talking parakeet.

"Every word," replied Mr. Myers.

Junior stared admiringly at the richly colored bird. "How does he stay alive?" he asked.

"That is what's wrong with this country now. People want to shoot every bird that tells the truth."

"I'll be," said Junior. He shook his head and gazed into an empty glass before him.

Mr. Myers took pity on Junior and poured him another shot.

"That's the purtiest bird I ever seen. Where did ya git that there bird, anyways?"

"He belonged to the last editor. When he got run out o' town, I got the bird. He was a real newspaperman. Just had one hang-up: printed the truth. They can tell you all about him over at the Crier office."

"I've been aiming to git over there," he said. He raised his arm for more exercise. "My brother is a reporter." Remaining on the barstool, he contemplated a visit to the Los Villas newspaper office in order to get a line on his brother.

In Mr. Black's office there was a discussion between him and his foreman, Roy Loftis. "I asked that hillbilly at the bar about the man he chased into quicksand," said Mr. Black "He said it was Walla Walla Wally. Miss Rush said that dumb hillbilly told her the same thing. Evidently he chased a man by that name into a puddle of quicksand. He wasn't far from Los Villas when it happened."

"How do you know Miss Rush so good?"

"I knew her in St. Louis before I left there. She got tired of waiting for me and met a man from Denver who was buying supplies. He gave her a big spiel about how he owned a big Colorado silver mine not far outside of Denver. He talked her into taking the Over Land Stage out there to be with him. She went out there and learned too late that he was merely a gambler, a poor one at that. When he lost everything he had in a poker game, they raided his room and took all his valuables. She had nothing left so she stole a horse and rode out of town. She headed straight to Los Villas, or at least tried to. After she hit that hillbilly over the head, she said she got lost for a few days. She was wandering around on the plains when Walla Walla Wally saw her and began to chase her. That's when the hillbilly showed up."

"What is she gonna do here, boss?"

"She can sing in the saloon when I get rid of Lil. Her mother used to sing in saloons in St. Louis, while her grandparents raised her on a small farm in Indiana. When she was sixteen, she left the farm for St. Louis, hoping to find her mother, but she never did, so she sang in saloons like her mother. Her grandmother, on her father's side, was a singer in minstrel shows and also sang on Mississippi riverboats. Singing seems to be in her blood."

"Do ya think we lost Walla Walla Wally, boss?"

"I'm satisfied we have. He should have been here by now. That hillbilly may be stupid, but he's no liar. That brings us back to what to do to get that pesky sheriff out of our hair. We've got to find somebody to do the job."

"Let me and the boys take care o' him, boss."

"We can't risk that, Lightning."

"Why not? The lead we shoot is just as good and will kill jist the same as anybody else's."

"There's a problem with that, Lightning. Longarm was a Texas Ranger. He may not be too smart, but he's steady and honest. If we plug him, every Ranger in Texas will come snooping around here. We'll have Texas Rangers not only coming from all over Texas, but from Kansas and Arkansas, too. We can't risk it."

"Gosh, yore smart boss. No wonder you got into Harvard. What puzzles me is why you didn't go to one o' them big, fancy, southern colleges like they got in Virginia. They're closer to where you growed up in Richmond."

"I couldn't get into a southern college."

"You got into Harvard and couldn't git into a southern college, boss?"

"That's right. You see, I couldn't get into a southern college because I'm a Black."

"Ah boss, you're uh pulling my leg. And the boys say you ain't got a sense o' humor. Was you joking about them Texas Rangers coming out of Kansas and Arkansas, too? And let me ask you this: What are you doing in a dusty, little cow-town like this?"

"I didn't get to finish college. I was in the middle of my third year and my father managed a bank in Richmond. He started taking out loans from Lee General Bank that they couldn't find the paperwork to cover. Needless to say, when the bank president found out about it, my college days were over. I became a pretty good poker player. I was so good that I was sometimes accused of dealing from the bottom of the deck. I had to keep moving and found my golden opportunity right here in Los Villas."

"Gosh, you're pretty sharp boss. I would work fer you with or without these here bullet holes I got up in Colorado and other places."

"Thanks, Lightning. We've got to get somebody to plug that sheriff. Let's go over the list once more. There's Philadelphia Phil."

"Philadelphia Phil is being seen with Pittsburgh Trilby. He's on the make and won't be available any time soon. Not only that, he's learning a new mayor how to use his office to earn money on the side. He is also helping to corral new immigrant voters in Philadelphia. What about Spokane Spike?"

"We can't risk it, Lightning. Washington Territory has already lost Walla Walla Wally. The territory couldn't handle another hit by losing such a valuable outlaw. What about Charlotte Sean?"

"No. He's chasing Altamont Alice. Ain't no way you're going to git him out here in the middle o' nowhere. Besides, them Southern gunslingers talk too slow to be really fast on the draw. Slow speech numbs the trigger finger."

"You're amazing, Lightning. How do you know all these little, juicy tidbits?"

"Heck, that's easy boss. I subscribe to the American Inquisitor," he replied. He pulled a current tabloid-like issue from under his shirt. Sure enough, there were large headlines above every story. A headline on the front page read, "Mummy born to Mexican Woman, Child in Quandary What to Call Mother." In smaller headlines on the left side of the page was a heading, "Who Blew Little Bighorn? Did Custer Try to Shoot the Bull?" Below it was a smaller headline, "Edison Glows over Prospect of Inventing Light Bulb; Evangelist Heralds Invention that will Fight Forces of Darkness." On a second page were more headings; "Lincoln Sighting in Cadillac," "Red Cloud Spotted in Painted Desert," and "Mayor Vows to Improve Corruption." There was an article about Philadelphia Phil under a large photograph of him and Cincinnati Cindy.

"So, that's Philadelphia Phil," mused Mr. Black as he looked closely at the picture.

"Yeah, that's him aw right."

"Why does the left side of his face have a shadow on it?"

"According to the article, that's a big birthmark. That's where I learned about him being active in Philadelphia politics. Heck, he jist about runs Philadelphia and the whole east coast for that matter. You may not git him out here unless they run him off."

"I see. Quite a magazine you have there, Lightning. I'm sure it will never be a success. The public would never be gullible enough to support a publication like that. One that prints hearsay, gossip, assorted superstition, and half-truths is a no-go. Just no way that folks would support it."

"Heck, people believe politicians, don't they?"

"You've got a point there, Lightning. I'll send a wire for Carlsbad Blackie. He can take care of that potbellied sheriff. Now, that hillbilly traded that Mexican's fabulous stallion. He said he traded it to a Colorado gold miner for that old, broken-down, jaded gray out there at the hitching post. I've got to have that big horse for stud purposes. I'm willing to pay five-hundred dollars in gold for that animal. If you can't buy it, steal it. I want that horse."

"If that horse was so valuable, why did you let the hillbilly git hold o' him?"

"Everybody has a little Oklahoma streak that comes out now and then, Lightning. Besides, I didn't know anything about that big Mexican's horse when he rode in here. I've found out that big, black stallion's won just about every horse race in Northern Mexico. What I want is that horse in my corral."

"Suppose you'll put him on yore Oklahoma Injun spread?"

"I've got other plans for that ranch. Besides, it's too danger-ous in Oklahoma. Some outlaw might try to steal him. No. I want that horse for my North Texas ranch."

"Well, Colorado's a dangerous place. I'm not shore you can find a man willing to go into that country. It's overrun with all them Injuns, outlaws, and men crazy with gold fever. A man might never come back out o' there alive."

"I'm counting on you, Lightning."

"Me!" he exclaimed. He recoiled at the thought of once again going into Colorado. "Go in that country agin, alone? I've got three bullet holes in me now from that train hold-up. I'd been a goner if that old miner hadn't found me after them mules scattered. These wounds are still a healing. You trying to git me killed?"

"You're about well. You can take Weasel."

"Can't."

"Why not?"

"I don't trust him. Besides, he's running fer public office. Got his eye on one o' them cushy courthouse jobs. He thinks he can run the whole state if he gits elected to a courthouse office."

"I wonder where he's getting the money to run?

"I don't know," said Mr. Loftis as he flicked some more cigar ashes into the floor.

"He might not be a good choice," said Mr. Black. He rested his right hand against his chin. "Somebody tipped off the railroad about us robbing that gold shipment. The army was there waiting for us like we were sitting ducks. Somebody squealed."

"Yeah, but Weasel didn't know nothing about it."

"I didn't say he did. Only you, Boomer, and I knew, a least in so far as I know. Somebody spilled their guts. When I find out, there'll be one more man for Morty to measure. Anyway, you can take Tumbleweed."

"Oh boss, do I have to? Ya know how people talk and gossip spreads around here. What will people say about me? Besides, he's spending a lot o' time with the padre now."

"Who do you want to take . . . Goldie?"

"Yeah, she looks like the cat that ate the canary."

"She just helped me out several thousand times. Speaking of birds, I want you to poison Gabby. The world isn't ready for a bird that spouts off at the mouth. I should have hung that loose-mouthed bird on Big Harry. I'd have been shut of that pest."

"Well, I can't go into Injun country alone after that horse. About all the boys got killed in the train robbery. Got to have some help."

"How about Ivory? He's a good man when he's sober."

"He'd be a lot better than that unreliable hillbilly. All that hillbilly is interested in is his next drink and places like Bell's. Ya jist can't depend on him. Ivory would be a lot better, providing I can keep him sober. Be worth a try."

"Ivory it is. One other thing: remember Frenchman's Folly?"

"That mine you spent a fortune on and never did hit pay dirt . . . at least not big time pay dirt?"

"That's the one. I want you to take this bag of gold. I want you to sprinkle it behind the last diggings to where it won't be easily noticed. Make it look as if it's in a vein deep inside that worthless old pit. I want you to take this other bag and come back through Roaring Springs. Drink, gamble, and flirt with the girls at the Red Fox Saloon. When the gold is gone, head back to Frenchman's Folly so you'll be followed. Stay there for a couple of days and then start looking for that fabulous stallion. Got it?"

"Shore. Salting a mine; you're a smart one, boss," he said as he flicked some more ashes from his cigar.

Chapter 5
The Visit to the Crier

Junior stepped through the crude wooden door at The Prairie Chicken Crier. Against a far back wall in the small, one room, high-ceiling, newspaper office, a young man sat pecking the keys of a new invention called a finger-stroke typewriter. Behind a high bar and four paces from the door, the tall, intelligent looking editor, Tom Wilson, was conversing with a rancher, customer Jack Bouknight who was standing across the bar from him. Both middle-aged men were about the same height.

Upon Junior's entry both men glanced in his direction. They turned to face one another once more, and Mr. Bouknight continued their conversation. He said, "Shore glad we broke that treaty with them Indians. We need more land for our cattle to graze."

"We've broken every treaty we've ever made with the Indians," replied Mr. Wilson. Tom Wilson was what most folks would call a self-made man. His grandfather, according to family lore, died at the Alamo, and his father, James Wilson, was raised by a single mother. James was a Confederate Veteran who, after the war, moved to West Texas to try his luck at cattle ranching. Tom was the oldest child in a family of thirteen. At an early age, he was apprenticed to a newspaper editor in Pecos, Texas, where he learned the business inside and out. To Tom, a newspaper was where the action was. He bought The Crier when it became available a few years earlier. He continued the conversation by adding, "Which treaty are you referring to?"

"Oh heck, Tom," replied Mr. Bouknight. "I keep forgetting that you side with them savages." Jack Bouknight was the youngest of seven children who was reared in the hills of Arkansas. He sought his fortune first on the Mississippi River by barging freight from St. Louis to New Orleans. He later worked as a surveyor and then as an engineer for the Overland Railroad where he earned enough money to buy a large ranch near Los Villas. He was no stranger to hard work.

"This is what I'm saying, Jack. The Indians were as free as the golden eagles and living close to nature. We took their land and what have we replaced it with? We're bridled with taxes, saddled with government, and spurred by demagogues."

"You ought to sell your papers to the Indians. You don't seem to think us civilized white folks count."

"You misunderstand how I feel, Tom. All I'm saying is that it should never have gotten to this point. The army is slaughtering innocent women and children in their sleep. I mean, there's such a thing as decency. We could have handled this Indian situation a whole lot better. In so far as I know, this is the first time in recorded history this has been done. We're employing a policy to exterminate a less developed people."

"You obviously haven't read in the Bible. Look how the Israelites took back the Promised Land. Besides, it's not our policy to exterminate the Indians, Tom. Show me where it's written."

"It doesn't have to be written, Jack. Those fancy talking, tea drinking, cunning Englishmen sat in their laced drawing rooms on the Thames in London. They looked down their devious noses at the rest of the so called uncivilized world. Their intention was to use all the force necessary against the unorganized, sparsely settled American settlements. They wanted to make their colonial system profitable by any means necessary. That was the policy at Jamestown, and it has continued to this day. There isn't a thing that we can use to justify what we're doing or have done to these people. Right now, all you hear is, 'the only good Indian is a dead Indian.' If that isn't a policy of extermination, I don't know what is."

"What about all our innocent people that were attacked and scalped. These savages showed no mercy when those innocent settlers were crossing the plains to Oregon and California. Doesn't that count, Indian lover?"

"What do you do, Jack, when you spot a trespasser on your ranch?

"I shoot and ask questions later."

"That's what I'm saying. If anyone owned this country before us, it was the Indians. They were here first. It's a national tragedy the way we've treated these people. There's no justification in law, warfare, or scripture for what we've done."

"Darn it, Tom, I just told you about the Israelites. Besides, we'll have plenty of time to repent . . . once the Indians run out o' land," he said while laughing.

"Maybe so, but the stain against our national character will never wash out. Someday, say fifty years from now, our leaders will sit on the world stage with other great leaders. We'll be reminded of our broken treaties and treacheries against these tribes. In fact, it wouldn't surprise me at all if some dictator cited us as an example. He could justify wiping out an entire minority group within his own country. He would then dare us to complain about it."

"Tom, you worry too much. Haven't you read that, 'he who is without sin cast the first stone?' There isn't a country in the world that hasn't committed what we've done or worse.

Heck, politicians can twist it to make it look like we done the Indians a favor. It wouldn't surprise me one bit if we tried to tell others how to run their countries. Our politicians could put a happy face on the Devil."

"That's the whole point, Jack. That's what will make us look foolish in the eyes of the rest of the world."

"Who gives a hoot about what the rest o' the world thinks. Let them mind their own business, and we'll mind ours. Besides, we won't have to break any more treaties . . . once they're out o' territory. Well, run that ad. I need some hands to drive a herd o' cattle into Arizona Territory. I'm hoping to get that herd out there before winter and before the range is completely fenced off. I'm paying top dollar."

Mr. Bouknight turned to face Junior, and said, "Here's a man that looks like he'd like to earn some money. How about it, cowboy? I'm driving a herd o' cattle into Arizona. I'll pay you fifty dollars for the drive. If ninety percent of the five thousand head makes it there alive, I'll give you a ten dollar bonus. How about it?"

"Mr. Bouknight is as good as his word," echoed Editor Wilson.

"Gosh, I don't know."

"Hey, ain't you the one that got that big Mexican's horse and wound up with a broke down gray?"

"Yeah, reckon I am."

"That gray won't last a mile out on the trail; no, sir. Doesn't have the stamina, or the savvy. Tell you what; ride with my boys and we'll cut you out a cow pony from my corral. He'll be smarter than half the cowhands that'll be on the trail with us. When we get back, he's yours."

"I don't know whether to go or not."

"Tell you what. Once this drive's over, I'll throw the biggest fiesta Texas has ever seen. There'll be dancing, barbecued grub, and all the liquor a man can guzzle."

"Got yoreself a deal! When do we start?" he asked while grabbing Mr. Bouknight's hand.

"Great!" replied the rancher. He began to rub his crushed right hand. "Be at my ranch come Monday morning and we'll get you started on the cattle drive. You can find my ranch; everybody knows where it is. My spread is the biggest one in North Texas." He turned to Editor Wilson, and continued, "Thanks again, Tom. Be sure to make that a big ad for cowhands. Quit worrying about them savages. The Lord's give us the land now. See you. See you come Monday morning, cowboy," he said as he was departing.

"What can I do for you, young man?" asked the editor who was slightly taller.

"Well, I'm a looking fer my brother who's a reporter. They said he use to work here. His name was Josh Justus. Back home we call him Dickens. He aw-ways wanted to be a writer. Heck, he even went to college at North Ca'lina University."

"Yes, I see a resemblance," replied the editor. After the initial shock of someone asking about the former editor, Josh Justus, at which time Mr. Wilson dropped his pen and the pecking on the typewriter suddenly stopped in the background, he continued his reply, "He was the editor here before I came. To the best of my knowledge when he first came here, he was well liked."

He strolled over to a stack of previously published Crier newspapers. "In fact, what few readers we have here in Los Villas found his headlines rather amusing. For instance, take this heading describing the burning of a Turkish national in Athens. Here's your brother's headline 'Turk Fries in Greece.'" He picked up another Crier in the stack, and said, "Or, take this one about Grant's interceding in an Arkansas governorship dispute. 'Grant Aids Baxter in Crossing Brooks at Little Rock.'" He picked up another that read "Polygamist Vows Celibacy, Brotherhood Pledges Assistance" and another, "Bell Sued over Phone." He laid the old newspaper back and said, "Your brother also did literary reviews." He picked up another paper and said, "Take this one, 'Tom Sawyer Marks Twain,' or this one, 'Henry James Unveils Portrait of a Lady.'"

"Some readers began to take offence. Take this headline 'Mule train Side Tracked by Crazy Horse' or, 'Squatters Stand against Sitting Bull' or, this one, 'Starving Indians Blamed for Reservation Stew.' And look at these," he said as he continued to flip through the stack to show and to read Junior the head-lines. "'Rangers Angle Bass at Round Rock,' 'Fate Deals Last Hand to Hickok; Cashes in Chips at Deadwood,' 'Mormons stay Young at Salt Lake,' 'Nast Unravels Tweed,' 'Liquor Sales to Miners Halted, Improper Aging Cited,' 'Indians Occupy Fort, Lawyer says Sioux,' and 'Blue Coat called Yellow in Black Hills by late Redskin.'

"Your brother had quite a sense of humor. He might have gotten away with all those articles had he not printed one particular short story. He wrote it and not one of the big eastern publications would take a chance on publishing it. So, since they refused to print it, he took it upon himself to run it right here in The Crier." He reached down into the top drawer behind the counter and pulled out another newspaper. He placed it atop the counter and opened it to the short story to which he was referring. Mr. Wilson said, "Here, read this article titled 'Calvin.' I'll explain it after you've finished. You can sit in that chair over there in the corner."

Junior moved toward a green, ladder-back chair as Mr. Wilson began to wait on another customer that just entered.

Junior sat down with the old newspaper in his hands. His lips started to move as he began to read silently.

Calvin

Author's Note: The following, classified by necessity as a work of fiction, is a true story. Only the names and places have been changed to protect the innocent and /or guilty.

A cold, clear, blue eye of a January morning stared down on West Texas. Tom Rains had an order pad in hand when he called on his first business customer in Hyattsville. He was a dry goods and grocery supply salesman who drove his route with four mules hitched to a creaky, antiquated wagon. Tom stepped briskly into a heartless, frozen Main Street and entered Mulls General Store where he hoped to find the owner, Jean Jordan. It was his first stop of the day and Mulls was the town's largest retailer. He spied two tall, slender, familiar male employees that were casually dressed in plaid shirts and Levi's.

Tom asked, "Where's Jean."

Jean Jordan, like Tom, was in her early forties. Eight years earlier when he began to call on her business, he thought that she was a very handsome lady. She had straw, blonde hair, a fair, smiling face, lovely figure, and carried on a friendly conversation that put friends, acquaintances, and customers at ease. On several occasions, she related to Tom that her husband, Calvin, nine years her senior, had a drinking problem that was a source of their conjugal unhappiness. His was a tender ear for her woeful tale.

For years, Mulls supplied goods to the growing Hyattsville area. Her customers were comprised of war veterans, poor Mexicans, struggling ranchers, miners, and younger folks moving into West Texas. Jean had a soft heart and sometimes sold items on credit to the down-and-out to the detriment of the business. Payments on store debts trickled in so slowly that it placed a strain on the bottom line; so much so, that it made it difficult to continue to operate. Only by shrewd management and cost cutting did she manage to keep the doors open. Tom respected Jean for being a successful and resourceful business woman.

"She's gone to the beauty shop to git beautified," replied Bob Collins.

Bob was tall and wiry, with dark hair and a light complexion. He was in his mid-forties and had been with Mulls even before Jean became the owner. He drew down one corner of his mouth when talking. This was one of his traits as was his nasal twang. His chief duties were stocking supplies, loading sold goods onto wagons, and doing most of the hard labor involved in operating the store. He also served in the unofficial capacity of supervising the man standing beside him, Lonnie Jones.

Tom knew the pair was competent and trusted employees. Jean relied heavily upon Mr. Collins for advice when it came to managing the store. Tom took a seat on a hard, wooden nail-keg near a warm potbellied stove that monopolized the middle of the rough, wooden structure.

With a sigh Tom said, "Poor Jean, has she still got family problems?"

"She'll always have family problems," Bob replied crisply. He had taken a seat on a bulky, wooden bench near a large window facing a narrow alley. His piquant, gray eyes were locked onto Tom's

small russet eyes. His partner, Lonnie Ray, was almost a carbon copy, at least in appearance, of Mr. Collins. Mr. Ray continued to stand beside the big stove radiating heat into the building.

"The last time I was here she was upset by a letter from her daughter. Did her daughter ever get a divorce?"

"Yeah, thank so," Bob replied.

"Poor Jean, it's a shame that Calvin stays drunk all the time," Tom muttered. "I don't see how she puts up with a husband like that. It seems a shame that a nice woman like Jean should have a husband like that."

"Who told you that?" Bob ejaculated with the force of a fired Remington rifle. His muscles became taut, and he balled his strong fingers into fists.

"Why . . . uh . . . er . . ." Tom stammered. He alternately turned red and then pale as though he had been discovered in a ladies', public restroom. "Everybody knows Jean has problems with Calvin because he's a drunk."

"Somebody told you wrong!" Bill retorted. "She was running around on him long before he ever started drinking. Don't take my word for it. Just walk-up and down Main Street here and ask anybody. Why, she's wrecked more Scott County homes than termites and house fires put together. Before he sold her this business, the old man Sylvester told me and Lonnie; he says, 'Keep close to the kitchen, boys fer she'll burn the beans.' She hadn't owned the place a week 'til I knowed what the old man meant. The more trashy and sloppy the character is, the better she likes 'im. Won't have nobody respectable. She made Calvin a cuckold long before he ever distinguished himself by becoming the town drunk." he concluded. His conviction was so firm that Tom dared not challenge it.

"That's the truth," echoed Lonnie.

Bob continued, "I hate to tell visitors these things about our boss lady. But you brought it up, and it's the truth. Oh, she's been good to us and treated us fair. We can't complain about that." His last words trailed off sadly.

"Well," said Tom who felt as though he had just escaped being caressed by a falling, two-hundred-fifty-year-old, oak tree, "I know some pious people who're the dickens to work for. There ain't no way you can please them or satisfy them by anything you do. I'd say, all in all, you fellows are pretty lucky."

"I suppose we are,' Bob replied. He glared tacitly at Lonnie, and they went about their work. They began to stack some large, heavy sacks of feed grain beside the entrance to the back office. With the conversation over, Tom departed.

Tom addressed his mules from his wagon seat. As a cold wind cut like a sharp knife into his bare, beardless face, he woefully thought, "I'll never see Jean in the same effulgent glow as before. No sir, it's like my dad once told me, 'You have no need to kill a man with a gun when all it takes is a loose tongue.'" His impression of her character was no longer like that of a tranquil, landscape painting by an Italian master. It was more like a bleak black-and-white photograph of a bombarded Civil War battle site. His perception of her was in ruins, and to him Hyattsville would never be the same.

Junior's lips stopped moving. With the reading of the article finished, he waited for Mr. Wilson to finish serving a customer, after which, he edged up to the counter and laid down the newspaper.

Mr. Wilson turned his attention to Junior and said, "After that article ran, other Texas Newspapers quickly picked it up and ran it. In fact, it was run in just about every newspaper from one end of Texas to the other. It even appeared in Colorado, New Mexico, and Kansas. Of course, they gave Josh the credit and told readers that it came from Los Villas' Crier.

"It wasn't long until about every business woman within a five-hundred-mile radius of Los Villas had an angry husband on her hands. They came swarming into town demanding Josh's hide.

"Local subscribers were outraged by some of his other stories. A committee of angry, local folks gathered in the Avalanche Saloon. They decided the best solution for all concerned was for Mr. Justus to leave town.

"Since Josh was an honorable man, he felt that he had done nothing wrong and refused to go.

"Rather than burn the newspaper office to the ground, some of the boys found where he was hiding. They took him out to a local ranch. They placed him aboard a huge, mean, never before ridden critter they called Big Harry. A group of cowboys, onlookers, curiosity-seekers, and well-wishers said their good-byes. They waved as pistols were fired into the air while Josh rode off into the sunrise. Witnesses said Tom tore off that ranch like a twisting tornado toward Topeka."

"Does anybody know where he's at?"

"Nobody knows for sure. I've heard various rumors from time to time. They say that he's in this place or that place; nothing you can pin down. I'd say he's still in the newspaper business in some capacity. That is if somebody hasn't shot him.

"You need to be careful with the *Truth* in this business. Some people don't like to be written about when they're put in a bad light. This newspaper business gets into your blood, and it can get you killed. I'm sure you know what I mean."

"Yeah. One thang I'd like to ast ya, Mr. Wilson," Junior said as he leaned forward on the counter.

"Sure, Mr. Justus."

Junior leaned even closer and whispered, "What's a cuckold?"

"It's a man whose wife is unfaithful to him. In fact, no one in town knew what the word meant until your brother came out with that story. I think that he taught his pet parakeet to say it.

"Some of the boys had never been interested in education in their lives. They beat down schoolmarm Henderson's schoolhouse door hounding her as to what the word meant. Boy, was that old maid schoolteacher embarrassed when they kept coming and asking.

"No, sir, few stories have captured this town's imagination like that one did. Speculation was rampant about who the characters in the story might have been. Everybody suspected it was Bill Matthews and his wife Peggy. He was the town drunk, and she ran a local saloon."

Thanks fer yore he'p," said Junior. "I'll check with ye from time to time to see if ya've heard anythang."

"Oh, before you leave, here is a short poem Josh wrote. I think that he was looking for a musician to set it to music. He was about to run it with a story in the Crier just before he left town. You might want to keep it."

Junior placed it in his pants pocket after silently reading the short poem. It read:

TEXAS IN THE HEART OF ME

From the Rio Grande to the Canadian,
From El Paso to the mighty Alamo;
Out where bluebonnet and cactus grow,
From Oklahoma to Mexico.

From the park at Big Bend,
I feel you deep from within;
In my soul you slowly grow,
And this much I know:

Chorus:
I've got Texas in the heart of me,
Blue skies open to eternity;
Oh, how I love being free,
I've got Texas in the heart of me.

I love that never ending sky:
In Texas is where I want to die.
That's how I want it to be:
I've got Texas in the heart of me

Junior left The Crier with a sad heart. He was no closer to finding his brother than before. He untied his horse from the newspaper's hitching post. He mounted and departed in the direction of the Avalanche Saloon. He stopped in the street to let an old man drive his three, frisky goats across the street in front of him. To the little, old man Riley "Papa Lode" Roberts who wore tattered clothes, Junior said, "Howdy."

"How'd ya like to swap that there hoss fer these here goats?" Papa Lode asked as he turned to face Junior. "I need to git back to them Colorado gold fields."

"I'm not inter-rested, Papa Lode," replied Junior. He knew Mr. Roberts because he often played cards in the Avalanche Saloon and was easily recognizable due to his manner of dress and short stature. Junior surmised that Papa Lode won the goats in a poker game. He claimed that he was raised by Indians and grew up on the Colorado frontier where he became a Kit Carson sidekick. He survived by hunting, trapping, and panning for gold.

The little man screwed up his dark eyes and contorted his face. He spat a week's collection of tobacco juice into the street, and said, "Swap ye two of my best goats fer that broke down, old nag. Got two real fine milkers here, Nina and Betsy."

"I ain't inter-rested," replied Junior who, without tobacco, matched the miner's spit.

"I'll even throw in my billy, Ringer. Be a real swap fer ye."

"Na, shucks, Papa Lode. I got to have my horse. Ain't got no use fer yore goats," Junior replied. He yanked the reins with his left hand to urge his horse on down the street.

"Tell ya what," shouted the little man through a tobacco-stained beard, "I'll give ya my two milkers, my billy, and a pint o' whiskey to boot. It's the best whiskey east o' the Rockies. That's my final offer."

"Got yoreself a deal," he replied. He pulled the reins to halt his horse in its tracks and quickly dismounted. Junior handed the old man the slick, worn reins and collected his pint of whiskey.

He attempted to drive his giddy goats down the street while the goatherd rubbed a sore right hand. It soon became apparent to any bystander that Junior was no goatherd. It took him over an hour to drive his new acquisitions to an open area behind the Avalanche Saloon, a distance of fifty-three paces. While driving the goats, he was in no hurry because he stopped at intervals. He felt compelled to sample the best whiskey east of the Rockies.

Lil watched Junior and the goats from her upstairs window. His new acquisitions were behind the saloon sampling the damp garments hanging on a long clothesline, knocking over rain barrels, and munching grain on loaded wagons. Junior was ineffective in dealing with the chaos.

He bent over to retrieve a plaid shirt where Ringer nibbled it enough to pull it from its mooring on a taut clothesline. He saw his opportunity to reward his new master by charging the juicy target that Junior afforded. While running at full speed, the billy butted Junior so hard that he landed in a watering trough several feet away. Only a malfunction in his slimy, water soaked six-shooter saved the rambunctious goat from a violent fate. Junior wasn't angry so much for the sudden butt as he was for the broken half bottle of whiskey mixing with the fresh water in the watering trough.

Only fifteen paces away, Ringer stood glaring toward Junior in the watering trough as several times his faulty six-gun hammer went click. He could not coax the six-gun to fire.

Lil rushed down from her room. She called the spry goats to her side and had mastery of them almost immediately. As Junior crawled from the watering trough, she asked, "What are you gonna do with these goats?" All the goats were behind her and were looking intently at Junior.

"Why, how did ya git them goats to mind ya like that?"

"I suppose some people have a gift," she replied while gently rubbing one of Ringer's horns.

He carefully considered his goat situation for a few minutes. At last he said, "Let's take them north to Whitey's ranch. He won't mind."

Junior and Lil drove the docile goats to Mr. Black's ranch two miles away. They herded them in a large, empty corral fifty paces away from the Black's sprawling, ritzy, Spanish style hacienda. They returned to the saloon where they passed a pleasant evening together.

Chapter 6
Return from the Cattle Drive

In the Avalanche Saloon, Saturday nights were always a lively bee-hive of activity. Under hot-blast kerosene lamp lighting, customers were drinking whiskey, playing cards, smoking cigars, telling lies, and listening to the cacophonous songs being vocalized by the new saloon singer Julie "Goldie" Rush. It was a convivial time in the relatively new western town of Los Villas. Mr. Jacobs could not wait to relate tall tales about rancher Bouknight's recently concluded cattle drive into Arizona Territory. He soon got his chance.

Miss Rush took a break from singing. Mr. Jacobs left his poker table and sauntered up to the bar, ordered a drink, and through the smoke filled and whiskey scented atmosphere, he faced the patrons who came from ranches, railroads, and mines far and near. "Junior," he began in a voice that boomed all across the crowded saloon, "you boys know him; he's that hillbilly that rode in here on a stinking camel."

"Yeah, we know him," replied a tipsy patron that was feeling no pain.

"The dumb one that rode in here and shot his foot off," shouted another.

"Yeah, that's him," Mr. Jacobs continued. "We got the herd to moving on the trail going down toward El Paso. Well, Junior got to chasing strays and come up on this old miner. This miner was going to hunt fer gold in Colorado. Well, sir, this hillbilly stops his horse; that's the one Mr. Bouknight let him have to ride on the drive. He traded that broke down horse he had fer some silly goats. Anyway, Junior halts his horse when he sees this old miner who seemed to have a problem with his mule. Junior ties his horse to a mesquite bush and sidles over to see what's the matter. The miner is all in a fuss about a horsefly that's just eating his mule alive. 'I don't know what I'm gonna do,' says the old miner slinging his hat at the fly. 'He balks so much, I ain't never gonna git to them gold fields.'

"Junior says, 'Let me take a look.' He walks around the mule to size up the situation. He stands in front o' that mule there in the blazing Texas sun. He spits out of the side o' his mouth and just misses the miner's leg. You know, I think all that whiskey he guzzles turns to spit. Anyway, he rubs his hawk nose and to the old miner, he says, 'Why, I kin fix that there fly.' You boys know how stupid them hillbillies talk.

"'You can?' says the old miner.

"'Shore kin!'

"Then the miner says, 'Do it then! I'd do anything to git rid o' that pesky, old fly.'

"So, Junior draws his six-shooter. He aims it right between that mule's eyes and pulls the trigger and plugs him. That's before the miner realized what Junior had been planning to do. Well, sir, that mule died right there in his tracks. That astonished miner couldn't believe his eyes. He rushes around, bends down on his knees and holds the mule's head in his hands. Where he's lying there a dying on the ground, the old miner's beside himself. He says, 'My gawd, you've kilt my mule. Not only that, you missed that cussed horsefly. Just look at the darn thing. He's still buzzing around his belly.'

"Ole Junior spits again and says, 'By golly, yore right.' Then he added, 'That fly may still bother yore mule, but he won't know nothing about it.'"

When the laughter ebbed, Mr. Jacobs continued with his story. "The Miner says, 'Oh, my precious mule.' With tears in his eyes, he said, 'I ain't got nothing to carry my supplies to the gold fields. He's my only company out there in them mountains.' While the miner was moaning, Junior was examining the ground where he shot the mule. On one knee he reached down and picked up that big, dead horsefly. He held it between a finger and thumb and raised it toward the sky. It had a bullet hole right through the side of its belly. It was in his right hand, and he turned it fer the miner to see. He said, 'Look a here! I did git him, too.'

"The miner dropped the mule's head and glared up at the hillbilly. He says, 'My gawd, you kilt my mule and there's still one a buzzing around my head!'

"Ole Junior reaches down for the gun in his holster and starts to draw. He says, 'Is that fly a bothering you?'"

When the laughter ebbed, he continued. "And the miner reaches out with his hands to hold Junior's hand on the six-gun to keep him from drawing it. He says, 'No! No! It ain't a bothering me.'"

When the laughter died, Mr. Rowe took up the banter with another story. He said, "We was on the way back from Arizona after we delivered all them cattle. One evening the foreman told Junior to help out our cook. The foreman says, 'Rustle up some grub, hillbilly.' So, heck, ole Junior leaves camp and is gone a long time. He's gone fer so long that ole Saddle Leather, that's the foreman, Bill Johnson, forgets about the hillbilly. Hours later, Junior drives three scrawny looking heifers into where we was camped. He sidles up to the cook, and says, 'There, I rustle them cows up fer ya. Now, we kin cook them.'

"Well, everybody was wondering where he got them cows. Sure enough, it wasn't five minutes until half the cowhands in the Pecos come swarming into camp. They was whooping and hollering and shooting it up. They were slinging lead everywhere and at everybody. Old Saddle Leather did one o' the coolest explaining jobs about that hillbilly you ever seen. He kept us all from getting strung up fer buzzard bait. Yes sir, that dim-witted hillbilly nigh got us all killed."

Junior made his way down the back steps amid the saloon laughter. He had been to see Lil and was headed for the front entrance of the Avalanche Saloon. Entering before him were two huge, rugged cowboys about to make their way through the swinging doors. Leroy Forbes was the cowboy on the left who noticed a scrawny, scantily clad Indian standing by the swinging doors just outside the busy saloon. To his big partner, he said, "There's a durned Injun." He approached the standing Indian, clinched his fists, and hit him with a big right, roundhouse swing. That barely conscious, battered Indian lay on the hard ground spitting out teeth and blood.

His partner Ronald "Bull" Simpson asked, "What did ya do that fer, Slick?"

"Heck, Bull, my parents was scalped on a wagon train to Oregon."

"Come on, Slick. I know better than that. Both o' yore parents are still alive. Heck, they live down in Dallas." After a short a pause, he continued, "I know what's eating you. Yore wife got wind o' you messing around that new place across the street. She knows all about the place that Miss Bell runs. That's the burr under yore saddle."

"Yeah, had a rough day. Had to take out on something, Bill."

"Why didn't ya take it out on that darkie we passed back down the street?"

"You kidding? I don't want to git in trouble and throwed in jail; darkies vote now. Besides, I didn't see him."

Before Junior entered the saloon, he lifted the little Indian to his feet. He helped to dust him off, and said, "Sorry this happen to ya little feller. Jist some thangs we can't do nothing about." After grunting, the disheveled, injured Indian regained his composure and looked appreciatively into Junior's eyes. He slowly moved his feet and quietly slipped away into the shadows.

Junior entered the saloon and ordered a drink at the bar. It was with the money he earned from the cattle drive. While Miss Rush was singing, Junior was drinking, and Mr. Jacobs was standing at the bar thinking. He was still in a bantering mood when at last he sidled over to the barstool where Junior was sitting. He took a barstool seat beside Junior and pivoted to face Miss Rush who was on stage. With a simper and for the consumption of the gathered saloon patrons, in a loud, bellowing voice, he asked, "How did it go on the cattle drive, Junior?"

"Purty good, except coming back," he replied, spitting into the floor. "Thought I was going to have to fight a darkie."

"Oh really," said Mr. Jacobs. He motioned for busy barkeeper Myers to slide him his usual foaming beer down the length of the smooth bar. Miss Rush quit singing and the piano music stopped.

"Yeah, I was down there in Texas near them big mountains. I got lost on the trail from the other fellers coming back. We was coming back from Arizona when I run into this little, skinny feller. He was so skinny a blacksnake would o' pass fer his brother. Anyways, he was standing by a campfire roasting a hunk o' meat. It was from a steer he kilt close by a little earlier. I rode up, got off uh my horse, and I says, 'Howdy, feller. Yore the first dark eye Mexican I've seen on the trail.' Well, he's got a gun point at me and puts it back in his holster; I thank he was scared o' me, I rode up so fast. He put his gun back when he seen I wasn't no threat. He drawed up his shoulders real puffy and frown real mean and ugly at me. He then turn the steak over and says, 'I ain't a Mexican. I'm a darkie.'" He paused to imbibe.

"Well, what happened?" asked Mr. Jacobs. His tone of voice indicated that he was now more interested in Junior's story than making sport of him for the patrons's benefit.

"Well," he said. He spit a tobacco-free discharge into the floor without hitting anyone. "I says, 'I'm a darkie.' That's an old mountain expression to show sirprise or disbelief.

"Anyways, he turn from tending to his steak, and I could tell he was real mad. He says, 'I ain't a Mexican, and yore making fun o' me fer being a darkie. He started to go fer his gun. Well, boys, from behind some big rocks beside the pass I hear a man's voice real loud and bold. He says, 'Wouldn't go fer that gun, Carlsbad Blackie. Not if ya want to go on breathing.' That's what this here big, tall feller said as he step out from behind some rocks. He had a big pistol strap on his hip that was as big as a cannon. He was ready to make a play. He was as cool as a blue norther.

"That darkie was real edgy and nervous. He says, 'Wyatt Earp!' When he said Wyatt Earp, my jaw drop to my ankles. I'd aw-ways heard about that famous lawman, but I never dream o' laying my eyes on him.

"Well, that darkie made a beeline fer his horse as hard as his scared legs could run. He jump a straddle of his saddle and tore out o' that place. He spur that horse like a spooky hant was a hanging onto his heels. He tore out o' there like a flush fox on far. Well, me and Mr. Earp got on our horses and give chase. We found him a few minutes later. His horse stop at a bobbed warr fence, and Blackie jist kept right on a going. We got down off our horses and check him over. He was deader than Cleveland's election chances. His clothes was tore off from that bobbed warr, and his neck was wrung lack a dinner goose. He didn't move no more. He couldn't even lift a fanger."

"That barbed wire is mean stuff," Mr. Jacobs said, nodding his head.

"Yeah," said Leroy Forbes who was seated at the end of the bar. "They say the whole range is going to be fenced off in five years."

"Blasted sod busters ain't going to keep me from grazing my Cattle," shouted Ronald Simpson. He was sitting by Mr. Forbes. His eyes were wild with a restless angst. "I'll graze my cattle anywhere I want to. Ain't no sod buster gonna keep my cattle from grass."

Those with unlimited power have numerous spies to keep them informed. Word of Carlsbad Blackie's demise quickly reached the ears of Mr. Black who was sitting in his office. He fretted visibly because his latest diabolical ruse to rid himself of the Los Villas sheriff had failed. At last, he dismissed his informant, Mr. Harry Warren, with a wave of his right hand. He then turned to his trusted foreman, Mr. Loftis.

A fuming Mr. Black said, "That clod's goats have eaten my exotic East Indian Shrubs. He's chased Walla Walla Wally into a bottomless sinkhole. He's squandered away the best horse in West Texas. And now they say he's creamed Carlsbad Blackie with the help of Wyatt Earp. There's just one thing to do with that witless hillbilly."

"Rub him out, Whitey?"

"No, no, no, Lightning. I want to kill two Indians with one arrow. I want Lil off my hands, and I want her to take those destructive goats and that stupid hillbilly with her. I know for a fact that they're keen on each other."

"How are you going to do that?"

"I will appeal to her woman's higher instincts."

"You mean tempt her with lots o' money, gold, and fancy clothes?

"Exactly, Lightning. I'm going to offer her money and my ranch northeast of here just below Kansas. I've got to get that ceaseless, incessant talker off my hands."

"Why, that's-no-man's land. It's Oklahoma Territory. Heck, Texas don't want it, and Kansas wouldn't have it. Washington can't even decide if it's there. Ain't nothing there but thieving outlaws, murdering Injuns, and miles-and-miles o' wasteland. Nobody in their right mind would settle in a place like that."

"We know that, but those two don't," said Mr. Black with his enthusiasm returning. "It would be an excellent place to raise goats and drink to forget where you are. We still have a problem with that dumb sheriff. He might accidentally stumble onto one of my schemes. He could spoil everything."

"I know you said you didn't want another gunfighter out o' Washington. But this Spokane Spike is really making a name fer himself out there in Washington Territory. They say he's the fastest gun ever to set foot on the other side o' them Rockies. Not only that, he ain't afraid o' nothing. He's married to Kennewick Connie but he killed Vancouver Chuck over Tacoma Trixie. Killed Chuck in Trapper John's Saloon in Colville. He's itching to marry Trixie."

"Lightning, I thought you said Spike was married to Kennewick Connie?"

"Heck, that don't mean nothing; Spike's a Mormon."

"I guess I'll have to swallow my pride, Lightning. It looks like Spokane Spike is the only hired gun that can get past that stupid hillbilly. I need him here to do the job on the sheriff. I'll dash off a telegram out there to get him to come here right away. By the way, where did you get this new information about Spike?"

"Oh, heck, that's easy. It's right here in the American Inquisitor," he said. He pulled the latest issue from under his shirt and opened it to the front page for Mr. Black to see.

The front-page headline read "Will South Dakota get rid of Deadwood for Statehood?" Mr. Loftis slid his fingers across another article on the same page entitled "Indian takes UFO ride Following Treaty Signing."

"Maybe I should get into tabloids where the real money is."

"What?" asked Mr. Loftis who contorted his face to indicate that he didn't understand.

"Nothing, Lightning. Now, I want you to go out there and see to it that the hillbilly gets to the Bouknight fiesta tonight. I don't want him to get so drunk that he can't make it. I'll see that Lil gets there with bells on. Yes, sir, I've got a feeling that Cupid's going to play tonight," mused Mr. Black.

"Cupid? I thought Mr. Bouknight had Bill Green's boys lined up fer the music. Why, he's got one o' the finest fiddle players in these here parts. Ole Billy Collins can scratch fiddle strings like nobody's business. Never heard o' them Cupid feller musicians."

Mr. Loftis departed to keep a watchful eye on Junior at the bar. Suddenly the saloon's swinging doors burst open and a slender, young man entered, saw Junior, and rushed up to him. In a high, strident voice, he said, "An old Indian squaw is here to see you. She's in an Over Land Stagecoach in front of the sheriff's office."

"What old woman, Tumbleweed?" asked Mr. Myers who was pouring Mr. Loftis a whiskey.

"I don't know. She looks like a dried up prune. I'd say she's a hundred years old if she's a day."

"Darn," shouted Mr. Rowe from a back table where he was holding a hand of cards, "I bet it's that haggard, old spook folks claim to see from time to time. Probably ain't nothing there. People that's seen her say she's that blasted old squaw. You know, the one that claims she helped Lewis and Clark explore the Northwest. Over Land supposedly gives her a free ride to anywhere she wants to go. If she even exists, bet she's so old that she knowed George Washington."

"That squaw's so old," added Mr. Jacobs, "that she was here when the Mississippi was a brook at New Orleans. I think you're right; she's got to be a spook."

"If she's the one, her name is Saka Jawea," said Mr. Myers who was staring straight at Junior. "But I don't get it. If it's Saka, she's been dead over fifty years."

"That's why they call that old squaw a spook, Guts," said Mr. Rowe.

"But they say the woman's smart," replied Mr. Myers. "They say she's the Dolly Madison of the Injun tribes. I don't know why in the devil she would want to see somebody like Junior. I guess it would take a spook to want to see him."

"Tumbleweed is always making things up. I doubt that there's anybody out there, spook or no spook," added Mr. Rowe.

"How in the devil would a spook know the likes o' you?" asked Mr. Myers as he looked down condescendingly at Junior.

"Probably got wind of ya having a sore elbow from pouring me drinks," Junior quipped tartly. He added, "She could have a brand new idea on how to keep ya from falling in the floor back there. Whitey ought to buy ya a mattress to fall on back there." He headed for the swinging doors.

Junior's vision adjusted to the darkness. His eyes began to take in the swarthy face of the wrinkled, elderly woman sitting in the stage's back seat near an oblong window. "I'm so glad that you could take the time to come and see me," she began. "I know how busy you must be. And you're the Junior Justus that Bent Birch and Mr. Earp told me so much about. They praised you so much that I just had to look you up. If all white men were like you and Mr. Earp, this country would be in wonderful hands. Say, I detect some Indian features in your face; Mr. Earp was right. Which tribe?" She spoke with perfect diction in a crisp, clear voice with neither a trace of a twang nor a hint of an accent.

"My grandma was a full Cherokee."

"How nice. That's the sophisticated, snobby Southern Tribe. Some of them marched into Oklahoma and have about taken it over. They drawl so slowly and stretch their sentences so subtly that one hardly notices how snobby they are. Oh, well, you're very nice though, and I won't hold your grandmother against you. Let me give you some advice, Mr. Justus. Don't hunt and fish for a living; farm the land. That's what you must do to survive. You see, the buffalo and wild game are practically gone. Some of the streams will be over-fished before long; the land is already over hunted. But just look at all these beautiful, rolling hills and fertile valleys. They're just waiting to be tilled, and they will support a superior civilization. Oh, there's a bountiful storehouse to be had. Farming this fertile land can provide you food for survival—are you listening to me, young man?"

When asked if he was listening, his attention was diverted. Music in the saloon suddenly stopped and several bursts of gunfire shattered the night air. Junior turned his head toward the Avalanche saloon where he saw gun and cigar smoke boiling through the swinging doors. He even imagined that he caught an offal whiff of the wafting, boiling stench. He turned his face back to her and replied, "Yeah, I'm a listening."

"You're so intelligent," she said. "That's what I'd expect from a Cherokee. Let me tell you something else, young man. I've talked with many of the chiefs and wise men of all the tribes. Do you know what they tell me?"

"No," he answered, feeling intellectually shallow.

"They tell me that on the plains there are some with a special gift. Those with a special gift can see right into the happy hunting ground. It's what the white man calls heaven. I believe that you may have that gift."

"Oh, really," Junior replied with a show of surprise. "I had an uncle with a gift. But my Aunt Gertie hate it. He didn't like it much either."

"Is that so?"

"Yeah, he had a gift aw-right. They call it the pox."

"I don't believe I've heard of that gift."

"Yeah, he had it real good. In fact, nobody would have nothing to do with him, especially my aunt Gertie. Shucks, she got mad any time she seen him. He slept in the barn most nights. Winter was purty rough on him."

"Well, it looks like they've changed the horses. I must soon be on my way young man." As the experienced driver and the agile, young man riding shotgun climbed atop the stagecoach, she added, "Remember young man, till the land. It means the survival of people like you." Several passengers boarded the stagecoach.

"By the way, I know Wyatt Earp, but who's Bent Birch?"

"Bent Birch used to stand over there by those swinging doors at that saloon. He was planning to sell wooden likenesses of himself to novelty stores all across America. He was testing how his presence would be received by folks at business places. He could envision a likeness of himself at every store and gift shop in the country. Since he got battered over there one night, he's scaled down his plans." Her lips continued to move but he did not hear her words. They were drowned out by a loud rebel yell and more bursts of gunfire that came from the competing Golden Clipper Saloon. As two men were carrying a body from the Avalanche saloon, she added, "I've enjoyed meeting you young man. You should go a long way in this world."

"Yeah," replied Junior, taking his hands from the narrow window embrasure of the slow moving stage that was beginning to pull away, "I've aw-ready been as far as the Rio Grand, Arizona, and the Colorado Rockies. Shoot, I come out here through the whole state o' Tennessee."

Soon the stage sank into the Texas night. Junior turned once more toward the Avalanche saloon where he passed the sheriff and a deputy making haste toward the competing Golden Clipper Saloon. It appeared to be a long, busy night for the Los Villas law.

He was met by Mr. Loftis outside the saloon. He said, "We ought to git on out to the Bouknight ranch for the fiesta. They've got music, lots o' barbecue, and kegs o' Kentucky corn whiskey. We wouldn't cotton to missing that, would we?"

Chapter 7
Junior goes to the Polls

A pow-wow was in progress in Mr. Black's office. Whitey brought the assemblage up-to-date. "We finally got Ivory sprung from jail. I thought I would never get him out. Longarm had him locked up for two months, Lightning. We've had to postpone that Colorado trip because of it. I never thought he would get drunk enough to smart off and take potshots at the sheriff the way he did. Longarm was more angry at him than he was with that drunken poker player who shot up the saloon and killed a man. I thought he would never let me get him out on bail. The whole thing was Longarm's fault from what Guts told me. He said that when Longarm told Ivory that with Goldie's singing and his piano playing, they ought to be performing in Cleo's Bordello in New Orleans. Ivory went completely loco. Longarm was just joking, but the comment had enraged Ivory. He grabbed ole Red's gun from his holster and nearly emptied the thing at the sheriff. Ivory was so angry that all he saw was red. He would have hit the sheriff with one of the shots, otherwise. I guess what Longarm said reminded Ivory of his wife's running away. She ran off with a gambler from New Orleans."

Lightning concurred. "It took a while to spring Ivory aw right." He stopped pacing, flicked his cigar, and faced Mr. Black squarely. He peered down into his eyes and said, "My wife ain't liking this here trip. She's really been giving me the devil."

"Well, Lightning, you've got to set your foot down. You simply can't let these hossy females boss you around. You've got to have a firm hand and show her who wears the pants. Women are weak and need to be bossed."

"I guess yore right, Whitey. My wife's pretty headstrong, though. Sort o' like a muley cow: can't handle her when she's riled. Ever git a line on that hillbilly that disappeared at Bouknight's fiesta? I had to leave early. What happened after I left?"

"I haven't heard a word. He met up with a stocky little man that nobody knew. That hillbilly was trying to impress and show him how he could handle his six-shooter. So, the clod starts to drawing and twirling the thing like a top around on his fingers. The next thing you know he accidentally squeezed off a round. I want you to know that scared the daylights out of the people at the party. The Honorable Judge James B. Colbert was standing with a glass in his hand by the punch bowl when the gun fired. His glass, punch bowl, and the barn mirror on the wall behind him were all shattered. During the brawl that ensued, the hillbilly and his friend helped themselves to two bottles of whiskey and hightailed it out of there. He hasn't been seen since he ruined the Bouknight party. In the two months he's been gone, his goats have been driving me to distraction. When I left home this morning, that white billy of his was astraddle of my roof. That thing was glaring straight down at me. He was munching on a shingle—a shingle, mind you. He had a big shingle in his mouth, Lightning."

"Ain't unusual fer a goat to eat a shingle."

"Terracotta?" After a pause Mr. Black continued, "I've got to get another wire off to Spokane Spike. He was otherwise occupied for a while, but he ought to be free by now."

"I've got to go to the polls and vote," declared Mr. Loftis. "Soon as I say bye to my wife and git ole Ivory out o' the saloon, we'll be going on to Colorado."

"I'll go with you to the polls." They eased by a large, bright, crepe draped stand where a rotund politician for the state legislature was delivering an oration to a spellbound crowd. Mr. Black was reminded by something the orator said and tuned to his foreman. "I thought I told you to poison Gabby," said Mr. Black.

"I put poison in his seed cup; he probably didn't peck at it."

"Looks like I'll have to shoot that bird myself," said Mr. Black. He stopped when he saw a familiar face in the crowd. "Hey, there's our friend." Mr. Loftis looked in the same direction as Mr. Black and saw Junior Justice and a short straw-haired man standing in front of the orator. They listened to the smooth-talking orator as he continued, "These are times that we need to be represented by men of strong will and uprightness of character—men who are honorable and honest. That's the kind of leadership we need for the great democracy that we've carved out here in the wilderness. Yes, we've got to have an honest government, by honest men, honestly doing the will of the peop—"

"Think I'll go and vote," said Mr. Loftis. He furtively slipped through the large crowd to make his way toward the polling station. Mr. Black remained to watch Junior, his friend, and the bombastic orator.

Soon the candidate finished his lengthy speech. Junior was in rapture as he made his way through the crowd to meet this worthy man. As he and his friend were making their way up the steps to meet the candidate, Byron Loggombottom, an aide whispered a few words into his ear. Junior and his companion continued to press forward where their persistent efforts were rewarded at last. Junior was now face to face with the neatly attired candidate in a dark, worsted wool suit. He grabbed his hand.

"That there was a great speech," said Junior. "What ya said was the truth. We need honest men in government."

"Well thank you, young man," Mr. Loggombottom replied. He retrieved what remained of his mangled right hand.

"If all our politicians was like you, this would be a great country."

"Well, thank you again. Since you feel that way, I want you to step back over here to my little, red wagon. Be careful going down these rickety old steps. Yes sir, you're a bright young man, and you'll go far."

"Heck, I've already been to the Rio Grand, Arizona, and them Colorado Rockies. Shucks, I jist got back from Idaho. Heard my brother was working fer a newspaper up there. We call him Dickens because he always want to be a reporter. Heck, didn't find him though."

"I'm sure you'll find him. Yes sir, it's men like you who will keep and preserve freedom in this great land." "Gosh, I don't know."

"Yes," continued the candidate, ushering Junior around his back steps to his big, sturdy wagon. He pulled from beneath the smooth, wooden seat a large, brown folder with several sheets of thin, white paper inside. "Now, I'd like for you to take this folder. Discard the folder and slip these sheets of paper through the slot in the ballot box when you vote. Make sure nobody sees you slip them into the box. You can greatly serve the cause of freedom and democracy."

"Gosh, I don' know if they would go through a slot in a ballot box."

"My good man, that slot in that ballot box is wide. It's wide enough to drive a loaded wagon and a team of mules through."

Junior began to fidget with the flimsy folder. Some of the thin papers fell to the ground, and when he picked them up, he discovered that they were ballots already marked. "Why, these here ballots are already check," said Junior. "Don't thank it's right to stick them in the box. That would be a cheating."

"My good man," said the politician unperturbed by Junior's discovery, "you'll be serving the cause of freedom and democracy. It's for this great country that we admire and love so much. You'll be voting for all those poor lost souls who were mercilessly slaughtered by cruel savages. You'll be avenging those souls we lost making their way across the plains to Oregon and California."

"Heck, they's enough ballots here to vote all them that ever made the trip to Oregon and California. And they's enough left over to vote half o' the folks that didn' make the trip."

"Tell you what I'm prepared to do for the cause of freedom. I'll pay you a fifty dollar gold piece to drop these ballots into the box. That's what I'm prepared to do."

"Sounds lack a real bargin," whispered Junior's partner, Oscar Ames.

"Can't do it. Ain't right," Junior said firmly and with finality.

"Tell you what I'll do. I'll throw in two pints of this homemade whiskey I've got right here in the wagon. These bottles will be waiting for you after you drop these ballots in the box. Yes sir, there is no end to the possibilities that this great new land offers. All we need are a few good men who are willing to make sacrifices for the common good. With men like you, freedom can ring from shore to shore."

"Where's that ballot box? I'm ready to do my part fer freedom and democracy."

"Put these extra ballots under your shirt so nobody will see them. Now, when you go into the polls," said Mr. Loggombottom, "take the ballot they give you. Don't tell them you've already got ballots. That would get us in trouble."

"Ya thank I'm dumb or something?" asked Junior.

"Go behind the curtain and mark the ballot they give you. You can put these extra ballots inside the one they give you and stick all of them in the box. Got it?"

"Okay, on that ballot they gimme, who do ya want me to vote fer?" asked Junior.

"It doesn't matter," said Mr. Loggombottom. "The important thing is to cast these already marked into the box."

After Junior and Oscar voted, they left the polling grounds. Mr. Black was waiting for them on the corner of Main Street and Baxter. "I haven't seen you around lately, Mr. Justus," said Mr. Black who casually accosted the pair.

"Heck, I run up with my Cousin Oscar here at the Bouknight place. He thought he had a line on my brother and shucks, we took off. Didn't find him though."

"I see. Well, do you have any work lined up?"

"Yeah, shore do," he said as he tugged one of the newly acquired bottles in his pocket. "Tumbleweed suggest fer me git on the railroad. They got about a hundred more miles o' track to lay on this here part of the line. That's before they move on up north. My friend here is going with me. We start work tomorrow."

"Well, that's certainly good that you have something lined up. We'll be seeing you boys around, I'm sure." Mr. Black parted company with the pair.

Junior and Oscar were left standing outside the newly finished Frontier Gift Shop. The two men observed a life-size, wooden Indian being placed by busy workmen just outside the front entrance. After watching the placement of the wooden Indian, they made their way down the street with some urgency because they had a mission to accomplish. They wanted to drain the contents in the whiskey bottles Junior received from the politician.

Mr. Black watched them from the entrance to the Avalanche Saloon as they disappeared.

Someone was waiting for Mr. Black in his office. "I'm surprised to see you this early, Julie."

"I just wanted to get by to see the wealthiest man in Los Villas; thanks to me."

"Well, my little sweetie, I know what you have on your mind. How much does my little darling need to tide her over a rough spot this time?"

"Well, Whitey, I need a complete new wardrobe. Thought I'd take the Over Land to St. Louis and pick out some new inexpensive frocks. That's where the judge's wife, Mrs. Bouknight, and some of the more wealthy ranchers' wives go."

"How much?"

"A couple of thousand ought to do it."

"I'll say this for my little singing canary, you have expensive tastes," he said while approaching her.

After holding her in his arms and kissing her once, she whispered, "I want to be your only singer, Whitey."

"I'll see what I can do. Lil will have to fill in for you while you're gone on your little shopping spree," he added and kissed her once more.

"See you, tonight," she said as she pulled away.

"See you tonight after we close. You're expensive, Julie; very expensive."

"Really?"

"Yes, you just cost me a thousand dollars a kiss."

"I know. And I'm worth every cent, am I not, Whitey?" she asked while she was leaving and closing the door behind her.

"I suppose so," he replied in a whisper as he stood staring at his closed office door.

Soon, Mr. Black had another visitor in his office. It was Mrs. Roberto Abernathy Black who sauntered through the door in a surprise visit. His wife seldom if ever visited her husband in the indecorous saloon. She didn't believe a husband owning an unseemly saloon added to one's social status. In other words, and to put it mildly, she didn't want to be caught dead in the Avalanche Saloon. Her ruffled appearance alerted him that she was in an ugly mood.

"James Black," she began, "I'm tired of being a prisoner to those stupid goats you brought in. If you don't get a handle on them, I will be forced to do something drastic. They've eaten my rare shrubs, and we can't leave a thing outside the house. The maid can't even hang out a wash anymore. Just this morning a nanny walked into the dining room where you left the outside door half open. Yesterday, my poor mother was working in her flower bed under the living room window. She was bending over and raking compost to cover some exotic bulbs she was planting. There she was defenseless when that white billy goat charged into her. It knocked her right through the big living room window. She bounced off a small table and slid across the floor. I'm telling you James Black: enough is enough. I'm not going to put up with this much longer. Do you hear me? Do you? Do something!"

Mr. Black had met his wife, Roberto Abernathy, in Kansas City, Missouri. Kansas City was one of his many gambling stops following his truncated education at the idyllic ivy-covered walls and hallowed whitewashed halls of historic Harvard. He had just left a high stakes card game at Cliff Kenerly's Saloon when he passed two young women coming toward him. As he approached the young ladies, his eyes fell upon a beautiful, petite, dark-haired, hazel-eyed woman who was strolling with her friend, freckle-faced Becky Crawford. He was so smitten by this young woman's good looks, attire and demeanor that he immediately did a u-turn across the street to watch where she was going. His eyes followed the young women as they passed the saloon he just left and continued to follow them on down the street. A few business shops past the saloon they entered Connie's Botique. He paced up and down the opposite side of the busy street until he observed them leaving the upscale boutique with their arms filled with several colorful packages two and one-half hours later. They left Connie's and strolled up the street in the direction in which they came.

Immediately, Mr. Black marched into Connie's. He inquired about the lovely woman and her friend who accompanied her. His spiel was so tactful, charming and artful with the sales clerk, that he learned the young woman's name, address, and some of her preferences. He also learned that she was from one of Kansas City society's oldest and most prominent families. Needless to say, James Black schemed to be introduced to her and chose Clarence's Café where she frequently had lunch. They immediately began to date, and against her devout Catholic mother's wishes—her had father died of consumption when she was sixteen years old—they were married three months later. Mrs. Black did not like to move about constantly with a husband who was a professional gambler. In fact, she felt that it was beneath one's social status to earn a living in such a manner. She was somewhat ameliorated when they settled down permanently, even if the location was the nowhere cow town of Los Villas. He built a beautiful home for her just a short distance outside the town.

Some years had passed and Mr. Black found other women to interest him. For him, some of Roberto Abernathy's allure had faded as she aged and her once petite figure began to expand quite rapidly. Lil Hutchins and Goldie Rush were but two of the women that lured him to stray outside his marriage vows. Sometimes he met Mr. Cliff Daniels, without his wife Carla, in a buckboard on the dusty road that led from his sprawling residence. These chance meetings on the road gave him a sneaking suspicion that Peddler Daniels was deliberately visiting his ranch while he was at his prosperous saloon or away on business. James Black prided himself on not being the jealous type.

Mr. Black had another reason for ignoring his suspicions. Roberto Abernathy's family and friends were influential socially and politically in Missouri and throughout the midwest. He respected his wife's potential power and extensive influence although he never expected or intended to use them for his personal enrichment. He desired to maintain his bonds of matrimony to Roberta in order to keep her influence and connections from ever being used to his detriment. After all, she was a practicing Catholic and the idea of a divorce was abhorrent to her. He knew that if worse came to worse in a nasty divorce, Roberto Abernathy had the potential to ruin him. That was the main reason he tolerated her icy side of the bed, which later morphed into sleeping in separate bedrooms at opposite ends of their beautiful mansion. He viewed divorcing Roberto Abernathy Black as an option of last resort. It would be up to her to broach the idea. He resigned himself to the fact that she never would grant him a divorce.

"Yes ma'am. I'll do something." He had the feeling that he was being indecorously pinned to the rough, wooden wall and being used for a dart-board. He added, "I'll get some wranglers to string some more barbed wire to keep them where they belong. I'll get on it right away. Honestly, dear, I'll do something; I will, really."

"Well, you'd better do something. If you don't, you'll be eating with a set of false teeth in your old age. My poor mother," she said with a sigh. "Oh, how embarrassed she was after that goat hit her. The nerve of that Dr. Witt asking her to pull up her dress to examine her," she added as she was leaving. She stormed from the room and slammed the door.

It was James Black's day for women. His wife had not been gone thirty minutes when his office door swung open once more. A big, knotty club in a scowling woman's right hand revealed that she was more upset than his wife had been. He felt threatened and intimidated because this woman appeared to be much larger than he. Not only was she larger than he, but she was wide between the eyes and had the appearance of a stampeding cow. She twirled the club as easily as if it were a toothpick, and her demeanor indicated that she would swing it at the slightest provocation. Her Latin temperament fueled his fires of fear to a fever pitch. Since she had the exit blocked, he was afraid to run. He couldn't strike her because she was larger and possessed a club. He had a pistol in his desk drawer but the laws of man, society, and nature dictate that a man can not shoot a woman, not without enduring the wrath of the law and public scorn.

He was relieved when she opened her taut mouth and began to talk. "How dare you seend my hombre back to Colorado, you heartless worm. He came back from the last treep with three bullet holes een him. He's had more bullet holes een him than a screen door. You got eighteen men keeled; seven husbands left children and grieving widows. The rest would have been married if they hadn't steenk so bad. I ought to keel you," she said as she raised the long, wooden club to strike.

"Now hold your horses, Hurricane. This is a safe job for Lightning this time. Besides, he does real well at taking care of himself. He's pretty resilient."

"He's not either. He's dumber theen a bluffed buffalo," she retorted while she relaxed her deathlike grip on the club.

"I pay Lightning well, Mrs. Loftis. Within a month he'll be back. I promise."

"It's Senora Loftis if you don't mind, Senor Black."

"Okay, Hurricane, it's Senora Loftis. You must not forget that I hired Lightning when you two were struggling to make a go if it. That job on the railroad didn't last forever. I hired him when you two were struggling to survive. The railroad couldn't use Lightning once the tracks were laid."

"He'd better be back, you sneaking, conniving, steeling scoundreel."

"Those aren't nice things to say to your husband's employer, Mrs. Loftis. I mean Senora Loftis."

"I know, but they'll have to do for now. Teel I can learn more descriptive, rotten words een English. You listeen, my hombre better back here safe witheen a month, Eef he's not, I'll come looking for you. I'll find you . . . you low down pole-cat." She waddled across the room and closed the wooden door behind herself with such force as to test the crafts-manship of the saloon's carpentry work. The slamming of the door reverberated throughout the empty saloon while reaming the Eustachian tube in each of his ears.

Mr. Black nervously reached inside his top desk drawer. Beside his loaded pistol was an unopened pint of ninety-proof whis-key. He pulled it from the drawer and turned the narrow neck opening to his lips. When he realized the gray, metallic lid was still attached atop the pint bottle, he quickly unscrewed it with his teeth, and, with the full force of his exhaling breath, he spat the light metallic lid against a distant wall. Once again he turned the bottle to his lips and let his Adam's apple play leapfrog with his throat while the intoxicating liquid sloshed into his stomach. With a gasping breath created by the fire in his upper alimentary canal, he thought, "Heaven help us if women ever get the right to vote. Tribades will run the country and little boys will be treated worse than the Indians. Our republic will become a matriarchy." Had he been there, Junior Justice would have said attaboy and asked for him to share the bottle.

Chapter 8
Off to Colorado

Like a relentless jackhammer, a torrid afternoon sun was pounding the Texas plains. Junior and his friend Oscar were riding their mounts to work through parched, short grassland toward Colorado. They approached and rode beside a stretch of completed railroad track when Mr. Ames pulled from his pocket a brightly colored, red bandanna to wipe away swatches of perspiration from his wide brow. To Junior, he said, "We come a long ways with this here construction since last week."

"Shore have," Junior replied and spit. "This railroad building's amazing. Why, these here rails are thirty-nine-feet long before they're bolted down. The tracks are four-feet-eight and one-half-inches apart. They are three-thousand crossties to the mile."

"Boy ya shore know all about railroads. It's amazing how much ya've learnt about this here business, Junior."

"Heck, it comes easy. All ya got to do is keep yore eyes and ears open. Amazing what a man kin pick up."

"Yeah, smart as you are about railroading, we ought to ast fer a raise. Big John seems like a good feller."

They arrived and tied their mounts to a thorny shrub at the worksite. They sauntered by some prickly bushes and dry,

113

brown grass to approach the busy foreman, John Bales. Mr. Bales was a heavyset man who was six foot six inches tall. He had dark hair, a twisted, weather-beaten face, and a stentorian voice that carried all across the tracklaying site. He stared at his two tardy crew members, rolled his eyes, and contorted his leathery face. "Good afternoon boys," he said in a booming voice. "You're just in time for the afternoon break. If you'd waited a couple more hours, you could have gotten here at quitting time."

"Yeah, we're a little late," replied Junior. He looked up into the heavier man's eyes. "Had some business to take ker of."

"Where was this business, in Cuba . . . dipping water from a sinking banana boat? You boys ain't showed up all week, and tomorrow's payday. You've only been putting in a day a week, if that, and taking off four. You were supposed to be here on Election Day and showed up a week and a half later. I got three days work out o' you boys in a month. The way you boys are going, durn Indians will take this country back, yet."

"Well, we been purty busy," Junior replied lamely.

"Busy, the devil; we've got a track to lay. We can't wait until lightning strikes for you boys to show up for work. My advice to you boys is to clear out o' here and find something else to do. We can't use you here no more. Just look at them durn Chinamen up yonder working their cans off. The way they're going, one o' these days this whole country will belong to them slant eyes. And they don't give no lip either."

"They work purty good," admitted Junior as he observed a tall Coolie driving a spike with a nine-pound hammer as on his knees a short partner, exhibiting no fear, was holding it upright for him to strike. Others were as busy as firefighters at a four-alarm fire as they performed tasks such carrying rails, keeping tracks in proper alignment the correct distance apart, and bolting the rail sections together. This railroad crew was organized like clock-work.

"Sorry, boys, can't use you no more. You're bad for morale. My advice to you is to get on a government payroll someplace. All you have to do is show up once in a while to pick up your paycheck. You'll never make it working for the man."

Soon the pair departed and was on their way back to Los Villas. "Ya know Junior," said Oscar, "we forgot to ast big John fer a raise."

"We shore did," he replied. He frowned while swiping at a swarm of gnats and three flies that were flitting around his face. "It seems a man can't thank o' such thangs at the time. It would have been nice to have got a raise before we was let go and fard."

They were riding into Los Villas on Main Street. They halted their horses in the street under in a dying sun because two men who were wearing large, white Stetsons blocked their approach to the Avalanche Saloon's hitching rail. One of the men was tall, wore a dark gray shirt with trousers to match, and he began to converse with them. "Howdy, boys, I'm with the Texas Rangers," he said. "I'm Lance McCoy. This here is my friend Les Reynolds with the Russell Detective Agency. We'd like to ask you boys a few questions."

"Yeah, anythang fer the law," replied Junior. He dismounted to greet the men who were standing in front of the hitching rail. Oscar did the same. Neither tied their horse to the hitching rail.

"We wanted to ask you about that gold you found," said Mr. Reynolds. "Think Sheriff Brooks said that you found four mules laden with gold out on the plains."

"Wasn't no lead on them mules. It was all gold in them saddlebags. I brought it right to the sheriff's office. Knowed it wasn't mine."

"I see," he said. "Did anybody know that you brought that gold into town?"

"Nobody but me and the mules and Miss Rush."

"Miss Rush?" he asked in surprise.

"Yeah, heck, that gold was too heavy fer her to carry in. So, I carried some into the sheriff's office. He he'ped me carry a lot of it in. It was real heavy stuff. I knowed that Longarm would know what to do with it."

"What about Miss Rush? Was she with you when you brought the gold in?"

"Yeah, she rode in with me."

"What did she do? Do you remember where she went?"

"I don' know where she went. Last time I seen her, she was heading fer the saloon. Heck, she got a job singing for Whitey right off. She ain't much of a singer, I don't thank. I ain't a saying that because she don't like me."

"Which saloon?" asked Mr. Reynolds.

"Why, this one right here that we're a standing at."

"Do you remember anything else about the gold?" asked Mr. McCoy

"No, except when I first got it, I was with Miss Rush. She had the gold fer a few days before I catched up with her. It was hard to know what she was doing. I couldn't keep up with her half the time."

"How did you come by the Mules?" asked Mr. Reynolds.

"Shoot, we didn't come by them. We rode right up to them where they was wondering around on the plains. There wasn't nobody in sight. They were jist wandering loose."

"So, Miss Rush was with you when you found the mules with the gold; is that correct?" asked Mr. Reynolds.

"Yep. She shore was."

"She was with you when you found the gold. You evidently entrusted yourself to take charge of the gold. And yet, you say that she had the gold for a few days. How did that happen?"

"Well, I waked up one day about noon, and I had a big hangover. It was jist like a hangover except the night before,

I didn't have a drop to drank. I went to bed sober as a judge. Next day, Miss Rush and the horses and mules was gone. I was by myself and start to walking. Catched up to her a couple of days later, and we come on into town. A mule must o' got loose and kick me in the head summers in the night. Say, you Texas Rangers do a real good job. Where's yore fishing pole?"

"Fishing pole?" asked Mr. McCoy. He gave Junior and Oscar a blank stare. He turned his head to his left and shared the same look with Mr. Reynolds.

"Yeah, you Texas Rangers must do a lot o' fishing. I seen in the paper where you boys caught a bass at Round Rock. You boys must be a lot like them mail-riders. They like to fish, too." He wiped the perspiration from his brow with the sleeve of his shirt, and added, "Heck, I dreamt about that mail-rider a fishing though."

Mr. McCoy looked at Mr. Reynolds as if to say, "This man's not with it. I wonder if anything he said is true." He then said, "If you remember anything else that might help us to find the missing gold shipment, tell Sheriff Brooks. We'd certainly appreciate it."

"Yeah, shore will," replied Junior.

Junior and Oscar tied their horses to the hitching post. After their chat with the ranger and detective, they eased inside the Avalanche Saloon. Shortly after they were seated on bar stools, Mr. Black approached the thirsty pair. He showed no outward agitation, but inwardly he was in knots due to his earlier encounter with a badgering Mrs. Loftis. She continued to be worried about her husband's safety; so much so that for several seconds that afternoon, she choked him by his shirt collar. He needed help.

"Junior, I need to talk to you for a minute."

"Shore, Whitey."

"You've been to the Colorado country. You're somewhat familiar with the lay of the land up there. Since you know my foreman, Mr. Loftis, I need someone with your skills to search for him and bring him back. He should be somewhere in the vicinity of Frenchman's Folly. That's an abandoned gold mine."

"Gosh, I don't know. Me and Oscar are purty busy right now, ain't we, Oscar?"

"Yeah, we jist come off a big railroad job."

"I tell you what. I'll give you a thousand dollars apiece if you boys find lightning and bring him back here within ten days. We're all worried about him, especially Mrs. Loftis."

"Gosh, we don't have no provisions fer that kind o' trip. I'm busted."

"Don't worry about that. I'll provide you with the mo—" he said. He stopped mid-sentence because he suspected the pair would use any advance money to buy whiskey. Because this was a most urgent business, he changed his sentence and continued, "a grubstake from the general store. You boys just go on over there and get whatever it takes for the trip. I'll have Guts to round up a couple of mules for you."

"Gosh, I don't know," Junior said with hesitation.

"Tell you what. Bring Lightning back here within ten days, and I'll give you boys a gallon of the best booze in the saloon. That's in addition to the thousand dollars apiece."

"Mr. Black," Junior said as he reached to grab the hand that Mr. Black pulled back in self-defense, "got yoreself a deal. We'll find Lightning fer ya; won't we, Oscar?"

"Shore will," echoed Mr. Ames.

Junior and his cousin made their way to the general store.

Mr. Black returned to his office where Mrs. Loftis was waiting for him.

"Where ees Lightning?' she asked in a demanding tone of voice.

"Well, he's not quite had time enough to get back. I'm expecting him back any day," he said.

"Of course you are. You seent him to the Colorado bad lands to geet hees head blown off. That ees outlaw and Indian country," she shouted and flashed a large, wide knife in front of his face.

"Well, Lightning can take care of himself. Besides, Colorado is a state now and things have calmed down dramatically."

"It ees steel a no-man's-land. I want my hombre back. Do you heer me, Whitey Black?" She shouted. With the gleaming knife in her extended right hand, she advanced directly toward his throat and again said, "I want my hombre back! I'm tired you geeting him filled full of lead. It's geeting old."

"I'm sending out two of the sharpest minds in Texas to find Lightning, Mrs. Loftis. Er, Senora Loftis."

"And who might that be?" she asked as she lowered her voice and the knife.

"Junior Justus and his partner, Oscar Ames."

"Sharpest minds in Texas!" she hooted. "The state's inhabited by idiots, theen. That loco fool rode een here on a steenking camel. He theen shot hees foot off een the saloon. That seelly heellbeelly spends every dime he geets on geeting drunk and puta."

"That's the point. No one will suspect his motives, and he'll get right through the Bad Lands. If anyone can do it, he can. He has the touch. He's got a gift."

"Huh! The only gift heel geet ees the pox from a puta. Well, you better geet my hombre back to me een one piece. That's all I've got to say," she said. She took the long knife away from his vest and stalked from his office.

"Why didn't they teach courses at Harvard on how to handle hussies," he thought. His trembling fingers reached into his wide, top desk drawer for quick shot of whiskey. Meanwhile, Junior and Oscar were at the general store. They were outfitting themselves with supplies such as foodstuffs, ammunition, and grain for their horses and the two mules fetched by barkeeper Myers. Their pack mules could not carry another ounce. Once the items were purchased, they had to wait for Mr. Clancey to get Mr. Black's approval. Junior had a reputation for being both honest and penniless.

They soon left Los Villas. After they rode two miles out on the parched trail, they met an old, wily miner. Mr. Willard Casey was returning with two mules from the Colorado goldfields where he struck a rich vein of pure gold and was most eager to return to his claim. Upon meeting Junior and Oscar, he saw an excellent opportunity to re-supply himself without revealing any of his secrets that might result in him being robbed, bushwhacked, or his claim jumped. He decided to attempt to barter with these two mounted men before him on the trail. He believed himself to be in luck; the two were abundantly supplied.

"Howdy boys," said the miner. "My name's Will Casey. I've been mining up in the hills fer about three months now. I'm looking to get some supplies. Where you boys headed?"

"We're out a looking fer a man from Los Villas. His name is Lightning Loftis."

"Don't know the man. What is ye name?"

"I'm Junior Justus and this here's my partner, Oscar Ames."

"You boys got some overloaded mules there. Shore hate to see them suffer from carrying such a heavy load. Tell ya what I'll do, I'll give you fellers this here bag o' gold if you'll let me have them supplies. I'll even swap my two mules fer yore two, and we won't even have to unload them."

"Gosh, I don't know," Junior said as he waved his hand at some gnats before his face.

Mr. Casey took the brown bag and poured some gold nuggets out into his open left hand. He held the nuggets for them to see.

"Tell you what," said Mr. Casey. "I'll up my offer and give a bag of this here gold to each one o' you boys."

"We got a long ways to go," said Junior as he pulled the reins to continue their journey.

"Tell you what, boys. Got one pint of whiskey left. I'll throw the whiskey in to boot," he added. He pulled a pint bottle from a pants pocket. He waved it around before Junior's thirsty eyes.

"Got yoreself a deal." In a flash junior dismounted and rushed up to the miner. He grabbed the whiskey bottle with his left and used his right hand to shake the miner's hand.

Mr. Casey took possession of his new purchase. As Junior and Oscar were sampling the contents of their new acquisition, the miner was rubbing his crushed hand. Mr. Casey said, "Gold will git ya killed in these here parts. When you boys start to cash it in, jist say you found it in, oh, say, Low Dyke. That's a valley up in Idaho. Tell them you just dug out enough for a big grubstake so you can git back fer a big haul. If you don't tell them something like that, they'll think ya stole it. Your life wouldn't be worth a plug o' backer if they thought that. These men are animals when they're hit by gold fever. Well, see you boys around."

They were in Roaring Springs, Colorado several hours after the trade. Once they were in town, Oscar took his horse and their mules to the blacksmith's shop to get a thrown shoe replaced for his horse. He tied the two mules outside the rough-boarded blacksmith's shop before joining Junior at the hitching post outside the Red Fox Saloon. There were five other horses hitched at the post when Junior tied his horse to the one remaining spot in the center. They sidled into the saloon where Junior tapped Oscar on the shoulder and with a simper, he said, "Cowboys put their savings where their heart is."

"Where's that?" asked Oscar.

"In a saloon," replied Junior with a chuckle. They seated themselves on barstools.

"You boys are strangers in these here parts, ain't ye? Looks like you've been on the trail quite a while. A man can really work up a thirst that way." said the barkeeper.

"Yeah, we shore are thirsty," replied Junior. "How about a shot o' whiskey."

"Better see the color o' yore money," said the surly, broad-chested barkeeper.

"How about this here stuff?" replied Junior. He crudely plopped down a brown bag onto the counter where five large gold nuggets spilled onto the polished, dark grained, wooden top. Every eye in the saloon was drawn to Junior's sack of gold.

An avaricious fever gripped the on-looking saloon patrons. Greedy eyed patrons observed the yellow metal on the counter and under their collective breath, they whispered, "Gold."

"Why, you boys can have anything ya want," he said. His eyes were glued to the yellow nuggets splashed on the countertop from the spilled brown bag. "You boys must o' found a gold mine. You know, you had better be careful with it. More than one miner has struck gold and never lived to spend it. That sack can bring you a lot o' trouble. Where did you fellers git it?"

"Oh, we can't tell ya that. If we told ya, half the men in this here saloon would beat us back to where we got it. Now, wouldn't they?" Junior said. He felt as important as a politician elected to public office for the first time.

Two men in the saloon approached the pair. They sat on stools on either side of Junior and Oscar, and each ordered a drink. "Where you boys from?" asked the man sitting beside Junior.

"We're from North Ca'lina. The mountains of North Ca'lina near Jewel Hill," Junior replied. He glanced at the man who was sitting beside Oscar on his left.

"Is that so? I'm originally from Fort Worth," said the man proudly. "You know, us Texans are a proud people. Before we joined the union, we made it on our own out here. We've got a lot to brag about. Why, we got the Alamo down in San Antone. You boys got anything like that in the Old North State?"

"We got a place call Blowing Rock. You kin throw yore hat off this here cliff and the wind will pick it up. That hat will come sailing right back up to ya."

"Is that so? Well, at the Alamo, nary a soul survived. A fistful of men held off the whole Mexican Army fer thirteen days. They saved the state o' Texas. What does that say fer yore Blowing Rock?"

"Well, they's a woman that jumped off, and she come back."

"Hey, that's pretty interesting."

"Yeah, she come back as a bat; I thank."

"Oh," the man groaned while the other patrons parted with their greed long enough to guffaw. After the laughter subsided, their eyes came back to rest on the sack of gold on the glossy bar.

"They name a place down the road after her. They call it Bat Cave," Junior said without smiling.

Greed swelled with each passing drink. A short little man sitting on the other side of Oscar swallowed a sip from his tall, clear glass, and said, "Nice sack o' gold ya got there, stranger. You can buy all kinds of things with it."

"Heck, they's all kinds of gold in the west. Jist got to know where it's at."

"Yeah, some men have the gift at finding where gold is at. Bet you found yours in Colorado."

"Nope. Found hit in Low Dyke, Idaho. Boy, that's a good mine."

The saloon became an animated whirlwind of activity. It was as if a Tornado sucked patrons from the saloon through the swinging doors. Those seated at the poker tables rose so rapidly that tables were overturned and chairs were scooted across the floor where they crashed into other overturned tables and the drab walls.

Other than Junior and Oscar, there were only two men left in the saloon, save the barkeeper. One of the remaining men's deep voices echoed against the walls and bounced off the ceiling when he said, "Low Dyke, Idaho! That's a long ways from here. Don't expect me to believe a yarn like that, do you? Ain't nobody would come this far jist to git a drink and then load up on supplies. Not nobody in their right mind."

"Had to wind around to avoid Indians and outlaws," replied Junior who was thinking faster than usual. "Had to worry about claim jumpers, too."

For a few seconds, the man absorbed the words while starring at Junior. Like the patrons before him, he made a darting dash toward the swinging doors. A remaining little man on the barstool emptied his whiskey glass with one last, big gulp that set his mouth, throat, and stomach ablaze. He too headed for the exterior doors. "Got another Injun treaty to break," he said. "Might as well git started. See ya boys around."

Oscar looked around the empty saloon. He said, "It ain't no fun drinking alone by yoreself."

"By golly, yore right, Oscar. What say we find us a place like Bell's. They ought to be one like hers around here summers."

Outside the saloon they glanced up and down a deserted street. It had been swept clean by gold fever. They noticed a large, elderly man and his skinny friend sitting in caned rocking chairs on a narrow porch outside Carl's Barbershop. These two sedentary rockers were hoping the pair from the saloon would approach.

"Oscar, these fellers might know a place like Bell's." They approached the relaxed men in their rocking chairs, and Junior asked, "You fellers don't know where a man could find some girls around here. Sort o' like Bell's place in Los Villas."

"No sir, shore don't," replied the big, glib man. This was the opportunity that he was hoping to get. "This here is a fine upstanding Christian town. Don't allow nothing like that to go on in these here parts, stranger," he said.

Five drab, mean appearing men slowly rode their mounts past them down the street. They hitched them on either side of Junior's.

"Oh, heck," said Junior. His countenance dropped as he started to drift away.

"Tell ya boys what," said the man. "You seem to be the kind o' boys a man can trust. Now, I know where a widow woman has two handsome, young lasses. They would shore like some entertainment. Entertainment like you boys got in mind. Now, this here widow woman jist left to visit her brother fer a couple o' weeks. He lives somewhere down around Fort Worth. For a small fee, I could tell these girls you boys are a coming. Heck, I'll even draw you boys a map o' how to git there."

"Well, I ain't got nothing but this here sack o' gold. Thank that's enough to tell me where them girls are at?"

"Gosh, I don't know," he said. He turned to his partner and asked, "What do you think, Jeb? Them ain't really bad girls. Heck, this ain't exactly doing the widow Murphy no favors neither. She thinks them girls are the finest that ever was."

"Yeah," said his partner. "Be awful to cause them girls to go bad, Zeke."

"Shore would," said Zeke as he agreed and shook his head horizontally.

"Tell ya what," said Oscar, breaking into the transaction. "I'll give ya fellers my bag o' gold, too. That's if ya'll tell us where them girls are at, and tell them we're a coming. How about it?"

"Think we ought to, Jeb?" asked Zeke. He turned and looked a long minute at his partner.

"Gosh, I don't know," Jeb said. "Shore hate to see them girls go bad."

"We could throw in them two mules we got at the blacksmith's, couldn't we? We won't need them a going after Lightning. That's about all we kin do, ain't it Junior?"

"Yeah, guess it is Oscar."

"They look like purty good boys," said Jeb. "Heck, jist this one time. The widow won't know nothing about it."

"We'll have to git a dollar back," said Junior. "Oscar's horse throwed a shoe and he's at the blacksmith's."

Zeke drew out a piece of paper from a shirt pocket. He steadied the paper against the dusty barbershop window and with a short pencil Jeb reached to him, he slowly drew a map. Zeke took the bags of gold and handed over the map. He added, "I'd suggest you git to that cabin around dark. Girls seem to git lonelier about that time."

Junior looked at the map. He asked questions about the distance, direction, and markings on it. He folded it and slipped it inside his soiled Levi's. Joy began to flow through his lustful veins, and he could have danced a jig right there on the wooden sidewalk that ran beside the dusty street. Had he thought about it, he would have yanked his harmonica from his pants pocket and played "Dixie" right there in front of the barbershop. He looked in the direction of his hitched horse down the street. He said, "Oscar, before ya go git yore horse, let me show ya what I learnt on that cattle drive. Watch me mount my horse like them real cowboys do. Here, hold my harmonica."

What did Junior have in mind? He would dash at full speed toward his mount and use both hands to hit the horse's rump to give his body an upward thrust so he could safely land in the tan leather saddle. His idea was to impress Oscar with his superior horsemanship. Little did he know there were forces working against his plan. Those five horses tied on either side of his were skittish and tense. Their extreme nervousness, like the influence of bad companions, had rubbed off and affected his mount. He was fifteen paces behind when he dashed madly for his tied, agitated horse.

His horse had no idea Junior was coming. All was going according to his plan until his hands touched his chestnut horse's rump; whereupon, he balked backward and thrust his head high into the air. With his tied horse retreating, Junior found himself in midair with his momentum out of control. He bounced over the saddle, hit the horse's head a glancing blow with his legs spread apart, and crashed through the pine hitching post. When Junior's capricious caper shattered the hitching post, he made a semi-somersault and splashed headfirst into the slimy watering trough brimming with fresh water. This action startled the five tethered horses beside his mount and they broke loose from what was left of the hitching post. They raced wildly in all directions through the empty street. Due to Junior's miscalculation, the skittish horses scattered and were out of sight within seconds. They disappeared completely.

Five fearless bank robbers suddenly appeared. In the wide bank door opening, two of them fired shots back into the bank while the other three fired their six-shooters into the air. They looked across the street and saw their four-legged transportation was missing for their intended rapid departure. There was only one horse tied to what remained of a saloon's hitching post. They quickly gathered around Junior's horse where an argument ensued as to who would have the honor of stealing the chestnut mount. A tall outlaw threw a money sack across the brown saddle and placed his black, left boot into the sturdy iron stirrup. Before he could straddle the horse to ride away, he was gunned down by a short, irate companion. Echoes of the shot had not died when two more outlaws promptly shot each another over who would have the pleasure of riding away on Junior's mount. They were unable to agree on which one was best suited for the sturdy saddle.

Only two outlaws remained standing. A sheriff and two deputies appeared and surrounded the desperadoes. These desperate men saw that they were trapped so they decided that it would be wiser to surrender than to die in a blazing gunfight. They raised their leather gloved hands into the air to surrender and were promptly led off and locked in a small jail cell at the sheriff's office across the street. Soon, the stolen money was quickly returned to a secure, thick, metallic bank vault. The excitement provided by the brazen bank robbers was over.

Junior was still in the watering trough. Oscar, a deputy, and the bank president helped a shivering Junior from the slimy goo to the empty street. Everyone was proud of Junior's part and nabbing the bank robbers. "This man is a hero," declared the bank president. "He scared those horses off so those mean robbers couldn't get away. Yes, sir, we at the Mother Lode Bank will forever be in your debt, young man. How in the world did you know to do that?" he added as he slapped Junior on the back whereupon water splashed in all directions and against his, new, blue worsted wool suit. "You'll go a long way in this world, young man."

"Heck, I aw-ready been to the Rio Grand and New Mexico. Also been to Idaho and the Colorado Rockies; that's where I'm headed fer now."

"Yes, young man. There's a party at my place tonight. I want you and your partner to come. We'll celebrate what you've done for the good citizens of Roaring Springs. It's at seven and out at my ranch not far outside of town." He pointed down the street in a south-easterly direction. "Anybody can tell you how to get to the James Wilson spread. You'll be able to make it, won't you?"

"Gosh, I don't know." Oscar tugged at Junior's arm in an attempt to remind him of another appointment.

"We'll have dancing, music and lots of food."

"I don't know if we kin make it or not."

"You ought to come. Yes sir, when I throw a party, everybody has a rip-roaring good time. There's nothing like it in Southeastern Colorado. We'll have music and dancing. Oh, I forgot to tell you there'll be plenty of good, hard liquor for everybody."

"We'll be right there," said Junior. He reached to shake the banker's hand.

Chapter 9
The Search for Lightning

Junior and Oscar set their priorities. They wanted to attend both the James Wilson gala and their premium-priced, pre-paid tryst at dusk. They had some time to kill, so they began to ride their horses at a leisurely pace toward the Wilson ranch. Just outside of town Junior brought his mount to a sudden halt because something of interest caught his eye. A short distance from town, he saw through the windows of a long, log building that was occupied by a woman and several children. Fifty paces from the edifice he and Oscar tied their horses on two spiny mesquite bush branches and stealthily crept toward a wide front window to view the activity inside. He had to satisfy his curiosity.

They peeped inside the rustic, elongated structure. There was a high ceiling, a rough boarded floor, a black potbellied stove supported by a thick, redbrick base, a few rough-hewn benches, an old, oak teacher's desk, and a cockeyed hanging, black chalkboard with a large hole in the center that was the size of a cannon grapeshot. Inside the circular hole in the blackboard was a large, active spider tiptoeing around a huge, green, ensnared fly. Both spider and fly were merrily dancing on the gray geometric web. Exhibiting the superior dance steps was the spider. A bespectacled, obese woman stood near the chalkboard. She was looking over her left

131

shoulder toward the children of all sizes and ages lined up behind her. They appeared to be deep into a class activity that she was conducting. All the children were participating except for a seated girl, a small boy propped against a far wall, and a large young lad who was meandering aimlessly about the large room. Each of the children lined behind the woman had two hands on the waist of child in front. At the head of the line, a tall girl had a hand on either side of the woman's waist.

Suddenly, the line began to move. As if on cue, they each simultaneously shuffled both feet forward. Periodically the woman turned her head to the left to look over her shoulder toward the children behind her as they shuffled their feet to move forward in a circle around the room. She would mimic the sound of a freight train rolling down the tracks with a *choo-choo* vocal sound. To mimic a whistle blowing, she would periodically voice a *wah-wah* sound as she pulled down her raised, crooked left arm with clinched fist. They would shuffle forward a goodly distance and then backward a few shuffles.

"What in the world are they a doing, Junior?"

"Why, they're social engineering. You see, Oscar, when we went to school thangs were different. Heck, by the time we did the chores around the farm and walked to school, class was about over. Most days we got to school in time to sweep the floor and dust the erasers."

"Social engineering? Don't they learn them the two Rs no more?"

"It's three Rs, Oscar: reading, writing, and romancing."

"'How does this social engineering work?"

"Well, Oscar, thangs are different now. In our day they made shore we learnt something. Now, they learn kids to be socially adjust. Them other thangs like the three Rs ain't important no more. Heck, the big thang is to build fancy new school houses ever' few years with more new tax money. So long as the buildings look purty, all the parents figure the kids git educated."

"Gosh, Junior, yore smart."

"Na, Oscar. I jist keep my eyes open. Let's bring our horses to this here watering trough. Then we kin be on our way."

They discovered that the watering trough was dry. Junior took a wooden, oaken bucket from its fastened position by the pine post beside the shallow well and dropped it down. When the chain stopped rattling, they heard a deep splash of the bucket hitting the water twenty-three-feet below. They drew several buckets for the watering trough and used the last one to drink and wash their faces. Junior poured the unused face-washing water from the bucket back into the well. Wasting water was abhorrent to him.

Junior and Oscar let their horses graze in high grass on an open field. It was near the Wilson spread and when they saw the first guests arrive, they rode in to avail themselves of the proffered hospitality. Mr. Wilson was most lavish in his praise while explaining to his guests, Junior's heroic deed in nabbing the bank robbers. This made him the center of attention at the planned gala. Junior and Oscar left early for their pre-paid tryst, but not before helping themselves to two bottles of whiskey, which Mr. Wilson graciously consented to give them. They reluctantly departed during the music and dancing.

An hour later they reached their tryst rendezvous. Junior folded the crude map he used to find the cabin and slid it inside his plaid shirt pocket. They dismounted at a rail fence near the cabin where they tied their horses fifteen paces from the front door that faced the rugged, jagged Rockies. They were only a few steps away from knocking on the front door of the humble cabin when their plans fell apart. There was a loud scramble inside the cabin; the door flew open violently on its creaky, rusty hinges, and a huge, big bruiser of a man with a long, dark weapon in his hands stepped forth on the tiny, creaky front porch. He had their attention. He fired a double-barrel shotgun into the air above the pair's heads who were expecting a different outcome. As the blast resounded across the plains and into the serried mountains beyond, the man shouted, "Ain't no hillbillies courting my daughters. I'll blast every dad-burned one of them." Junior and Oscar were inclined to agree.

For a few seconds, they froze in fear. Then, like scared cottontails, they scurried down the seldom used path from the cabin. They raced from the scene only to return, stealthily, a few minutes later to retrieve their tied mounts and ride away into the creeping twilight of coming night. Their fright and fear subsided once they were deep into the cavernous labyrinths of the mighty Colorado Rocky Mountains. They stopped to rest their weary animals in a steep wooded area near the trail taking them deeper into the rugged terrain. As they were sitting on a large boulder, Junior mused, "Ya know, Oscar, we ought to stay at the party the banker throwed."

"That's looking back," replied Oscar. "It's too late to git back there now. Might as well go on and hunt fer Lightning and Ivory. Let's rest right here fer the night."

They moved deeper into the precipitous Rockies the following day. At last, they came upon a secluded cove where they saw in the distance an old man, presumably a miner, carrying a huge timber into a wide, gaping-mouth opening near the base of an almost vertical mountain. He was under a great strain as he entered the mine and disappeared from their view. Here was some information for the asking. "That ole feller might be able to tell us where Frenchman's Folly's at," said Junior.

They approached the mine opening and dismounted. Junior entered the mine shaft and yelled, "Hey, I'm a loo—"

He didn't finish the sentence. As his words echoed inside the deep cavern, from far inside the tapering deep, dark mine passage, there was a report from a blazing rifle that sent a bullet flying in Junior's direction that went ricocheting off a rock by his short, sandy hair. It did not take him long to realize that he was not welcome. He fled in haste, mounted his horse, and he and Oscar galloped rapidly away in a westerly direction. It was a wise decision because Junior's yell into the mine and the report from the miner's rifle set off an earthquake type rumble. Those vibrating sound waves triggered a mine cave-in. "Thank we ought to go back and see about that miner?" asked Oscar.

"Na," said Junior. "He kin shoot his way out."

As they rode, Junior recovered from his close call at the mine. In the distance later that day, they spied a stocky, red bearded man chopping a large standing pine tree. He swung the axe in a slow arc that struck into the dark bole of the large fir tree and when the man withdrew it to prepare for another swing, they heard the echo from the previous chop. He appeared to be completely exhausted. As they slowly approached him, Junior said, "Now, let's approach real slow. We don't want him to git the drop on us. That last miner nearly got me kilt."

On horseback they quietly approached the man closer and closer. He was so intent on felling the tall tree, that he didn't notice the pair's presence behind him only a few paces away. He was so surprised to see the visitors that he dropped his heavy double-bitted axe. He rushed up to the mounted horsemen and offered them a friendly, outstretched hand. "I'm Jim Burgess," he said, grinning and then grimacing when he was unceremoniously yanked two feet off the ground by Junior's hearty handshake. "You're two men who could help me out," he said as he felt for feeling to return to his right hand. "You can help build-up the country by chopping down some trees for me."

"Build-up the country by chopping down trees?" Junior mused under his breath as a big question mark as wide as the French Broad River spread across his face.

"Oh, yes," said the man as he straightened his tired back to relieve the muscular discomfort, "I've about finished my cabin as you can see." He pointed to a big neatly stacked rectangular formation of logs. "All I lack is raising three more logs for the walls. Then I'll finish with the rafters, sheathing, and shingles. It's going to be a long, rough winter. I could sure use a hand."

"A rough winter?" asked Junior. "How do ya know?"

"It's the woolly worm. He's much darker this year. I even saw one dragging a set of earmuffs and a wool blanket," he said while chuckling. "I could sure use some help to finish it," he continued. "If I could get seven more trees cut, I can finish it myself. I'll pay you boys two dollars apiece to cut them."

"Gosh, we've got to find Frenchman's Folly Mine. We ain't got a lot o' time. We don't know where it's at though."

"I tell you boys what. If you'll help me, I'll tell you where that mine is, plus the two bucks."

"We've got to be going. Besides, ya ain't got no crosscut saw."

"Oh, yes, I do! Please, won't you fellows help me? It'll only take a few hours to fell these fir trees. I can do the rest myself. Sure could use a helping hand."

"We've really got to go," said Junior as he pulled the reins.

"Listen, boys," he said in a pleading tone of voice, "it ain't much, but it's all I got left. I'll give you boys the two dollars apiece and a pint of real whiskey to cut these trees. What do you boys say?"

"Where's yore crosscut saw? Which way do ya want them thangs to fall?"

With a sharp crosscut saw, they felled the trees in short order. These trees began to crash to the ground quickly in spite of the fact that Oscar was doing what most men in Jewel

Hill would have considered the unpardonable. He was riding his end of the saw. They pocketed their two dollars and soon afterward Junior bashed an empty whiskey bottle against a bulging canyon boulder as they made their way along a narrow, twisting mountain chain toward Frenchman's Folly Mine.

Three days later they were winding through late evening shadows on a colorful Colorado trail where it crossed a steep mountain gap. They saw before them a vast, sandy desert covered with prickly pear cacti. With their eyes sweeping across the desolate landscape before them, they spied what appeared to be an old, ragged miner crawling on his hands and knees toward them. Above, buzzards were circling to exercise their gliding skills.

They approached the disheveled, crawling man. His white beard dragged the ground and it appeared he could crawl no further. Under his breath, he whispered, "I need a drink." He was elated to see the men before him. Junior and Oscar dismounted and stood directly in front of the bedraggled man. "Got a drink?" the man asked.

"No," replied Junior. "We drunk the last drop a while back there on this here trail." They heard no more from the man as they mounted and rode past him.

Three rods beyond the dying man, Oscar asked, "Why didn't we he'p that feller?"

"Heck, Oscar. All he want was a drank. You know I can't stand a drunk."

They continued to follow Mr. Burgess's directions to the mine. That evening they were only three miles from the mine entrance when they pitched camp. Over an open fire they roasted some pheasants Oscar felled with his rifle. After a tasty dinner, they retired for the night.

They continued their journey the following morning. They had ridden only an hour when, eight rods away, they spotted a man standing by an improvised livestock pen. He was busy feeding his animals that included two brown mules and a large, black horse. He appeared to be standing only fifty paces from the Frenchman's Folly Mine. He was holding an elongated pan to feed the black stallion. "It's Frenchman's Folly," Junior whispered.

They approached the unwary man. "Hello there," Junior shouted.

Startled, the man reached for an upright, high-powered Winchester Rifle. It was leaning against a low, broken-down, rail fence where the livestock were corralled. They saw that the man was in an agitated and frightened state when he grabbed the rifle, cocked it, and placed the butt against his right shoulder. He began to fire the shiny weapon in their direction.

They immediately saw that their lives were in peril and dove from their horses to take cover behind some large boulders.

Four shots were hastily fired from the rapid firing rifle, and large boulders and assorted debris began to crash down from the tall mountainside behind the man. Junior and Oscar saw the flying boulders, loose soil and sliding trees cascading down the mountain.

They quickly rushed to a safer location away from the huge, rumbling, thundering landslide. The miner stood helplessly while the black stallion broke through the flimsy enclosure to race for safety. Their eyes surveyed the damage inflicted by the assorted rocks, loose soil, assorted vegetation, and stifling dust that engulfed the hapless miner. A long look at the mountainside above the fallen debris was enough to convince the pair that the perilous rockslide was over. They did not expect further catastrophe from a second dangerous landslide.

They cautiously advanced toward the flying dust and fallen debris. Junior felt a gentle tug from behind on his right shoulder as they neared the randomly piled rubble, small trees, and loose soil that partially covered the miner. Junior turned around and said, "Hey, right here's that black horse that belong to the big Mexican and me. Glad to see me, boy?" he said, while gently rubbing the horse's flank.

Oscar located the bloody, bruised body of the mangled miner. "Do ya hurt?" asked Oscar.

"Jist when I wiggle my toes," he replied with a deep groan.

"Anythang we kin do fer ya?"

"Shore could use a drink. It's times like these when a man needs a drink the worst. Gitting mauled by a rockslide shore works up a thirst. I don't know what a man could do out here if he didn't have a drink now and then."

"I'll git my canteen."

"No, no, not that filthy stuff," he said with a scoff. "I want whiskey. Out here whiskey is better for you than water. It's cleaner at least. It'll help kill this dust I've been breathing."

"We ain't got no whiskey. Drunk the last drop we had back there on the trail."

"Got a pint in the mine," he said. "It's on the ground to the left as you go in."

Oscar entered the mine opening, which hadn't been blocked by the slide. He returned to the man's side with the bottle in his hand. He sloshed the contents in the half full bottle and the sound inside the bottle did not escape his partner's perceptive ears. As Oscar was uncapping the lid to give the mangled miner a drink, Junior converged on the gory scene. He rudely reached for the bottle and said, "We better check this here stuff out. We don't want to give him nothing to hurt him." He turned the bottle to his lips and consumed half the remaining contents. "Here, Oscar," he said, "you check this here stuff out."

There was a tacit contempt in the miner's dying eyes. He groaned in despair as Oscar drained half the remaining contents in the bottle. He heaved his chest in spasms in an attempt to gain their undivided attention. Finally, Junior looked down upon the landslide victim, and asked, "Where did ya git that there big horse?"

"Gimme a drink o' my own whiskey, and I'll talk," he replied as he writhed in agony.

"Gosh, I don't know. Oscar, what do ya thank?"

"Well, we're looking fer some information," he replied while he felt a furnace like fire in his mouth, throat, and stomach. "Seems like a fair swap fer a couple of swallows o' whiskey."

"Let me have that bottle," Junior said to Oscar in a demanding tone of voice.

"Wait!" said the miner in a weak, squeaky voice. He knew the bottle wasn't safe in Junior's hands. "I'll tell you what happened. Two men was working this here mine, and they had three hosses and two mules. I followed them here from Roaring Springs on the plains. We had a gunfight and I drove them off. I managed to roundup and keep their black horse. They went south," said the miner as he attempted to point with his mangled arm and fingers. "I winged one of them purty bad."

"Must o' been Lightning," said Junior.

Oscar elevated the man's head for two last swallows. The man sighed, smiled, wheezed, and then dropped his head to the side one final time. As the crushed man lay dying in the rocks and debris, Junior said, "Now, that's dying in style. If a man's got to go, there ain't no better way." He concluded by spitting in the rocks beside the man's crushed leg where he lay.

They sniffed the clear pine-scented Colorado air. They headed in the direction provided by the miner. While passing through a long, narrow arroyo, they saw dazzling mountain walls the color of vermilion and sienna. They had not been long on the winding trail when several rods ahead of them, they heard faint reports and echoes of several rifles firing. Junior spurred his strong, black stallion up a rocky, steep trail in the direction of the ruckus while holding the reins of his former mount that followed along behind. At the rim of a long, rugged ledge over a canyon, he beheld Ivory holding off a war party of hostile Indians. Junior and Oscar slowed their horses to a walk as they approached the battle scene. They approached the crest of the ridge near the battle site. From the canyon rim, Junior could see on his left that Ivory was outnumbered by several armed Indians who were in a facing stone field that was peppered with scattered, green shrubs and dry sagebrush.

Tall mountains, blue sky, and a cool breeze formed a backdrop for the deadly standoff as Junior tied his two horses a safe distance away. After crawling on his belly for the last few yards to get near a pinned down Ivory, he was only four feet away when he whispered, "Psst, hey Ivory. Need he'p?"

A perturbed and surprised Ivory whirled his smoking rifle toward Junior. Junior shoved the dark barrel upward as Ivory fired the weapon. Once he recognized Junior, he trained his rifle back toward the real enemy, and said, "Boy, it's great to see you. I'm afraid we don't have a Chinaman's chance, though. We're really outnumbered."

"Where's Lightning?"

"He's back over there behind us in some rocks. We've had a rough day. First, we got dry-gulched at Frenchman's Mine, and now we're pinned down by Indians. Lightning caught two more bullets and an arrow."

"Don't know if Lightning kin survive an arrow," said Junior. "I'm not worry about the bullet wounds."

"Some varmint jumped our claim back there. He was waiting for us."

"Yeah, we met him," Junior said without expression. "He had some real good whiskey, didn't he, Oscar? We should have look in the mine. He might o' had another bottle or two stash in there summers. Shore was some good swigging he had."

"Shore was! Heck, dranking like this is what makes the West worth fighting fer. Really been some good swigging out here," he said as bullets and arrows ricocheted off the irregular rocks above their heads.

"Don't worry, Ivory. Me and Oscar will git us out o' this here mess," said Junior as he reached into his front pants pocket.

"What have you got in there, explosives?" inquired Ivory.

"Nah, something better," he replied as he pulled a shiny harmonica from his pants pocket and pressed it against to his dry lips. "Shoot I kin break up a crowd anytime I want to with this here thang. Jist watch me."

"That won't do any good against them Indians. You'll get us killed."

"Jist relax, Ivory. We'll be out o' this here mess in no time." He turned from Ivory to Oscar and asked, "What do ya want to sang fer them Redskins?"

"How about 'Red River Valley?'"

"Na. We're too fer north fer that one. We need one that's more fitting for this rugged setting. We need a song that reflects the open air of the mountains. A tune that inspires and uplifts is what we need."

"How about 'Home on the Range.'?"

"Yeah, that's a dandy. It aw-ways breaks up a crowd."

Junior began to play a few bars on the harmonica. Oscar began to sing with the music and before long the Indians stood as one, lowered their weapons, and began to insert long, lean fingers into their musically bombarded ears. They exhibited a defeated demeanor. Ivory sought to avail himself of an opportunity to shoot some of the unwary warring Indians, so he took aim at an amply feathered chief. From the corner of his eye, Junior noticed that Ivory's action would be detrimental to their plan to escape. With his dusty left boot, he kicked the long rifle barrel upward to cause Ivory to fire wildly. Junior glowered down at Ivory's inappropriate action. He got the message.

Except for the music, the battle scene was quiet. Amid the harsh-sounding music, two Indians again rose from the inclined field of strewn stones. As the chief and sub-chief began to confer, Junior walked across from the rim of the canyon to join the pair standing among some large boulders that jutted above some prickly shrubs. He caught them before they could slip away into the vast wilds of the endless Rockies. With a disarming drawl, he said, "Now, hold yore horses chief. You boys can't jist git up and walk off like this. I can' let you fellers go away mad. Heck, ya've got to learn to be good sports."

"Chief Two Feathers no stand-um music. Bad for ears. Bad for head. Bad for stomach. Bad for braves."

"That's no way to talk about mine and Oscar's music talent, chief."

"Hey, you Junior?" asked the chief, contorting his facial features as he pointed a short, bony finger into Junior's face.

"That's me," he replied. He wondered what the chief meant by contorting his face. Furthermore, he couldn't fathom how the chief knew his name. "Shore good to meet a real live Indian chief. Used to know some in the mountains back home. Heck, most of them got kilt—not by whites—by each other. Boy, they like to drank, fight, and cut each other up. How do ya know me, chief?"

"Saka Jaw—," he began but was cut short by the report from a cracking rifle. A bullet ricocheted off some rocks above their heads.

Scantily clad Indians scattered for cover in all directions. Junior faced in the direction of the immediate danger where his eyes fell upon a tall man holding a smoking rifle, and he was riding a big, slow moving, sorrel horse. He took a giant stride in the tall, ugly man's direction, and shouted, "Hey, what are ya doing, feller? Ain't you got no respect fer nobody?"

"Trying to kill a durn Injun. Git yore ugly, Injun loving carcass out of the way."

"Listen feller, I don't know who you are, and I don't care. I've aw-ready disarm these here Indians. Now git the devil out o' here before I git mad!"

"Why, I'll blow yore blasted head off yore slimy shoulders. Yore jist a brainless, lily-livered hillbilly. All yore type is good fer is pushing up daisies in Boot Hill. I'm gonna blow yore brains out, yellow-belly."

"No, you won't either," shouted Ivory. He was in the rocks near the man on horseback.

Surprised to see Oscar and Ivory with cocked rifles leveled at him, the man dug his spurs into his huge horse and continued his journey down along the steep, winding trail. As the man's mount began to move into a slow trot, he looked back over his right shoulder and shouted up to Junior, "That's all right hillbilly. I'd kill ya in a fair fight. You won't aw-ways have yore friends hiding in ambush to back ya up. I'll blast ya one o' these here days, you jist wait and see. Yore as yellow as a Chinaman. They don't come no bigger coward than you are," he said as he continued to make threats and shout imprecations. He continued his bombastic bellowing as he faded from sight. Finally, his echoing threats stopped when he rode out of earshot.

Junior turned his attention to the chief. He was hiding behind a large boulder. "Sorry this happen, chief. Ya know how anxious some o' these here white folks git."

"Ugh me know-um well, Junior. You man with-um gift to see gods."

"I guess it runs in my family. Had an uncle that had a gift. He saw stars. His wife nigh kilt him with a cast-arn skillet fer branging home a gift. They call it the pox."

Chief Two Feathers looked toward the sky and continued, "Me see-um in you that gift."

"Not me chief. Ain't never had the pox. Been lucky I guess."

"You always be Indian's friend. You must-um be Indian."

"My grandma was a Cherokee," Junior said proudly. "She was working in a trinket shop in North Ca'lina when she met my grandpa. He come through the area a selling wholesale trinkets fer shops to retail. She was a clerk in one of the trinket shops that sold authentic Cherokee trinkets label 'Made in Denmark.'"

"Ugh," he said as he contorted his nose with seldom used facial muscles, "haughty Indians. But you-um good Indian," he said as he smiled and reached out with his hands to bring Junior's arms close to his side.

That night Junior, Oscar, Ivory, and Lightning camped on the protruding rocky ledge. As best they could, they patched and bandaged Lightning who had three new wounds, the worst being an arrow through his thigh.

For comfort and ease of traveling the following day, the three riders placed Lightning on an improvised travois to pull along behind Junior's extra horse. They traveled all day and at dusk they were passing a remote Indian burial ground where they spotted some fluorescing Indian gravestones. Oscar and Ivory were terrified by the unusual phenomenon. A calm Junior merely made light of the unusual sighting that spooked the tremulous two.

"Heck, a man with a gift kin see right into heaven," boasted Junior. "Yes sir, I kin see right into heaven."

"I believe we've all got the gift," replied a quaking Oscar as he continued to view the eerie phenomenon.

Chapter 10
The Gunfight

Mr. Black needed a respite from his persistent problems with three perplexing women. Not wishing to incur the wrath of Mrs. Loftis, not wishing to listen to a contentious wife complaining about the marauding goats that were taking over their well manicured, posh residence, and not wishing to be seen near Lil by Miss Rush; Mr. Black, for long, quiet, peaceful hours, retreated to the complete solitude of his remote, quaint, four-room hideout in outlying Buzzard Canyon. He was informed periodically by one of his trusted messengers about the progress of his vast operations. In solitude he could plan stagecoach holdups, cattle rustling, and an occasional bank robbery. Now and then he cautiously sneaked back into his profitable saloon to keep an eye on a thriving business and consult with the lead carpenter who was building his new Los Villas hotel. He also came back sometimes at night to see the luscious Miss Rush when she wasn't in St. Louis refurbishing her extensive, expensive wardrobe and buying costly jewelry. He knew that he had to remove the pesky goats from his ranch due to his wife's incessant insistence, and Lil from singing in his saloon due to Miss Rush's. He had to act to protect his sanity.

Late one evening Mr. Black visited Lil. He furtively stole up the rough, back steps of his rustic saloon hoping Mrs. Loftis

147

would not spot him. "I know I'm not carrying your child," she said as she pressed her small fingers against her slightly distended stomach. "I've never said I was carrying your child. I've only said I carried one of your children. I don't know why you would ever think that I would ever think I was carrying your child. You're the last person in the world I would ever think that would think that I was carrying your child. You're the last person in the world I would expect of being the father of this chi—"

"Darn it Lil, that's not the point," he said, interrupting her while uncharacteristically raising his firm voice. "The fact is that it's over between us. I've got Goldie singing in the saloon now. I've got a bunch of goats I'm keeping just for you that are driving me to distraction. There's simply no longer any need for you to remain in Los Villas. I know you like that hillbilly, and that he's the father of the child you're carrying. And I'm willing to make all the necessary sacrifices to see that you two are happy."

"You mean that Goldie has your heart. Go ahead and say it. She's the one you're spending all your time with. She's the one that wears expensive jewelry that I never go—"

"Listen Lil," he said, breaking into her soliloquy again. "I'm willing to give you a big spread in the Oklahoma Territory. What's more, I'm offering you a thousand dollars to help you over the rough spots of resettling, and a twenty dollar allowance each month for the support of my child," he said as he glanced over to a curly dark-haired, fair-skinned, little toddler named James Joshua Hutchins who was asleep on a small elevated cot in the far corner. He added, "There's a nice log cabin on that ranch, and it can be developed with a little work. It has the potential to be a cattle ranch or a nice wheat farm. I just want you to get those blasted goats off my hands so that I can go home again. I'm tired of being attacked by my wife, mother-in-law, and that blasted billy goat."

"Well, I can see that I'm no longer wanted, Whitey. I'm not blind to who you're after. I kno—"

"I'll make sure that hillbilly finds where you are in Oklahoma Territory," he said interrupting her once more. "Even if he doesn't show up, you'll have the ranch and a thousand dollars, as well as a twenty dollar a month allowance. If he's still in one-piece, I'll even have him dropped off at your Oklahoma ranch when he gets back from Colorado. I'll have your things moved for you. I'll send the goats, and I'll even throw in that crazy camel I bought off Morty. Here's the deed; I've already signed, and it's been notarized. The ranch is yours."

Mr. Black didn't explain the Oklahoma Territory deed's exact status to Lil. He had a surveyor to enter the Oklahoma panhandle to survey six-hundred-forty acres of prime grassland and had a deed drawn up to specify the boundaries and acreage. For the purpose of legitimizing his claim, he even dug a shallow well, a storm cellar, and built a small floorless cabin on the property. He hoped that when the dust settled on the area in question and Oklahoma Territory became a state, his deed for the property would be recognized and recorded by U.S. and state authorities as being valid. His claim to the Oklahoma Territory property was questionable under the most favorable of circumstances. One thing Mr. Black had in his favor was his extensive political connections in Texas and back east. In 1879 Oklahoma Territory was not a state. It was considered to be Indian Territory.

"Very well, Whitey. I'll be ready by two o'clock tomorrow afternoon. No use of prolonging the agony for you any longer. I don't mind leaving when I'm not wanted. It's become a bore around here for me only getting to sing when that Goldie is on a shopping spree back east. No sir, I don't want to be tied to a place where I don't feel that I belong or fit in. No, I don't want to—" Mr. Black left the room and closed the door. He descended the back stairs.

Early the following afternoon, three goats were tied behind a large, two-horse-drawn wagon. This transportation was parked outside the Avalanche saloon and sent by Mr. Black to remove Lil and her possessions from Los Villas. When the wagon was fully loaded with all her belongings, one of the hands helped her into the front seat while the driver was climbing aboard on the other side.

With the leather check-lines in hand, the driver was preparing to move the horses into an easterly direction when a tall man emerged near them from the Saloon and fired his six-shooter into the air. His shot startled the movers. Most startled was Ringer. He jerked loose from the rope with which he was tied behind the wagon and dashed under it with horns and shoulders a *thump a bum-a-tee-bump bump* that continued to bump until he rammed his curved horns into the traces of two hitched horses. These two fine draw horses were so startled that it immediately transformed them into a wild state of bestiality. Lil and the driver were hardly settled in the front seat when these spooked horses lurched forward so quickly that the unsuspecting driver and an unwary Lil were flipped heels over head into the back bed of the fully loaded wagon. Ringer raced past the horses and down the street.

A runaway wagon soon sped after Ringer. Pedestrians, horsemen, chickens, and dogs parted like ocean waves to make a path for the runaway horses. Boxes bounced and trunks tumbled in the jolting wagon bed. A large front, iron-rimmed, left wheel hit a rather rounded rut that contained a jutting rock, which caused one side of the wagon to bounce high off the ground in the busy street. This jostling and jolting caused a dancing trunk to spring ajar. An open trunk spilled her personal effects that included white panties, pink petticoats and scanty dresses that scattered and emptied into a stiff breeze. A long petticoat flapped from the wagon's tailgate while panties wafted and flew from the precipitous pandemonium all together. It was a wild ride leaving lingerie items strewn along the dusty street.

Ringer turned aside from the runaway team and wagon. He remained in town and was intent on more mischief. Now free from the taut rope that bound him, he began to gad about for some excitement—something to sink his hard, stiff horns into. It did not take long for him to spot a hefty, tempting target. It was in the form of a rotund blacksmith, Sam Jones, who was minding his own business as he was bending over to nail a new shoe onto the held hoof of an unsaddled cow pony. Ringer surveyed the tempting target that had his back to him. He pawed the ground twice to psyche himself for the impending impact that was imminent. At full speed from thirteen paces away, Ringer put all his weight behind his ramming horns that smashed into Mr. Collins's broad buttocks. He went sailing through the side of the loosely boarded shed that housed his cluttered Jones Blacksmith Shop. Ringer stood for a few seconds to admire his handiwork and then silently trotted away. He pranced out of town toward the southwest.

A dazed blacksmith Jones sat up outside his damaged shed. He found himself in the company of two scantily clad lovers covered by a faded, motley blanket. They were in a compromising position that caused them to immediately flee for more friendly confines. What prim prude would let this sort of hanky-panky happen in the sparsely populated part of the west? It is refreshing to note that, in the Wild West, men were kissing more than their horses.

After Lil's hasty departure, Junior and his party arrived later that afternoon. Ivory took Lightning to see Dr. Witt while Junior and Oscar hastened to slake a thirst in the Avalanche Saloon. As they were entering the swinging doors, a tall man watched them from a small bedroom widow at Bell's.

Earlier in the day he had fired a shot into the air outside the Avalanche saloon that startled the team of horses taking Lil to Oklahoma Territory. He fired the shot in anger because Sheriff Brooks, the man he was hired to eliminate, was investigating a cattle-rustling complaint that took him ten miles from town. Whispering to his lady friend, the malicious man asked, "Hey, who's that tall dumb-looking feller heading toward the saloon? I can't wait to fill him full o' lead."

"Oh," she replied as she softly slipped from the crumpled sheets to stand by his side, "That's Junior Justice. He comes in here pretty regular."

"Ya better tell the lady o' the house to start looking fer a new customer. He ain't going to be around long, I'm gonna fix his wagon," he snarled as he scurrilously scowled from the left side of his contorted lips.

Junior was spending his two-dollars at the bar. To disturb the relative tranquility of the smoke-filled saloon was hastily moving Tumbleweed Adams, who came bursting through the swinging doors from the street outside. He made an ear piercing yell, and said, "Man out here! He wants to see Junior Justus in the middle of the street. He's got blood in his eyes and looking for trouble. Says his name is Spokane Spike."

"Pay no attention to Tumbleweed," said Mr. Myers as he rubbed a clear glass with a white cloth.

"What makes ya say that, Guts? I ain't found the boy in a lie yet."

"The rest of us have. The first day he come back to town from California he busted in here and started a stampede. He yells, 'Boys, Seth Maynard's discovered loose gold in the O'Brian Canyon!' That's why you can't believe him."

"Yeah," replied a cowboy at a back table. "I was three miles out o' town before I realized there ain't no O'Brian Canyon. The boy durn near started a panic."

"That's not what I said," responded Mr. Adams. "What I said was, 'Boys, Seth Maynard's discovered loose coals in his outlying mansion.' I couldn't set everybody straight about the misunderstanding. I didn't get a chance because I got trampled in the rush to get to the gold fields. I was bruised all over and laid up for over a week. That caper broke two Indian treaties. Of course, nobody minded that. What burned everybody up was the fact that we got five good men killed in the frenzy. And all that happened while Ole Seth's house was burning to the ground. Nobody was left to fight the fire."

"Well, you ought to learn to talk without a lisp," said barkeeper Myers.

A customer peered over the swinging doors, and said, "They's a man out in the street, all right. I'd say he's itching to kill somebody. He could probably do it with his nasty looks. Boy, he looks mean, like a real gunfighter."

"See, it's just like I said it was," said Tumbleweed as he trod on tiptoes toward an unoccupied barstool.

Junior took a long gulp to empty his shot glass. All eyes were on him as they wondered what his response would be to a vengeful dare that could mean life or death. He slammed his empty glass hard against the solid oak counter top, and said, "Durn shame a man can't kill a thirst in peace. No! He gotta kill some dumb dolt before he kin enjoy hisself." He spit into the floor, rotated his body around on the barstool, faced the swinging doors, and added, "Jist one way to find out about this, boys." He slowly strolled across the floor, flicked the swinging doors with both strong hands, and ambled out into the street. He was there to face the fate awaiting him.

"Hold it right there, Junior Justice," said a stern, harsh voice seventeen paces away. Spokane Spike stood in the windy street under moving dark, thick, heavy clouds that were rapidly rolling across the heavens.

"Hey, yore the smart aleck we met on the trail. And heck, tried to shoot an innocent Indian chief to no avail. You flap yore mouth like a windmill."

"That's exactly right, and now I'll cut ya down like a blight. I've heard enough of that yapping o' yorn. Now, I'm going to plant ya like a grain o' corn."

"Wrong time of the year to plant a corn crop. I thank yore full o' evil, hateful crock. Heck, the best time to plant is in the sprangtime. That's when all the flowers bloom and the birds sang real fine. Ain't nothing like the smell o' lilacs and wild onions and scent pine."

"'Enough of yore almanacking yakking, today. I'm ready anytime ya want to make a play," said the tall man whose clothing swelled as a result of a strong, dusty breeze from behind. Thus harshly spoken, he used the wide street for a private spittoon to make a spurious spit, and added, "I'm ready anytime ya are, son. So, go ahead and jerk yore gun, Justus!"

Junior was not a man to back down. He and Spike were ten paces apart when Junior firmly replied, "Boy, ya jist think that yore mean. Spite's spark yore spunk, Spike. Now, I'm gonna split yore spleen."

"Why, ya jug head son of a jackass disguise as a joker. Go fer yore gun."

"Hold it, hold it!" shouted Sheriff Brooks. He had just returned from investigating a cattle-rustling incident on the Rocking T & C Ranch. He slung his hat onto the ground before the crowd gathered on either side of the street. "Looks like I'm going to have to run you boys in."

"Ain't no law agin gun fighting," said Junior who kept a wary eye on his unwavering adversary.

"That's right!" added a voice in the crowd. "The Second Amendment guarantees it."

"I know the law better than you boys do. Don't mind you boys killing each other; that's not the point. You boys don't have a poet's license. Yore pitiful poetry is persecuting these poor people; it's pathetic," he said as he turned from the pair to face the crowd on the Avalanche Saloon side of the street.

"Yeah, don't you boys draw yet," said Washtub. "I've got to finish placing my bet."

"Yeah, me too," said another as the crowd nodded as one in agreement and began to buzz by placing bets.

"I keep hearing that Justus has a gift. He's the only man in Los Villas that gits along with the Injuns. He always seems to come out on top. I wouldn't want to draw agin the hillbilly," Mr. Rowe whispered to Mr. Jacobs in a low voice.

"Why not?"

"Junior is one lucky hillbilly. Be afraid lightning would strike Spike deader than a hammer. Jist look at them black clouds. Besides, he's already put three Mexicans in Boot Hill without even firing a shot. I believe that he really does have a gift."

"Yeah, I want to place some bets myself," said Spike as he stepped toward the crowd that was a beehive of discussion about how to bet on the outcome.

"Me too," said Junior as he approached a tall man with a slick, dandy appearance. His countenance was accented with a cynical grin on a greedy face. "Want to make a bet?" asked Junior.

This man that Junior approached was William "Word Twister" Jackson. He was the son of an Ohio Methodist Minister. His family wanted him to become a minister of the gospel, but William had other ideas. With his gift of gab, mental agility, and ability to see all sides of an argument, he was ideally suited for the legal profession. He apprenticed under an unscrupulous lawyer William Collier in Memphis, Tennessee, and wandered west after an irate client threw Mr. Collier into the raging Mississippi River one moonless night. Mr. Collier was never seen alive again.

"How do you want to bet?" asked Mr. Jackson who was standing beside a friend.

"I bet ya a thousand dollars. That's what I've got coming from Whitey. I bet ya that Spike's dead within the hour,"

"That's a bet," said Mr. Jackson hastily. He faced his friend storekeeper James Clancey who was standing beside him and asked, "What time is it, Shortchange?"

"I got a quarter to five, Word Twister," he replied to his lawyer friend.

Bets were placed, and the crowd awaited the resumption of the gunfight. Weasel Warren furtively slipped up to Junior's side and whispered, "Whitey's planted an old miner to come up behind you, and shout, 'I've struck gold!' When you make a move to turn around, Spokane Spike plans to plug you. He's here to rub out the sheriff."

"Thanks Weasel, ya've probably save my life," said Junior as a rolling tumbleweed in the undying wind caressed the faded pants of his right trouser leg.

Once again the pair slowly sidled into the middle of the street. They prepared to slap leather to participate in deadly gun-play. Suddenly a stentorian voice shouted, "Hold it, boys! I've got to get a picture." A feisty, tall, slender, gray-haired man stepped from the gathered crowd. It was photographer Philip Parham, who was originally from Philadelphia, Pennsylvania. He was working for The St. Louis Sentinel whose editor, Riley Smith, wanted vivid pictures taken to reflect the realities of life in the sparsely settled west. Mr. Parham was carrying a large, black case and a heavy tripod toward the two combatants. All eyes were on the photographer.

"I don't know," said Junior as he glowered at Spike.

"Don't thank it will work," added Spike as his upper lip twitched in a nervous tremor.

"Of course it will," said Mr. Parham. "Future generations will want to see the gallant men who fought and died so bravely here today. Who knows, thanks to you boys Los Villas may be a top future Texas tourist trap. Now come on in here closer to me. Let me get a picture of you two together."

"Guess we could fer an honorable cause," Spike said as he stepped closer to Junior.

"Might as well," Junior added.

"Great!" said Mr. Parham. "Now come closer. Come in toward me. That's right. Put your arm around Junior's shoulder, Spike. You're taller."

"Heck," said Spike with a whine in his voice, "I can't do that."

"Of course you can do that," said the photographer as he took Spike's long left arm and slung it across Junior's back where it landed on his left shoulder. "See how easy that was."

As Mr. Parham was positioning himself under the black canvas behind his tripod, Junior said to Spike, "Where ya from?"

"I was born in Tennessee. I was the youngest of eighteen kids. I run away from home at sixteen and tried to join the army. They said I was too young to be killing Injuns. So, when gold fever hit, I come out west to try my luck. I hunt fer gold all over the Rockies where I kilt my first man. I like to kill so good that I decide to do it fer a living. If I hadn't made a living a killing, it would o' been a great hobby. Women shore take a liking to gunfighters."

"Gosh, I envy ya Spike. I growed up in a place call Jewel Hill, North Ca'lina. It wasn't even a town. More like a place on a map to hold it together. We had a farm and there was twelve of us kids. It was a hard life raising corn, backer, and cane. I would of stay, but I come out west hunting fer my brother. He's a writer; we call him Dickens."

"Okay boys, frown," said Mr. Parham.

"Jewel Hill? I was born jist across the ridge in Pigeon Forge, Tennessee. Heck my pa drove cattle, hogs, and turkeys through Warms Sprangs, Lapland, and Altamont on the way to Charleston. Believe they call it Drover Trail or even the fancy name Buncombe Turnpike. Is Jewel Hill anywhere close to Warm Sprangs and Lapland?"

"Heck, Spike, it's half-way between them two places."

"Shoot, I bet it ain't ten miles from Jewel Hill to where I growed up. Bet we're akin. In fact, we had a preacher that run off with our organ player. They run off to North Ca'lina. Ole Revern Kenny Barton and Miss Rosy Bradley. That was a scandal and a half. Made me not want to be a Methodist no more. Heck, I become a Mormon. Ya kin have more women that way. Be less hypercritical, too."

"Okay boys, one more shot. Look real mean; that's it," said Mr. Parham.

"Ole Reveren' Barton! Why, he come to a church down the road from us. Did ya know he dump Miss Rosy? He run off with Deacon Wagner's wife. Hey, we growed up close together and didn' even know it. I bet we really are akin. My grandpa come from Jonesborough—James Hawkins."

"Hey, he's my grandpa too," said Spike.

"Well, I'll be doggone," said Junior.

"Okay, boys, take your positions," said Mr. Parham. "I'm through with your mugshots. Let me get my tripod set-up in the middle of the street before you draw on each other. Want to get an action shot of the shoot-out. It'll only take a minute."

"Don't know if I kin go through with this or not, boys," said Junior as he shrugged his shoulders.

"Me neither," added Spike as he kicked a littered beer bottle with his black boot.

"Oh, come on. You boys ain't yellow, are you?" asked Mr. Clancy. "We got a lot o' loot riding on this here gunfight."

"Yeah," added Mr. Jacobs, "ya fellers are acting like a couple o' lily livered hillbillies. Don't you boys think we deserve some excitement? If it wasn't for gunfights and gold rushes, we'd die of boredom. Besides, if we don't see some gun-play, we'll call you boys yellow."

"That's right," added another. "Don't disappoint us. We ain't seen a good shoot-out in over a week. An outdoor gunfight is a treat."

"Might as well git on with it, Spike," said Junior. "Looks like we're outnumber, and opinion's agin us."

"Yeah, can't disappoint honest, God-fearing folks in these here parts," Spike said with finality.

So, once again with steely eyes the pair stared at one another in the windy street. They stood ten paces apart while the dusty wind tugged and stuffed their shirts while flapping their trail worn trouser legs. Both knew that one unnecessary slip on his part could be the difference between survival and six-feet beneath the red clay soil atop Boot Hill. They were careful and deliberate so as not to make a false move that would excite the other into a quick, premature draw. Tension filled the air.

"Hold it! Hold it," shouted a man who stepped from the crowd to break the silence.

"What now, for Pete's sake?" asked Shortchange as men in the crowd murmured their disappointment.

There was another delay. A little, shifty-eyed, bespectacled, spry man practically sprang before the restless throng. His was a risky act to stop the crowd's lust for blood that the two gunfighters presented before them. "Gentlemen, please let me have your attention," he began in a shaky voice. "Please allow me to make it possible for you to buy some souvenirs to commemorate this day's event. My assistants are setting up a souvenir table as I speak. We're also setting up a refreshment stand for cold drinks, fresh popcorn, and roasted hotdogs." Before he finished speaking, two aides began to pass through the crowd. These aides were holding up tee shirts of which some read, "Gunfighters Take the Lead," "Lawyers from the

Lip, Gunfighters from the Hip," "Gunfighters are Straight Shooters," "Support your local Gunfighter, Don't Draw," and "Tornadoes and Gunfighters Blow you Away." Another aide with a box of refreshments made his way through the crowd. He was yelling, "Peanuts, cold drinks, popcorn!"

"Please bear with me a couple more minutes," said the enterprising little vendor. "For those of you who can wait around, we're printing tee shirts to reflect the winner of this gunfight. They'll either read 'Spokane Spike Got Justus,' or 'Justus Nailed Spike.' These commemorative issue print shirts use America's finest cotton fabric. They're mass produced in our most efficient New England sweat shops with abundant, cheap kiddie labor. They'll forevermore mark this day's momentous event in your mind."

"Yeah," said a deflated Mr. Jacobs, "let greed prevail." After a pause, he turned to James Clancey and asked, "Who's that little feller selling all this here stuff, Short Change? What's his name?"

"I don't know. Let me ask Word Twister," said Mr. Clancey. He turned to Mr. Jackson and asked, "Who's that enterprising little vendor, Word Twister?"

"He's a foreigner from Holland that illegally came to America. He jumped ship in Charleston. Nobody could say or pronounce his name, so he changed it to Major Parker. He's quite a promoter," said Mr. Jackson.

"Why didn't he change it to Colonel Parker?" asked Mr. Jacobs. "Colonel Parker sounds a whole lot better."

"I think he wanted to save the name "Colonel" for one of his grandsons," said Mr. Jackson. "He's hoping that a promoter grandson will come to America later. He figures that with population growth, new inventions, and times getting better, a grandson could mop up. That is with the right product like a talented song and dance man. With somebody like Daddy Rice, an enterprising promoter could make a killing."

Soon the excitement of the new souvenirs and sold refreshments subsided. Once more the anticipating crowd cast their anxious eyes on the two combatants who positioned themselves ten paces apart. While the crowd held their souvenir tee shirts, munched hotdogs, and drank their refreshments, they waited on either side of the street to witness this deadly shoot-out. Foreboding of the lonesome tombstones on Boot Hill flicked through each gunfighter's mind with each flash of lightning and the rumbling of distant thunder that followed. Each gunfighter was prepared to test who had the more nerve and the quicker hand when, as Weasel forewarned, an old miner crept behind Junior. "They's a gold strike on Carson Creek!" he yelled.

Gold fever quickly consumed the accumulated crowd. Wild-eyed, animated men began to scurry in all directions. "Ain't you fellers going to wait and see who wins this here gunfight?" asked Junior.

"Heck, no," Red replied as he rushed for his horse. "Yore's is child's play. This here is a chance fer some real excitement."

"Yeah," added Washtub Jacobs, "we can break an Injun treaty and kill dozens o' Injuns. While we're at it, we might find time to pan fer a gold nugget or two."

"See ya fellers," Junior said to the departing party of frenzied gold seekers. Without turning his head to the man behind him, Junior added, "Nice try, Papa Lode. I ain't falling fer none o' yore tricks."

"How did ya know it was me, Junior? You ain't turned yer head."

"I don't have to see ya. I'd recognize yore smell anywheres," he replied as he glared unceasingly at Spike. "How come ya done it, Papa Lode? How come ya tried to git me kilt?"

"Nothing personal; Whitey made me do it."

"It seems he's always making fellers do thangs. It must be nice to have lots o' money to throw around. How much did Whitey pay you to make ya do it?"

"Two-hundred dollars."

"That's what I thought."

There was a frenzy of activity on Main Street. Wildly, the gathered throng scattered and hastened toward the new gold strike. They mounted horses, buckboards, and any convenient conveyance that would speedily carry them to Carson Creek. When Junior finished his short conversation with Papa Lode, he and Spike were almost alone in the windy street. "We ought to call this thang off, Spike. Don't like the idea o' killing my cousin, not unless we was drunk." Junior said as he spat into the street.

"We could call it off, Justus, except fer one little detail," he said as he also spit into the street. Spike and Junior possessed similar spits, which indicated a genetic link to a similar family tree.

"What's that?"

"Yore worth five-thousand dollars in gold to me. That's after I plug you right here in the street. Yeah, Junior, yore going *down* is going to allow me to live it *up*. Plugging you is gonna provide me a powerful payday."

"Spike, you mean ya'd kill yore own cousin?"

"I like ya, Junior. But when it comes to a payday, money spends better than blood."

They continued to glare maliciously at one another. One question remained. Which man would draw first? Behind Spike, Junior spied an out of control, thundering herd of cattle rumbling down an almost deserted street. They were excited, had fire in their eyes, and would tear asunder anything in their path. They were moving like a Kansas tornado when Junior said, "Spike, they's a herd o' cattle coming behind ya."

"That's the oldest trick in the book, Justus. That's a rumble o' thunder. Don't expect me to fall fer a trick like that, do ya? I expect better from a cous—" Spike never finished the sentence as he made a fast move to draw. Before he could level his six-shooter to plug his stationary adversary, a set of sharp-pointed longhorns had his unsuspecting, helpless flesh on their wildly, charging cusps. A premature shot from his pistol ricocheted off the scorched street between Junior's feet. As Spike disappeared under racing hooves and in the boiling dust, Junior dived for cover on the front porch at Bell's to escape the rumbling, trampling stampede. He peeped from a position of safety behind a sturdy, front-porch post and watched the thundering herd race past him down the street. Soon the stampeding, thundering herd was gone.

All was quiet in the street as heavy rain began to pour from a black sky. Morty and the sheriff began to scrape Spike's remains from the damp, empty street while Junior and Oscar strolled into Bell's. Unnoticed in the excitement was a white billy goat that was affirmatively nodding his head and proudly standing at the south end of Main Street. He had a satisfied look on his placid face as he surveyed his most recent handiwork. Only a few minutes earlier he butted the lead bull's favorite cow to start the just-concluded stampede mayhem. Soon the billy goat trotted away.

Junior and Oscar entered Bell's. Once inside, Oscar sauntered up to and sprawled his short torso across the counter. In a slow Appalachian drawl, he asked, "Do ya give gunfighter discounts?"

By early that night, gold fever in Los Villas had abated. Men were returning from the gold rush and gathering in the Avalanche Saloon to drink whiskey, play poker, and to tolerate Miss Rush's musical talent. Mr. Warren was bored with the drinking and banal chatter about the earlier gunfight, so he slipped into Mr. Black's office. Mr. Black was in deep thought as he sat at his desk idly twiddling his thumbs. He was staring straight ahead and thinking about sending a wire back east to learn if Philadelphia Phil were available for some gunslinging. Spokane Spike's demise had put him in a morose mood.

Mr. Black looked up at his visitor and in a low voice, he said, "Wonder where that hillbilly is?"

"He's over at Bell's. That's where he's been since the gunfight."

"He's what? I thought he had been carried away in the stampede. That low-down, lucky varmint. I'll fix him. Where are the boys?"

"They got restless. After the Colorado train robbery, what's left o' them are getting ready to do some mischief. They're getting a crowd together to do a little vigilanteing. They're going to torch The Prairie Chicken."

"Why The Prairie Chicken?"

"Everybody agrees the editor is an Injun lover."

"I could put them to better use. Oh, well, they're probably already worked into a fever pitch by now. Let me know when they get back. In the meantime, I want you to take Junior's horse over to the hitching post at Bell's. And take that smelly camel that I got from Morty, too." As Mr. Warren was leaving, Mr. Black added, "And Weasel, take Gabby and tie him across Wheeler's back. I want rid of that pesky, trouble-making parakeet."

Mr. Warren tied Wheeler to the long hitching post at Bell's. A crowd dressed in white sheets and matching hoods began to gather in the street between the two competing saloons as Mr. Warren was returning to tie the covered parrot's cage across the calm camel's back. When the crowd became increasingly noisy, Junior's horse became nervous while the camel remained calm. A sudden, strong, gusty breeze blew the cover off the talkative parrot's protective cage. An intoxicated crowd began to move slowly down the street past Bell's when some of them heard, "*Squawk, squawk,* Shorty's a cuckold, Shorty's a cuckold, *squawk, squawk,* Whitey's a crook, Whitey's a crook, *squawk squawk,* Lil's pregnant, Lil's pregnant, *squawk, squawk.*"

"Heck, everybody knows that Washtub," Mr. Rowe ejaculated.

"I didn't say nothing, Red," came a reply from beneath a white, pointed hood with holes for eyes, nose, and mouth.

"Listen you dummies," said Mr. Clancey. He, too, was dressed in a white sheet with a hood. He faced the two men under white garments, and continued, "That stupid sheriff heard every word you boys said." With his right hand pointing toward the camel, he added, "Why go to the trouble of wearing these hoods if you're going to tell everybody your name. Why not climb on top o' Bell's and shout it out to the whole durn town?"

An inebriated miner stood at the edge of the crowd near Bell's. He observed the camel's profile and said, "These fellers ain't going to give you no trouble. You jist wait here, and you won't have a bit o' trouble, Longarm."

A tardy, white, hooded figure emerged from the dark shadows beside the saloon. He stepped high as he joined the naughty group. "What's the plans for mischief tonight, boys?" he asked

"We're going to torch The Prairie Chicken," a voice replied from beneath some sheets.

"Why, you boys can't do that!"

"Why the devil can't we?" came a reply from a hooded man holding a lighted torch.

"We wouldn't know where to find work. That paper is one of the town's most valuable assets. Why, it provides news from all over the country. It also lists valuable job information," replied the newcomer to the motley, assembled group.

"Shoot, none o' this bunch wants to work no way," said Mr. Rowe. "Besides, this here is more fun than work."

"I know, but if we burn down The Prairie Chicken, there will be no more cartoons."

"Durn," they murmured in disappointed agreement. "He's right," muttered some of the others, as they shook their hooded heads to concur.

"Well, since we're all dressed up, we ought to do something constructive," Mr. Jacobs said as he kicked some mud off the bottom of his dark boots. "It ain't no fun to git all worked up like this fer nothing. Heck, it's a lot of trouble keeping these sheets hid."

"Ah heck, I'm going to Bell's," said a voice as its owner broke from the crowd.

"I've got some serious drinking to do," added another as he departed for the Avalanche Saloon.

"I'm going home," announced Mr. Rowe as he headed for the Avalanche Saloon's hitching post where his horse was tied.

"Heck, you can't blame ole Red," said Mr. Jacobs. "His old lady will snatch the rest o' his hair out if he ain't home by ten. Next thing ya know, she'll brand him like a steer. Heck, she'll even have him keeping banker's hours." His chiding Mr. Rowe brought laughter from the remaining members of the mischievous crowd.

"Well, I feel mean," said Mr. Forbes to Mr. Simpson as they left the small remaining crowd. They slowly ambled over to the newly erected Panhandle Souvenir Shop. Mr. Forbes sauntered up and stopped to face a stationary, wooden Indian standing outside the closed shop. Alcohol exuded from his breath so strongly that it could thin lead-based house paint as he stood there staring at the silent figure facing him. "Come on and fight me, you gutless Redskin," he said. Unmoving, the quiet statue stood there facing straight-ahead. As the seconds passed, Mr. Forbes became angrier with the unblinking Indian and at last he pompously boasted, "I'll show you, you savage." With a mighty swing of a huge, doubled up fist of a big right hand, the bullying cowboy connected with the solitary statue's wooden jaw. Both Mr. Forbes fist and the Indian's head cracked simultaneously.

Mr. Forbes writhed in pain as he grabbed his throbbing fist. A wooden Indian's frame lay flat beside the souvenir shop while his head went dribbling down Main Street toward Bell's. "Oh! Oh, that gutless Redskin. He's kilt me!" he cried.

While Mr. Forbes writhed in pain, the Indian's wooden-head dribbled away.

Two of the last hooded men still in the street saw the wooden-head come bouncing by them. "Don't want no part o' this," one said. "Me neither, I won't be able to sleep fer a whole week," added the other. They quickly departed for the Avalanche Saloon where they could burry in a bottle what they just witnessed.

Mr. Warren ignored the commotion in the dimly lit street. He was busy getting Junior's attention by softly pecking on a back bedroom window at Bell's.

Junior finally looked over the rumpled bedcovers where he was lying and rose to answer the light, tapping noise at the narrow window. He raised the window slightly and asked, "What do ya want, Weasel?" There was a female giggle from beneath the plain, cotton counterpane and clean, white sheets.

"Can I talk to you a minute?" he asked as he raised the window slightly higher.

"Shore, I ain't doing a whole lot right now," he replied. There was another titter from beneath the sheets.

"Whitey's planning on seeing that you're run out o' town. In fact, he plans to send you into Oklahoma Territory. He's give Lil a cabin, and he's planning to dump you there. Some o' his boys will be over here in a few minutes. They're going to work you over and ride off with ya."

"Took Lil to Oklahoma Territory?"

"Yeah, Whitey's give her a spread up there. He wanted to git her off his hands. Didn't want her around no more after Miss Goldie got here."

Mr. Warren dropped the window, or allowed it to slip and caress his fingers. "Oh, darn," he moaned aloud as he gingerly rubbed his reddened fingers while leaving the premises at Bells. His hands hurt worse than had they encountered a Junior Justus handshake. As he was entering the Avalanche Saloon, three of Mr. Black's burly bruisers made their way by him on their way toward Bell's.

Thirty minutes later these same three burly bruisers returned from Bells. These badly beaten, bloodied bruisers sat and watched Mr. Black seethe behind the desk in his dimly lit office. He listened to a detailed account of how the ferocious hillbilly fought them like a cornered, rabid wildcat.

Finally, Mr. Black said, "Enough, I've got a new plan that I should have thought of before. There's more than one way to deal with a real hillbilly."

Just before midnight there was another light tap on the window at Bell's. Under an unblinking eye of a full, lover's moon, Junior raised the window again for Mr. Warren and a companion. "Here Junior," he said. "Look here what we brung you." He handed Junior six bottles of Mr. Black's best West Texas whiskey from atop a wide shelf behind the bar in the Avalanche Saloon.

Junior was most grateful for Mr. Warren's generosity and thanked him profusely as his accepted the dark, round bottles that were handed gently through the partially open, drafty window. He could have imbibed the contents right there with his thirsty eyes without ever opening the bottles. A gleeful Junior rubbed his hands together with delight. He felt like dancing a jug and singing "Dixie."

Those six bottles of free booze worked their inebriating magic. Before sunrise the following day, two mounted men on horseback were unobserved as they were leaving town. One rider was leading a droopy dromedary with a snoring

Junior and a black cloth, covered birdcage strapped across its back while the other was leading a saddled sorrel horse and a frisky billy goat. This atypical caravan made its way up a quiet Main Street headed in a northeasterly direction. Mr. Warren waited until late afternoon to inform Oscar as to Junior's whereabouts.

Chapter 11
Musing on the Range

A month later, a stiff breeze waved the dry shortgrass like a flapping banner in the hot Kansas sun. Junior had a wide, round stem of brown grass in the corner of his mouth while he stretched out and relaxed in a never-ending rolling plain. Oscar was also lazing in the scorched grass as both were looking toward the fluffy, white clouds floating across an endless sky. Their horses were tethered nearby and they switched at flies with their long, stringy-haired tails in an unceasing motion. Now and then gaggles of wild geese filled the sky high above. As they streaked southward toward their southern winter harbor, these graceful geese periodically darkened the sky. A recently purchased jug lay between the two.

"Ya know, Oscar, a man like me or you could be somebody. Somebody say like a Mr. Racketguy if we only had a chance."

"Ah heck, Junior, fellers like me and you don't know where we're going. We don' know where we are when we git there. And we don' realize what we had until it's gone. We're like a crazy dog a going around in circles chasing his tail. We'll never have nothing. Never be nothing."

"You could be right, Oscar. Some of them Indians thought I had a gift, though. Even some of them white folks said I was going places."

"Maybe so, Junior. I suppose when a dog comes down with the distemper, he thanks he's got something. Or a calf comes down with the blackleg; he thanks he's got something."

Junior pulled a worn, brown piece of paper from his front, pants pocket. He rolled half a turn while taking care not to tear the wrinkled paper that he smoothed out against his pants leg. "Right here's a poem my grandpa had. It's entitle 'Speaking Truth.'" He read the poem aloud.

Somewhere tonight someone is speaking truth;
Just like it is and trashing some uncouth.
No evil words from lips of aged or youth,
From bar, rostrum, pulpit, or a sequestered booth.
Unknown to all, someone's a being plumb,
Not counting on the other's being dumb;
A soothing balm a being spread aplomb,
The words are plain like sounded on a drum.
And yet a rhythm sound of lies that soothe
The endless evil poison coated sweet;
Deceiving one or crowds that sway and move,
A sound that neither stops nor ceases beat.
So, when I sit me down in Glory Land
To singing, shouting in eternal youth;
With all the blessed joy of heaven grand,
E'er hear echoes of someone speaking Truth.

"Boy, that's a nice poem Junior. Say yore grandpa wrote it?"

"Yeah, it's from a book o' poems he had. Thank he wrote them."

"Yeah, I remember it now. Yore grandpa was some smart feller. They read another poem at yore pa's funeral. It shore was a dandy. I'd shore like to hear it agin. I'll never forget that funeral until the day I die."

"Ya mean us gitting there late?"

"We shore did, Junior."

"Heck, I got that poem right here Oscar. Thank it's the best one grandpa ever wrote. It's on the backside o' this one I jist read. It's called 'He Left a Little of Himself along the Way.'" He read the second poem aloud.

They came to carry his body away,
I heard a neighbor whisper words that day,
All they're getting is a shell; just clay,
He left a little of himself along the way.
All through the years from his childhood at home
His wife and children loved him twas known.
With love he cared for them with toil and play;
He left a little of himself along the way.
By helping folks out in the neighborhood,
Throughout his life he kept a doing good.
As solid as a rock, not just Sunday;
He left a little of himself along the way
Seems at the church there were only a few,
A couple friends, his mother, those he knew.
His funeral was one December gray;
He left a little of himself along the way.
It's been so many years since his paid debt,
O'er that time in my mind echoes reset.
What that neighbor and preacher would relay;
He left a little of himself along the way.
Now with the angels sing so far away
A light is dim and yet relit today;
In glory land eternal now so gay,
He left a little of himself along the way

"Yeah, boy that's a nice poem. We'd been out on a three week drinking spree. Nobody knowed where we was. Yore ma didn't know where to find ya. I never will forget you being up on top o' that twenty-five foot haystack. You was holding onto that locust pole that was sticking through the top. You was holding that pole with both hands and kicking the sides of that hay stack with yore big brogans. You was shouting, 'Gitty up horsey, gitty up!' And I ast, 'Junior, what in the world are ya doing up there?' And you said, 'I'm trying to make my horse go.' Well, I said. 'That ain't yore horse, Junior.' Ya look down at me, and said, 'It ain't?' That's when you turn loose o' that pole and come sliding down off o' that haystack. Ya slid on yore back twenty-five foot and hit right on top o' yore head.

"Old Grant Thorpe come along about that time and seen you on the ground. If he hadn't told us about the funeral, we would o' miss it. Senior had already been dead fer two days.

"We was late gitting to the funeral. I remember when we got there, the family was outside the church. Me and you was standing in the hall when they come in. They didn't even thank you'd be there. They had been talking about who would take yore mama to her seat. They settled on Josh to walk her down to her pew. When yore ma seen ya at the back o' that church, she went wild. She elbow Josh in the ribs and give yore oldes' sister a hip to git by her. She want her Junior to usher her to her pew. You gitting to yore pa's funeral made yore mama forget about Senior dying. Her elbowing Josh and giving Ruby a hip at the funeral was the talk o' Jewel Hill fer weeks. That was some funeral."

"Yeah, we shore had some good times back then. Never will forget. I was fourteen and ya got hold of some blackburry wine. We sample that stuff until it was all gone. Boy, that was some good swigging. When we come from behind pa's barn, we look like a pair o' sick pups. At least that's what Uncle Lester allow."

"Yeah, from then on we was like two peas in a pod. Old deacon Rogers said I was too old to be running around with ya. Me drinking and all. Said I was a bad influence. Me being ten years older."

"Yeah, that was right before he run off with his best friend Jack Johnson's wife Nell. Boy, Oscar, we've shore had some dillies, me and you."

"I've got to git a letter off to my folks. Why don't ya ever write yore ma, Junior?"

"I don ever thank about it, Oscar. I guess it's jist a habit o' me not taking the time to write. I kin never think o' nothing to say. Besides, I'm usually going into or coming out o' something. Never seems like the right time to write."

"Yeah, it's hard to thank of stuff between hangovers. Reach that jug back over here, Junior." He took a swig and added, "I'm going to have to git a haircut."

Junior gazed into the far distant regions on the open, rolling plains. In the heat rising from the weaving grass, he saw a wavy object pinned against the endless horizon. It appeared to be a wiggling, shimmering image making its way toward them. It was similar to one's distorted reflection in a funhouse mirror. He said, "Yonder comes somebody that'll cut yore hair."

Oscar looked in the same direction as Junior. "I don't see nobody," he said as he laid the half-empty jug between them in the grass.

"Well, there is. Ya know, Oscar, sometimes I thank life is like a mirage. By the time you git to where ya thank it's supposed to be, it's moved on ahead. Ya never kin catch up to it."

Oscar was squinting to see the figure Junior described. He knew that Junior had the stronger distant vision and was usually right. At last he saw the figure approaching them, and it appeared to be a staggering, injured Indian. "Don't want no haircut from him. I know how them Indians cut hair; they scalp ya."

"It's Two Feathers. I told ya, I had a gift."

Two Feathers had extreme difficulty in walking. At last he stumbled up to the reclining pair on the fertile plains. Twelve paces away from them Two Feathers saw Junior and said, "Me get-um shot."

"Didn't thank ya was drunk," Junior replied without laughing. "Let me he'p ya, Two Feathers."

"Ugh, white man help-um too much now. Took all land, kill buffalo; help-um self to squaw. Nothing left for Indian but tall grass."

"I want to he'p ya, chief," said Junior as he reached for the jug beside Oscar.

"Me no drink-um firewater. Go loco."

"I ain't offering ya a drank, chief," he replied as he turned the bottle to his lips to allow the fiery nectar to play with his Adam's apple. When he removed the mottled jug from his lips, his contorted face had an anguished appearance.

"White man make-um me convert."

"Yeah, Mr. Colt and Mr. Winchester really done a number on ya chief," Oscar said with a chuckle as he jerked the jug from Junior.

"No. Me convert," he said with agitation in his voice as he pulled a Holy Bible from beneath buckskin covering his loins. "Missionaries come and give-um Bible. Bring word of Great White Spirit."

"I'll be durn," said Junior aghast.

"Say-um not to steal, not kill, not tell lie. Wise words. White man's book. Why him kill-um Indian, buffalo, and take land?"

"Well, chief, thangs ain't what they seem," said Junior. "Most white men more or less use that Book fer convenience. You know, when someone wants to do some meanness to somebody else, they leaf through that Book. They hunt to find a scripture passage to justify their devilment. It's sort of like a tool. Yes, sir, that Book gives white folks fits too. It says the Jews is God's chosen people. Baptist preachers have had one hell of a time explaining that. Yeah, chief, it says first the Jews and then the Gentiles; that's the white folks. You Indians ain't even on the list. Ya don't rate a smell. Tell ya what, chief, you'd be better-off to write yore own scriptures and Bible verses. That way, if the words git twist, it'll be you fellers a doing the twisting. It'll keep it in the tribe, too. That is if ya know what I mean."

"You say-um Bible no apply to Indian?"

"That's right, chief. Why, jist look at yore people," Junior answered with the expressive aplomb of a prophet. "Yore people are about wipe out. Land gone. No food. Yore people starve in stockades. Do ya thank a God that loves you would wipe ya off the map? Of course not! No sir. Ya need to write yore own book."

"Why white man treat-um Indian worse than Black man?"

"Well, chief, the Black man votes and don't own land. Now, you own land and don't vote. That's a bad sign." Junior said as he nodded his head negatively. "What's more, the white man's newspapers paint you fellers as evil. It paints ya as having horns. It calls you savage."

"What must-um we do?"

"You boys need to give up the rest o' yore land. That's if there is any land left. Ya need to become civilize, learn to vote, and you'll be treat fair."

"You mean-um go to school, church, and make-um better life?"

"Oh, no. Ya need to learn to hold yore liquor, play poker, and mug folks in dark alleys. It may take a few years to get the hang of it, chief. But I know that yore people are smart. You kin pick up the white man's ways purty quick."

"Yeah, lie, cheat, and steal," Oscar added with a chuckle.

"Um, and pale face call-em Indian savage," mused the chief aloud.

"Yeah, and we didn't even mention fornication," opined Oscar.

"That's the way it is, chief. There's some good stuff in here. I'm jist saying nobody does much practicing o' what it says. Right now, yore dying. If you'll let me see that Book, I'll read ya the Twenty-third Psalm. It'll be a comfort to ya while you're going to yore hunting ground."

Two Feathers handed Junior the Bible. He began to leaf through the pages. "Got it upside down, Junior," whispered Oscar.

"I know that, Oscar. I got a little school housing."

While Junior was reading, the chief fell into a swoon and fainted. Junior laid the Bible aside to examine the unconscious chief and found three bullet holes in his naked back. Beyond a reasonable doubt, they decided that he was dying. His pulse was faint as he lay at death's door.

Two Feathers lay helpless in the grass. Junior and Oscar observed the dying man a few minutes when Junior said, "Ya know, Oscar. We need experience taking out bullets. Never know when a man may need to take a slug out when they ain't no doctor around. Two Feathers won't know nothing. He'll be good to practice on."

They took turns passing the brown jug and Junior's gleaming Bowie knife. Junior was the less squeamish of the two about the gore of flesh and blood oozing from under and around the knife blade while operating on the chief. He carved wide gashes as he cut deeply into Two Feather's back to remove the embedded, bullet slugs. Finally, he wrenched the last one from deep in the chief's back whereupon he took a big swig to celebrate. Since Two Feathers twitched, they decided that he could possibly survive if they poured whiskey into the wounds and wound some bandages around them. They celebrated the successful surgery with several more swigs.

"Ya know, Junior," said Oscar, "his laying there that way reminds me o' one morning at Lil's. I woke up laying flat on her front porch. Seen through them slats holding the rail and thought I was in jail."

"Yeah," said Junior, "ya look into Wheeler's face, and said, 'Morning Longarm.' Boy, did ya tie one on."

"You can't say nothing, Junior. You was a wallowing in puke and spit all over that porch. Then ya start arguing to yoreself about Lil's being fairly faithful. If that wasn't enough, ya roll out into the yard. That's when you and Ringer begin to butting heads. Shore had a good time, didn't we? Still don't remember how we got there. Glad Lil lets me sleep in the storm cellar."

"Thank nothing of it, Oscar. What's that a coming yonder?"

"I don't see nothing."

"It's a band o' hostile Indians. They're coming to check on Two Feathers here. We'd better git on into town and deposit Lil's thousand dollars. That reminds me, I gotta git my money from Whitey that he owes me. I also want to collect my gunfight bet with Word Twister. That's two-thousand dollars I got a coming to me."

Chapter 12
The week in Wedgewood

Junior and Oscar rode into Wedgewood, Kansas. They tied their horses to the low hitching post outside the Prairie Dog Saloon and were on their way inside for some big time beverages. Before they could reach the wooden door under an outward, leaning awning that also served as a front porch for the large saloon, they were accosted by a morose middle-aged preacher who was clad in a baggy black wool suit. "Young man," he said to Junior, "don't you see what sin and evil the Devil works within them walls of iniquity? Yes, my good man, he's at work in there." He pointed an extended index finger from a long, bony, right arm toward the wooden door, and continued, "Souls are lost, dying, and going to Hell because of the evils of drink that's served in there. It's the work of the Devil; I tell you." Junior continued to take steps toward the door as if he hadn't heard a word from the mournful man. "Don't you have any plan for your life?" asked the preacher.

"Shore do," Junior replied as he stopped and wheeled around to face the surprised melancholy man.

"You do?" he asked in surprise. "Yep, I'm going to see the Indians wipe out."

"Your existence is based on seeing the savages destroyed? The Redman so desperately needs the word o' God. Your

181

one goal in life it to see him wiped out? Come man! Let me pray for your soul."

At that point Junior released his right hand from the black doorknob. He slowly stepped toward the surprised preacher and looked deeply into the man's mournful, dark eyes, and said, "Wiping out the Indians ain't none o' my doing, preacher. Ain't never kilt a one of them to this day. So, pray fer somebody else's soul. I merely state a fact. I'll live to see the Indians wipe out."

Oscar, who had a deep, unspoken phobia about preachers and preaching, moved rapidly through the large door while passing Junior and the perplexed man of the cloth in a wrinkled dark wool suit.

A very puzzled preacher watched the wide saloon door slowly close as it also absorbed Junior.

"Some preacher," Oscar said as he attempted to adjust to a dim grotto like atmosphere.

"Yeah, shore makes the whiskey taste a lot better when they preach agin it." Amid the odor of tobacco smoke and whiskey distillates, Junior spied a well dressed Travis Tillman sitting at a center table. He appeared to be enjoying himself in the company of a young woman that he also recognized—Mona. This lightly-freckled, full-figured female was more voluptuous than he remembered. "Well, I'll be doggone," Junior whispered under his breath to Oscar.

"What is it?"

"I he'ped that swamp rat git out of a Colorado mudhole. Then he has the nerve to leave me high and dry on some rotgut whiskey. It's time to git even. Don't be surprise if I beat the devil out o' him."

He ambled around some round tables to approach Mr. Tillman. Junior swaggered to a stop and with the left heel of his big, brown boot, he gave a quick mule kick to a vacant, flimsy chair behind him that sent it flying five table spaces across the partially patronized saloon. He favored his left leg because his injured right toe still bothered him. In an intimidating tone of voice from the back of his throat and for all to hear, he said, "Bought any legislatures, lately?"

Mr. Tillman showed no outward sign of fear. In fact, Junior was taken aback when, in a smooth, commanding tone of voice to the barkeeper's helper, Mr. Tillman said, "Hey, young man, bring us two of your best bottles of whiskey for my friends." He apologized profusely to Junior concerning their first encounter while they waited for the slender server to reach a high, wooden shelf behind the bar for the whiskey bottles and bend under the ebony, wooden bar for two shot glasses. "I appreciate your helping me to get on with my business in Colorado," he said. "I couldn't have made it further west without your help. I'd appreciate it if you boys wouldn't say anything more about my buying legislatures. Most of these sodbusters and cowpunchers think they have total freedom. That's fine. Let them crow while they tug at the ropes binding them to an eternal treadmill. They'll help to build America as long as they think that way. So, we don't want to upset our new republic with minor trivia, now; do we, boys?"

"No, I guess not," Junior muttered as he ogled Mona's comely, plump bosom. He and Oscar became more comfortable when the two bottles arrived. While pouring himself a shot of ninety-proof whiskey, Junior spilled a goodly amount on the table because Mona's cleavage was garnering more attention than his shot glass. Mr. Tillman excused himself and Mona as they took their leave from the table before Junior finished two gulps from his clear whiskey glass. "Ya know, Oscar. He ain't such a bad feller,"

"Yeah, especially since you was in the notion o' smashing his face in and knocking his brains out."

"Yeah, but heck, a man's got to be flexible. Know what I'm gitting at?" "Guess yore right, Junior."

"Heck, a man kin drink anytime. I feel lucky. Shore would like to git in a card game," he said after spitting into the floor.

Junior's last remark was overheard by a tall, relaxed cowboy two tables away. He called over to Junior, and said, "They need another player over at that far table to make four. They'll probably be happy to let you in to play a hand or two." He pointed to the table occupied by three idle poker players.

"See ya in a few minutes, Oscar," he said as he slowly rose, picked up his round, brown, bottle and clear shot glass and quietly strolled toward the poker table.

Oscar sat alone at their table after Junior departed. Three men entered the saloon and saw that Oscar occupied their favorite table in the establishment. They furtively moved toward Oscar's table. A rotund man in the party approached and politely asked to join him.

Not one to say no, Oscar said, "Shore. By the way, I'm Oscar Ames." To the big one who took a seat across from him, he asked, "Where ya from?"

Instead of answering Oscar, the man called across the saloon to the barkeeper's helper. "Hey, St. Pete!" he said.

"Oh, he's from Liberal," said the man who took a seat on Oscar's right.

"But I'm a conservative," replied the man to whom Oscar originally directed his question.

"I see. Where are you from?" he asked the man on his right.

"He's from Republic," answered the man seated to Oscar's left.

"But I'm a democrat," the man replied.

"A democrat from Republic," Oscar mused.

"That's right," replied the man in a strong, proud voice.

"Where are you from?" Oscar asked the slender man on his left.

"Oh, he's a Redwinger," replied the server who was standing near the table to take the new arrivals' orders. His footsteps were light and he seemed to appear out from thin air.

"Don't ya mean he's a left winger or a right winger?" Oscar asked.

"No," replied the man. "I'm an anarchist."

"That's right," replied the man across from Oscar. "We all git along real good. You see, we don't take our politics out here too serious. If we did, there would be a gunfight over politics every day. We're quiet, peaceful people living out here on the prairie."

Oscar looked at the young server, and asked, "Why do they call ya St. Pete?"

"That's for St. Peter," replied the big man across from him who gave a crude, chortle laugh.

The two other men seated on either side of Oscar joined the coarse laughter.

"Let me see if I got this straight." To the man across from him, Oscar said, "Yore a liberal from Conservative?"

"No, I'm a conservative from Liberal. My name's Radical Free. In fact, most of the people who live in Liberal are conservative. Not only that. There are a bunch of Frees and folks related to the Frees that live in Liberal."

To the man on his right, he said. "Yore a republican from Democrat."

"No, I'm democrat from Republic. My name is Liberty Free. There are lots of democrats that live in Republic. We would change the name of the town if it was named Republican. To us, *republican* is a bad word."

To the man on Oscar's left, he said, "Yore a redwinger from Anarchy?"

"No, I'm from Redwing and I'm an anarchist. My name's Independence Free."

Oscar took a few stiff quaffs that he poured from his tall bottle. These stiff drinks refused to let him grasp the names, politics, and residences of his guests. He glanced at the three once more and with a perplexed look on his bewildered face, he said, "If ya fellers would excuse me. I'm not feeling too well." He stumbled to his feet, picked up his bottle and shot glass and shambled away. He weaved around six tables to join his partner.

Oscar took a standing position behind Junior at the corner poker table. With glass and bottle in hand, he peered over Junior's left shoulder and saw his fantastic hand—a royal flush.

"Thank I ought to bet on this here hand, Oscar," he whispered.

"Anythang wild?"

"No."

"What about jokers in the deck? Are ya playing by any rules that I don't know about? If a man knows the rules, he shouldn't be surprise by something that comes up at the last minute. A man could lose his shirt if he didn't."

"No. Ain't no hidden rules."

"I'd bet my life on it," Oscar whispered.

On his turn to play, Junior confidently pushed all the chips for the rest of Lil's thousand dollars into the pot. Directly across the table from him, the dealer called Juniior's bet and asked, "What ya got?"

"A royal flush," said Junior proudly as he spread his cards on the table.

"Ain't good enough," said the dealer as he spread five aces on the table cluttered with whiskey glasses, playing cards, and poker chips before them.

"Why, I had an ace with my hand," said a flabbergasted Junior. "And here you got five?"

"I had two with my hand," said the man on Junior's left. "In fact, I throwed them away with my discards. I was hoping to draw some better cards to go with my hand. You know, poker is one crazy game."

"I had three aces myself," said the man on Junior's right.

"Eleven aces. I don't understand," said Junior as a strong, sinking, emotional feeling swept over him.

"Well," said the dealer as he unhurriedly raked in the huge pot of chips, "it must be a problem with the manufacturer of these cards. It's probably a quality control problem. Back east it's hard to get good help. It's a big mess with all them ignorant Micks and uneducated Wops working in all the factory jobs. All the smart people are moving west, you know."

"I feel like I've been cheat," Junior exclaimed as he frantically fidgeted in his flimsy, wooden chair.

"I certainly wouldn't cheat a man at cards," said the dealer. "Heck, I'm from St. John."

"Don't think he would either," said the man on his left. "I'm from St. Paul."

Junior turned to the man on his right, and said, "Looks like you fellers are covering all the saints today. With the saints on yore side, it's a wonder you fellers don't have a Baptising. I suppose yore from St. Peter?"

"Heck, no. I'm from Paradise," he replied as he and his two partners began to laugh heartily.

After the laughter ceased, Oscar added, "He's right. St. Peter waited on my table. He works here."

"Well, something is cockeyed," Junior said in a riled tone of voice. He nervously rose to his feet while simultaneously kicking his light, wooden chair with a swift backward thrust from his left boot. Every eye in the saloon fell on their table as Junior placed his right hand on his pistol in anticipation of a bloody, brutal shootout. As he prepared to draw his six-shooter, he took a step backward without looking and tripped and fell over his overturned chair. As luck would have it, the dealer fired his small derringer that missed Junior's chest as he was falling backward. He fell flat of his back into the dirty floor. He went sprawling on the filthy oak floor near the damp spot where he had been spitting.

Oscar bent over his fallen cousin, and said, "These fellers have got us. The table I left had a monopoly on politics. This table's got religion corner. St. Peter serves from the bar. Ain't no way in hell we kin beat them. I say we git the devil out of here while we're still in one piece."

Junior was not inclined to argue with either Oscar or the dealer's friends that had their six-guns pointed at him. An angry Junior and a consoling Oscar left the saloon.

Out in the slippery, muddy street, Oscar had to restrain his frustrated friend. They could hear roistering and guffawing from inside the Prairie Dog Saloon where Junior just gambled away Lil's money that he intended to deposit in the First Jayhawk Bank. From a side door of the saloon, the short, neatly dressed proprietor, Albert Wright, emerged and slowly approached the pair where Oscar held Junior by the arms to restrain him from storming back inside. Mr. Wright seemed calm, serene, and sincere.

"Listen boys," he began in an apologetic tone of voice, "I'm sorry about what happened in there. When the sheriff gets back, I'm going to have that filth run out of town. If it's any consolation," he said as he looked directly into Junior's angry eyes, "here's fifty dollars. It's not much, Maybe it'll get you home."

"Don't want it," said Junior.

"Maybe ya ought to take it," Oscar said. "Lil won't like yore losing all her money like that. It'll be hard to explain, especially when ya was going to put it in the bank. She's the real loser."

"Yore probably right, Oscar. I don't enjoy being cheat though."

"Good! Good," said the proprietor as he handed Junior a gold coin. "Here, let me give you your bottle of whiskey you left on the table in there. Since you boys have been good sports about this, I'm going to give you some redeemable stamps. I think some folks call them coupons." He reached inside the coat pocket of his dark, worsted wool suit and pulled out a large wad of various colored little booklets. "Here's some to stable your horses at Horace's barn," he said as he took a yellow-covered one from the stack and handed it to Junior. He continued to flip through the roll. "Here's some for you to eat at Riley's," he said as he handed him a green booklet. "Here's some for you to room for a week at the Open Range Hotel," he said as he gave Junior a blue one. "And now," he said with a cheesy grin that became a sly smile, "here's a booklet with a week's pass for each of you boys to Annie's place. It's just down the street." He pointed to a large building fifty paces away. "It's adult entertainment," he added with a knowing wink and a licentious smile, "if you know what I mean. When you go in, if you want a really good time, ask for Shy Ann."

"Cheyenne?" Oscar asked. "Sounds like an Indian to me."

"You just ask for Shy Ann; you'll see. Yes sir, you may get cheated in my saloon, but nobody can say that Big Al doesn't have a heart," he concluded as he handed Junior one last turquoise colored booklet from his assortment.

Big Al disappeared back inside the saloon. They were flipping through the flexible coupon booklets with their fingers as they began to establish proprieties. After much discussion, they decided that they had everything they needed to spend a week in Wedgewood—everything but the most important thing—whiskey. How could they spend a whole week in a strange town without a necessity like whiskey? They began to view the free coupons with a jaundiced eye and contemplated that these free, complimentary tickets might be like newly found fool's gold—a curse. "I know," Oscar said, "I'm a good blacksmith. I kin find work in town with my skills. They's aw-ways a demand fer a blacksmith, and it pays good, too." So, the pair decided to spend a whole week in Wedgewood.

Junior was adamant in wanting to protect the fifty dollars. He firmly insisted that the fifty dollars not be fritted away and needlessly wasted. He wanted to find a place for safekeeping so the money would not be squandered. He decided to deposit the money immediately in the First Jayhawk Bank early the following morning to ensure that these fifty dollars would not be spent superfluously on frivolous fun. His firm resolve was finally to do something right.

Oscar wanted to test the validity of the coupons for Annie's the following morning.

Junior insisted on being the custodian of the coupons for safekeeping, because he feared Oscar would let them fall into the clutches of a greedy female. So, Junior had most all the coupons and fifty dollars as he made his way toward the First Jayhawk Bank while leaving Oscar a single coupon for Annie's.

A rough oak floor, high ceiling, a large lobby, and several iron barred teller's cages greeted Junior inside the town's only bank. As he stood in a long line of patient customers who were being assisted by two friendly tellers behind the bleak, black iron enclosures, he inched slowly forward on a creaking floor. He was the second in line at the left teller's cage when a thunderous noise from behind him startled everyone in the busy, crowded bank. A masked outlaw and four accomplices burst through the outside door and stormed inside the bank as terrorized customers and bank employees alike screamed and cowered in fear. For a few, frenzied seconds afterward, everyone in the bank was frozen in stunned silence.

"Jessie James!" ejaculated a man. He was standing at a small customer service desk that was against a bleak outside wall to the right of the armed outlaws.

While facing the outlaws, another gentleman quickly raised from his right side toward his face, his right arm with an index finger extended.

From the corner of his eyes, a masked man noted the sudden movement and fired a deafening pistol shot into the tall, slender patron's chest at close range.

In agonizing pain, the man slumped into the dark wooden floor.

"Anybody else moves and they git the same medicine," said a gruff voice from the adrenalized masked man who had fired the deafening pistol shot.

"Why, he was unarm," Junior said in disbelief.

Quickly, the vicious villain rushed to the helpless man's side. "I'm sorry," said the outlaw in an apologetic tone of voice. "I thought you was going fer yore gun."

"No. I was just going to pick my nose," he said with a groan. It's a bad habit, you know. This ought to cure it, though. Wife's been nagging me for years to quit the habit. This will end her being embarrassed, dagnabbit," he murmured.

"I'm sorry," the outlaw repeated. "I'll see that your wife is taken care of. I'll make shore that she gits ten dollars."

"Thanks Jesse, that's fine. Of all the bad outlaws, you're the most kind," the man said in a tone of adoration.

Jesse's armed confederates were busy scurrying behind the teller cages. Terrified tellers stood by helplessly as a masked outlaw rummaged through cash drawers while two accomplices stashed stacks of yellow gold coins and green bills into large brown sacks in the narrow bank vault behind them. Nervous, frightened customers were not exempt from the bold heist. An outlaw began to frisk those customers in line to take their money, jewelry, and any item of value. From the man ahead of Junior, he took a black wallet, a gold watch, and a diamond studded, gold wedding band.

To all, it was obvious that this was going to be a complete pillage.

Junior was the next to be robbed. When the bandit took the fifty dollar gold coin from his front pocket, Junior said,

"That fifty dollars is all I got. It's to git me and Lil through the coming winter."

"I'm a doing the robbing," said the outlaw gruffly. "Besides, I'm robbing from the rich and giving to the poor. If a man can afford to put money in a bank, he don't need it."

"Ya sound like a North Ca'lina tax man," Junior muttered softly.

"What?" asked the outlaw as his attention was focused on his robbing associates behind the teller's cages.

"I said take these here coupon books," he replied as he flipped through the coupon booklets that he removed from a pants pocket. He proffered them in the direction of the gun-wielding outlaw.

"The poor can't appreciate the finer things," retorted the outlaw. "All they know how to do is spend money." He rudely refused Junior's most gracious offer. When the robbers had finished, they gathered briefly in the spacious lobby and soon fled out the front door. Gone was the marauding band of robbing masked outlaws.

Attention turned to the wounded man lying in the floor. Junior rushed quickly to his side and knelt near him to raise his head into a lap formed by his dirty shirt and his discolored Levi's.

Two tellers moved frantically to slide windows upward.

"Thanks," said Junior. "This here man needs lots o' fresh air."

"We're not doing it for him," said a skinny female teller. "Heck, this is for us."

"Yeah, the James gang stinks," said the other male teller. "Got to get the odor out."

"If they don't get you with a bullet, they'll get you with body odor," said a deflated fleeced customer.

"Don't worry about a thang, feller," said Junior to assure the lanky, rangy, wounded man with the solid muscles of a hardworking farmer. "I'll git that bullet out of ya in no time.

Since there ain't no doctor in town, I kin operate. Jist be still and relax."

He drew out his big, wide Bowie knife. It was in a scabbard attached to the back of his leather gun belt. This was the same bloodstained knife that he used to operate on Two Feathers. With its tapered tip pointed toward the ceiling, Junior slowly raised it into the air to make it perpendicular to the boarded floor. His movements with the huge knife were as though he was in a sublime rapture. Then, as if snapping from reverie, he lowered it into a horizontal position level with his chin whereupon he puckered his lips and spit on one side of the knife blade. He took his thumb and forefinger of his right hand to spread the fresh saliva evenly across the sharp blade for uniform dampness. He drew the blade across his dirty, blood-spattered shirt sleeve to clean one side. He repeated the procedure for the other side of the sharp blade, spit into the floor beside the patient, and then he rolled the words from the back of his throat to proclaim, "I'm ready to operate."

"What do you think you're doing, young man," asked a middle-aged, perky-lady, bank patron. "What makes you think you're qualified to operate?" This middle-aged lady was standing over Junior and the wounded man. She had just entered the bank to make a large deposit and was accompanied by her short, slender, timid husband. She was tapping her foot and had a contemptuous look on her face.

"Why," he replied as he spit into the floor near her shoes. He looked up at the prim, neatly dressed woman, and said "I took three bullets out of a feller jist the other day." He reached into his plaid, flannel shirt pocket and withdrew three battered lead bullets. He held them up to show her and continued, "See. I done it, and he didn't say a word. Heck, they say I got a gift."

"Humph, you'll never operate on me," she said with disdain in her voice as she stuck her nose high into the air and snapped her head sharply upward.

"Well, ma'am," he replied; then he hawked from deep inside his throat and spit a wad of slimy mucus beside her left foot. "I hope that if you ever git a bullet in ya, they won' be no need to operate."

She was beside herself with raging anger when once more she said, "Humph!" She stalked out the battered bank door and into the dusty, blustry street.

Before her short, neatly dressed husband could turn to follow her, Junior said, "That yore wife, feller?"

"As a matter of fact, it is," he replied contemptuously.

"Well, if you'll hurry, you kin catch up with the James Gang."

"Why would I want to catch the James Gang?"

"Being married to a hant like you got would make an outlaw out of anybody. They ken probably make room fer ye. You'd be better off with them than ya would be at home. So, if ya'll hurry, you kin join up with them."

Quickly, the insulted man left. "The nerve of some people," he muttered as he barged across the floor to leave the bank.

Junior turned his attention to the dying man on the floor. To free his hands, he struck the point of the knife blade deep into the seasoned oak floor. He then prepared to position the farmer for the impending operation. He lifted the man's shirt high on his chest to remove it from the area around the round, bleeding wound. He then reached for the knife but twisted and jerked it so awkwardly that the torque motion from his powerful hand on the knife handle caused the blade point to break off in the hardwood floor. Undeterred, he lifted the awkward knife to operate.

"No! No! Don't want to sound like an ingrate," said the wounded man. "But please mister, oh please don't . . . don't you operate!"

Junior looked at his pointless knife blade, and said, "Guess I could git another knife."

"No, no," the man said in obvious pain. "Tell him, Jim," he said as he cast his eyes upward toward a new arrival that was standing over them. Jim Long was the local editor of the Wedgewood Post.

"Don't guess he wants the bullet removed, stranger," said the neatly dressed, slightly overweight, bespectacled editor.

"That's right," said the wounded man. "Jesse James has a chance to be remembered and famed. I dare say that he'll be the only one of us that folks will sing his refrain. As long as there's a Kansas, let everybody know about Jesse James. When they list them that he shot, there'll be a wide range. So let me die as uh sacrifice so that his name will be known. Then I'll be remembered as one of the victims his bullets have blown. I'll gladly give my life for his fame. Let the world never forget this outlaw, Jesse James."

"That's right noble," said Junior as he stared at the local editor. He turned back to the farmer and asked, "Don't ya have a wife and kids? I mean, what's to become of them?"

"They'll make it," he replied. "Jesse is giving them ten dollars, you know. Besides, d'ya think I want to slave for the next twenty years or so, only to leave a thankless wife and ungrateful kids to follow." He sputtered and gasped for breath. He continued, "If I'm remembered at all, it will be for slaughtering the grass-eating plains buffalo. They'll say I slayed innocent Indians who were here since the get-go. Why, I destroyed this virgin plains grassland with a vile turning plow. Let me be sacrificed and die for a *man's* man who's endowed, a man who looked Hypocrisy in the eye, took its money, and blew its brains out. There's a man who didn't base his reputation on an Indian pow-wow. He didn't blow the buffalo away or rape the virgin prairie with a turning plow. So, let me die for a man who made something of himself on these crazy plains.

I'll have immortal fame as a man slain by Jesse James." His eyes rolled as he lay lifeless on the floor.

Editor Long checked his pulse with his fingers and declared, "He's gone. With his passing, Kansas has lost a pretty potent poet from the shortgrass prairie plains."

"He didn't want to live," said Junior with a sigh.

"Probably took a good look at your operating knife," quipped the editor.

"Don't understand, wanting an outlaw like Jesse James to be famous."

"Not really," said Mr. Long as he looked at Junior through firm, wise, steely brown eyes. "What we have here is basically a decent man. He could have lived to be a hundred and fifty years old, and nobody would have appreciated his worth. Now, on the other hand, there's Jesse James. He's a murdering, robbing, stealing thug. They're calling him Robin Hood when in reality, he's a hood out robbing. He'll always be remembered.

"Now, I can take this man right here in the floor as an example. I can take a few of his minor flaws and turn him into a vile monster. Yes sir, my friend, that's what I can do. I can do it with the printed word in my newspaper. For instance, if he's honest and paid his bills, I can say that he was too timid to take a chance on indebtedness. If he's a nice man, I can say that he was a softie and his wife henpecked him. If he was a religious man, I can say that he was a wild-eyed, rip-roaring, Bible-thumping, religious maniac. See what you can put in print for people to peruse?"

"I s'pose so," Junior replied in a tone that conveyed a doubtful understanding.

"Now, let me get back to Jesse James. I can say that he only robbed from the rich. I can point out that those rich being robbed are robbers themselves. If he gave a few coins to the poor, I can point out in print how generous he was to the needy. Why," he said as he looked through a bank window into the distant blue sky, "you paint him as a daring, colorful Robin Hood. His sole purpose in life is to redistribute the nation's wealth by taking it from the greedy and giving it to the needy. You can make it appear that his type is doing a public service for the country. You can have every young lad in America wanting to be just like Jesse James."

"I see," said Junior who had a puzzled look clouding his face.

"You see," said Mr. Long. "It's not whether a man is good or bad, it's how he's made to appear in print."

"You reporters kin play God, can't you?" said Junior as he rose to his feet.

"Yes, we come about as close to playing God as doctors do. Well, I'd better go and write-up this story. I've got to tell the world what a glorious deed that was done here today. Jesse James's memory must be etched into the endless annals of eternity."

"Hey," Junior asked as the editor turned to leave, "ya wouldn't happen to know my brother? He's a reporter."

"What is his name?" the editor asked as he turned to face Junior.

"Well, back home we call him Dickens. He aw-ways wanted to be a writer. His name's Josh Justus. Heck, he went to a big fancy college in North Ca'lina. He graduated and become a reporter."

"Yes, I've heard of him. Think he went back east to get a line on the James boys."

"Boy, he would a seen them if he'd been here today! I'm shore he would a love to write up this story. Shoot, back home we all knowed that Josh was going places. He's what they call an honest reporter. So, he went to git a line on the James boys."

"Oh, not these James boys."

"Not Jesse and Frank?"

"No, Henry and William."

"I see," replied Junior with another puzzled look. "I ain't heard of that bunch o' James outlaws. I don't guess they come this far west. Maybe they'll head out this way before long."

"Say, if your brother is anywhere in these parts, he'll be at the newspaper awards convention in Los Villas next spring. If he's not there, somebody will have a line on where he is. It's the first week in May."

"Los Villas? Why, that's nothing but a hole in the prairie. It holds the map together till you kin git to where you're going. Why would anybody sensible want to meet out there?"

"Nobody said newspaper reporters were sensible. Reporters settled on Los Villas because it is a little out of the way. There shouldn't be any trouble. And Bell's place is famous all over the country, and they have two fabulous saloons. One saloon in particular has a piano player that's known far and wide. He's supposed to be the best piano player to ever to cross the Mississippi and come out west. The sheriff may not be a genius, but he's honest and runs a good town."

"Yeah, Longarm's a good sheriff aw right."

Oscar found work at George Preston's Blacksmith Shop at the edge of town. He went immediately to Mr. Preston's shop following a rollicking three hour stay at Annies. Junior found work the same day at the Wedgewood General Store where he stocked merchandise and loaded and unloaded supplies from cumbersome, unwieldy wagons. Both diligently labored for two days and took the next three off to celebrate their good fortune in finding steady employment. They planned to leave town on the sixth day because they were running short of ready cash. Also, their resumes were now full of holes due to their early retirement from their two day's work earlier in the week.

Oscar determined that their horses were lethargic. They only nibbled at the hay and snorted at the grain provided by

Horace's Barn. Both he and Junior agreed that green forage would act as a needed tonic for their ailing animals.

That evening when they ate at Riley's, Junior had a plan. He wanted healthy horses for the homeward journey to Lil's ranch. They filled their plates with steak, potatoes, and a salad from the salad bar. As they were sitting at their dining table, Junior took a long look toward spacious tables spread with salad bar delicacies that included yellow vegetables of all descriptions, different types of tasty melons, leaf lettuce, kale, and assorted greens. He fixed his focus on the green, leafy foodstuffs.

Junior got the attention of the proprietor, Mr. Roy Chatham. He said, "I'd like to have an extra he'ping from yore salad bar,"

"It's not covered by your coupons. It will cost you twenty-five cents extra."

"Heck, I kin swing that," said Junior as he rattled some loose change in his right front pocket.

"Me too," Oscar added.

"Everybody loves my salad bar. It has a most exquisite assortment of fresh fruits and leafy green vegetables found anywhere. There's not another like it in the entire west. It will suit any connoisseur's palate," said Mr. Chatham as he looked across the dining area toward his many paying customers. His chest swelled with pride.

"Heck, don't matter so long as it's green. Old Trail Blazer will eat anythang that's green," Junior said as he and Oscar each gave the owner twenty-five cents.

Old Trail Blazer, Mr. Chatham thought, as he retired to the kitchen, was Junior's referring to himself.

Mr. Chatham returned thirty minutes later to check on his many customers. He stood aghast in the dining area where he saw serving tables stripped bare of the cornucopia of assorted green foodstuffs.

"My gawd," he ejaculated as he approached Junior and Oscar, "what happened to the five bushels of greens that were out here?"

"Oh, heck," Junior replied. "I fed old Trail Blazer with them. Dobbin like them, too. Them greens really perk them right up. Got any more left? Shore like to have another he'ping. Thank I kin come up with another quarter."

"Another helping!?" exclaimed the agitated proprietor. He looked first at Junior and then Oscar and groaned, "Oh, my gawd."

"Heck, don't take it so hard," said Junior as he spit into the floor. "I kin probably go fifty cents fer another he'ping. Heck, I'll even set yore galvanized washing-tub back inside fer ya. Shoot, we want it to be jist like back home. We want to be good neighbors."

"Yeah," said Oscar, "I'll take another he'ping too. I kin go another fifty cents."

"Ooh," Mr. Chatham moaned as he left for the kitchen in tears.

"Strange feller, Oscar." They walked outside Riley's where Junior reached down to pick up some of the long stem greens that had fallen from the big washtub they had carried out to feed their ailing horses. He raised the lid and deposited the loose greens into a large, red, white, and blue container.

"My lord, Junior. Know what ya jist done?"

Why no, Oscar. What did I jist do?"

"You jist threw them greens into a Unided States Post Office letter deposit container. That's what ya jist done."

"I'll be doggoned," he replied, displaying surprise. "So that's what them red, white and blue cans are fer. Heck, I never use them. I didn't know. It'll jist make a little more work fer them boys over at the post office, that's all. Heck, I'll git them greens out o' that can," he said as he yanked the wide lid open and reached his long arm down into the deep throat of the metal container. "Don't want them government boys to be overwork."

"Don't mess with it, Junior. They'll put ya in jail fer tampering with the U.S. Mail."

"Them fellers are finiky, ain't they?" he said as he withdrew his swallowed arm.

"Say, Junior. Why didn' Josh write yore ma? That way ya wouldn't have to hunt all over the West fer him. He got plenty of school housing at Ca'lina and he's smart. If he'd wrote yore ma, ya wouldn't have to hunt fer him."

"My ma told him not to write. She said that post master Miller might find where Josh was at. Then he'd have the sheriff to fetch him back. She didn't want nobody to find him. That's why she had me hunt fer him. She wanted to find where he was without anybody else knowing."

"Yore ma's purty dang smart, Junior."

A huge, overweight woman came waddling toward them. She appeared to be in her early thirties and carried a large axe on her right shoulder. She was wearing a drab, cotton print dress that covered her huge, vibrating body. Her facial expression told the pair standing by the letter container that she intended to use that gleaming axe as did her shaking, quivering body. As she passed by them, she turned her head to the right and with a scurrilous frown, maliciously eyed Junior. Then she ogled Oscar.

Oscar fawned and to his partner, he whispered, "Have I been dranking too much?"

"Why do ya ast, Oscar?"

"I'm either a shrinking, or women or gitting bigger. Boy, she's a big one. I ain't never seen an elephant, but she would probably pass fer one. Shore hope what she's got ain't catching."

"I've seen oxes that would be afraid o' her."

"Boy, she's as big as an ox," Oscar mumbled.

They watched her waddle toward the Prairie Dog Saloon.

She approached one of two pine posts that held the cedar shingle roof that served both as an awning and porch cover over the front door. She stopped, lifted the axe from her shoulder at which time she felt with her chubby fingers, the glistening point of the sharp blade. She blew on it with a deep breath. Then she drew back the axe and with a mighty swing, the blade slashed into the square four inch post with such a strong force that it tore from its loose bottom mooring and the low, short roof. As the post lay on the ground from the axe blow, the postless end of the awning undulated between three and five feet above the ground. She tried to withdraw the axe from the felled post where it lay on the ground and in so doing, she almost fell. She freed the stuck axe blade and waddled over to the other upright post that was still holding up one side of the awning. She addressed the standing twin pole in same threatening manner as the first, and, with another mighty swing, she felled it as well. With no support, the awning like roof slammed against the front entrance door facing and rough, wood boarded wall of the saloon. It hung there for several seconds while vibrating and slowly working free from the rusty, iron-nail fasteners that held it in place. Finally, it worked loose from the saloon boards above the door. It fell and tipped over to expose sharp nails on the roof's underside where it lay flat on the ground. With the awning gone, the saloon looked like a hat without a brim. A jocular cowboy might have said the Prairie Dog Saloon without the awning was like a dog without a tail.

Saloon patrons became suspicious concerning the noise outside. A short, skinny man raised a narrow window and shouted, "What are you trying to do? Get the dickens out o' here, Big Kate!"

"I'm going to get rid of every saloon in the west," she shouted in reply. She waddled over to the window where the man addressed her. She drew back the axe and gave a mighty swing that shattered the narrow windowpanes above his hairless head. Shattered glass shards were sent sailing inside and outside the saloon as splintered wood from shattered clear window panes and painted framing went flying about the outside yard area.

Fortunately, the little man had a wary eye on the woman and quickly ducked under the swinging axe. Although he wasn't injured, he didn't feel safe.

Mr. Wright appeared inside the shattered window. "What in devil do you mean, Big Kate; wrecking my saloon?" he demanded.

She replied, "Saloons are evil and the work of the Devil. Too many men have gone bad, and too many good women go hungry. Saloons are why so many children suffer. They deserve to be destroyed."

"If all women are like you, it's no durn wonder men spend all their time in saloons."

"Well, there won't be any saloons in Wyoming Territory. Women up there can vote."

"Why, heck, go to Wyoming Territory then," he shouted loudly in reply. After a lengthy pause, he stuck his head cautiously through the shattered window as she began to chop down the front door. "Heck," he shouted, "here's a twenty dollar gold piece." He took a gold piece from his pocket and tossed it out the window. It landed near the doorframe and bounced back onto the downed awning. "Take the next Over Land Stage to Wyoming!"

Big Kate's axe handle shattered with the third blow against the tall, wooden door.

Perplexed patrons were relieved when they learned that a splintered axe handle was all the huge woman now wielded.

A little man stuck his head through the shattered window. Upon seeing that she was limited in the damage that she could inflict with a broken axe handle, he began to horse-laugh her joyously while pointing his index finger at her.

Big Kate angrily slung the axe handle at him and when he ducked, she grabbed him by the neck and pulled him through the window opening. She ran her right hand under his wide, tan belt just above the seat of the pants, and with her left hand, she grabbed his shirt collar at the nape of the neck.

He was completely helpless as she carried him to the wooden door.

She began to swing him back and forth as if he were a pendulum on a grandfather clock. She addressed the oak door with his shiny baldhead and began to use him for a battering ram. After four stiff blows with the stationary door not budging, his shirt collar ripped loose from his white cotton shirt, which caused Big Kate to lose leverage with her left hand. This made her angrier because she could no longer use him for an improvised battering ram. She threw him back through the open window where he slid across a dining table and landed face-down in the wide saloon floor. In all her frenzied activity around the downed awning, she never once experienced the pleasure of piercing her heavy feet by stepping on a rusty nail with her tan leather loafers. She began to retreat in the direction whence she came.

Big Kate barged straight toward Junior and Oscar who were observing her. She stopped within three paces of them. With eyes of ice, muscles as taut as a strand of stretched barbed wire, and in a voice as hard as annealed steel, she said, "You men are fools to farm, look for gold or fence cattle. The smart money out here is in distilling liquor." She took a step in Oscar's direction, glowered down into his cowering eyes, and added, "A little shrimp like you would drink it faster than it could ferment." Big Kate waddled away from Oscar and Junior and soon disappeared between two wooden buildings. A blow for temperance had been struck; in fact, several blows had been struck.

What they had just witnessed made them thirsty. Junior and Oscar carefully navigated and crossed the exposed nails in the downed awning. They joined saloon patrons who felt they had earned the right to some serious drinking. As they were sitting at a table, a trio of Kansas ranchers entered the saloon and asked to join them. There was no objection, so the three pulled up chairs, one of which was borrowed and scooted from an unoccupied table. St. Peter took their orders for drinks.

"Where you boys from?" asked the tall, red-faced man across from Junior.

"We jist come up from Texas a few days ago."

"Texas," replied a man sitting on his left. "Why, that's like saying you're from Hell. A place has got to be bad if the Mexicans wouldn't' have it. Nobody in their right mind would live in Texas."

"More water in Hell," said a third, "and less heat."

"Heck," added the first, "Bow-legged Texans have to import Mexican men to take care 'o their women."

"We're living in Oklahoma Territory, now." added Oscar.

"Good night, that's worse than living in Texas. Kansas didn't want it and Texas wouldn't have it. Why, they ain't nothing but outlaws and wild Injuns running wild down there. Heck, it ain't even a state yet."

"Oklahoma Territory is downright dangerous," said the leader.

"Don't seem to have a monopoly. I met some outlaws in the Jayhawk Bank a couple o' days ago. It was the James gang."

"Well, the James gang is good outlaws," said the leader. "They rob from the rich and give to the poor. Seen it in the paper."

"Yeah, the feller they shot thought so too," Junior said as he looked intently into the big man's round, russet eyes. "He rob me of fifty dollars and made me porer. I could either give'em my money or git shot. I never consider muself wealthy."

"Well, ole Jesse will make it right," he added. "You married?"

"He's wigwamming," Oscar replied.

"Yeah," laughed the big man with a red face. "Why buy a cow when you can git milk free?" They all laughed but Junior.

"She work any place?"

"She use to pierce ears," Oscar replied.

"Pierce ears?" asked the leader. "She must o' sold cheap, costume jewelry. I say that because I'm just looking at you boys. Of couse, she could've worked in one of them places where they sell all kinds o' expensive jewelry. Did she sell expensive jewelry?"

"Heck no," Oscar replied with a laugh. "She use to be a saloon singer."

"Hey, that's pretty good. Where's she from?"

"West Virginia," Junior replied as he gave Oscar a pained look.

"West Virginia," ejaculated a little man who was sitting by Oscar. "They have an annual West Virginia celebration every year to celebrate the break from Virginia. They celebrate like there ain't no tomorrow."

"What's so unusual about that?" asked the big leader. "Lots o' states have special days they celebrate. In Texas they celebrate whipping the Mexicans. In Massachusetts they celebrate the Pilgrims. I'm sure West Virginians look forward with pride every year to that special day."

"Who said anything about West Virginians celebrating? These are Virginians celebrating gitting rid of that worthless hunk o' real estate." They all laughed.

"What are you laughing so hard about, Pee Wee?" The big man said. "You're from the dumbest state in the union."

"I am not," he replied as he took offense. "I'm from Tennessee."

"That's what I mean. They're so dumb they fly their flag upside down. It took a visiting Yale law professor to tell them that they was a flying it all wrong. He told them they ought to flip it over."

"I happen to like Tennessee."

"The only thing good I can say about Tennessee is that the Mississippi runs by it." Turning to Junior, he continued, "If you boys plan to live in Oklahoma, you ought to consider statehood. It'll help you clean up them outlaw gangs. It will also help you with your schools, and you'll have a place to throw your trash."

"You mean a place to throw yore garbage . . . like a dump?"

"Heck no; throw it along the roadside right o' ways."

"With statehood, "added the medium build man, "you don't have to worry about all them treaties we signed. You can march right through Injun land and look for gold, hunt wild game, or graze yore cattle. Statehood will give you a license to screw the Injuns."

"Looks like we're a doing purty good without a license," Oscar replied with a wide grin.

"Just think boys," said the big man, "with statehood, the government furnishes you with everything. If a man loses his job, the government will find him one. Don't even have to work unless you want to. Government provides lots of pensions, post offices, free school housing, and all kinds o' free stuff. You jist don't git them things otherwise. Statehood is like having a big brother watching out for ya."

"Who pays fer all them thangs?" asked Junior.

"Heck, the rich do. Yes, sir. It's like having Jesse James working for you. Nothing like statehood."

"Well, if statehood's like having Jesse James working fer ya, I know who'll pay," Junior said sarcastically. Then closing one eye while leaning across and setting his elbows on the table, he looked toward the server. He whispered to the big man, and asked, "I want to know something?"

"What's that?" he replied in a whisper.

"Why do they call that kid, St. Pete?"

A peal of laughter from the three visitors went unceasingly for two minutes. "Hey, kid," said the big man who finally called over to the young server. "This hillbilly poker player wants to know why they call you St. Pete?"

Upon hearing the question, the young man they called St. Peter blushed red and alternately pale. He made a desperate, unscheduled, half-hearted swipe with a soiled cleaning rag on a nearby, vacant tabletop and hastily retreated behind the serving bar. Oscar and Junior upon hearing the word "hillbilly," felt they were being used for sport. They rose, paid their bar tab, bought a bottle of whiskey, and left the saloon. Once outside, Oscar said, "It's my night fer Shy Ann."

"Yeah, if ya don't mind taking a number and standing in line."

Chapter 13
Oscar Takes a Squaw

They sat in the shortgrass. Their tired, tethered horses munched in an endless dry grassy field. Junior and Oscar were in Western Oklahoma Territory near the spot where Junior performed the operation on Two Feathers. With their trip to deposit Lil's thousand dollars in the First Jayhawk Bank an abject failure, the duo was returning to her sprawling Oklahoma Territory spread. Junior lay musing as his eyes searched the horizon of the dry grassy plains while his cousin turned a pint bottle to his parched lips. Junior muttered, "Do ya thank we done right by the Indians? You know, taking their land, killing the buffalo, and putting them on reservations."

Oscar removed the bottle from his burning lips and gasped for air. He felt as though his insides were torched from his burning mouth to his fiery stomach when he replaced the small metallic bottle cap. He replied, "I didn't have a thang to do with it. I ain't got an inch o' land to call my own. It's jist like right now. We're setting on ground that once belong to the Indians. The way I see it, Junior, is like this. Ya got Indian blood, ain't ye?"

"Yeah, my grandma was a full-blood Cherokee."

"Well, so have I. My grandpa was a fur trader with the mountain Cherokee, and he took a squaw. Now, the way

209

I figure it is like this. If we got Indian blood, we can't steal our own land. A man can't steal from hisself, kin he, Junior?"

"By golly, yore right Oscar. I hadn't thought of it like that. I feel better now." He reached for the round bottle and took a swig. As he was recapping the brown bottle, he saw in the vast distance on the far northern horizon what appeared to be two forms on horseback. Ever so slowly this small image was getting larger as it was moving toward them. "Thank my gift's coming back, Oscar. Yonder comes two Indians riding a paint pony."

"I don't see nothing," Oscar replied.

"You will. They'll be showing up in yore eyeballs in a few minutes."

Oscar finally saw the pony slowly approaching. "But they's only one rider on that paint. Thought ya said they was two. Sometimes I thank ya see more than is there. You need to adjust yore gift."

"They was," Junior said, as his focus was following a flock of fluffy geese flying across an endless sky.

"Well, they's jist one. Ya only got half a gift," Oscar replied as he chuckled.

At last, a pony and rider stopped before them. A slender, tanned Indian dismounted and stood in the shortgrass as he looked down upon the reclining duo. He held the pony's leather bridle and said, "Me look-um for Junior Justus."

"I'm Junior Justus," Junior replied while rising to his feet. He spit to the left of the dismounted Indian's scantily clad leg and cast a haughty glance of superiority in Oscar's direction.

"Ugh, me friend of Two Feathers. Me-um Chief Long Smile. Ugh, Two Feathers say you wise man for white man. No try to cheat-um Indian. You save him life. You Indian friend."

"Ya mean, Two Feathers made it?" asked Junior in disbelief.

"Ugh. Him going to live. Thank-um Junior Justus. Wise man white man. Chief Long Smile come to see-um wise man white man with gift."

"See, I told ya," Junior said as he looked around pompously toward Oscar who was still lazing in the short, dry grass.

"Indian in heap big trouble. White man kill-um buffalo, kill Indian, steal land. We starve and have no place to go. Great Spirit give-um no answers for Indians. We come to wise man Junior. What must-um Indian do?"

"Well, Chief Long Smile, it's like I told Chief Two Feathers. Looks like you boys have piss God or somebody off."

"What have-em Indian done?"

"I don't know, chief. Heard a Baptist Preacher once say that suffering's cause by sin. Now, whether he knowed what in the devil he was a talking about, or not; I don' know. But that's what that preacher beller out in church."

"Indian no sin. Do what always done. Still get-um bam bam from army fire sticks. No understand," he said in a fit of contorted discomfort.

"Look chief," Junior said as he placed his arm around the smaller man's shoulder. "Sometimes a man jist can't win. The deck is stack agin him. I mean the white man's greed is going to swallow yore land. If ya git in his way, he'll distroy ya. So, ya may as well let him take it. At least, that way you'll git to live."

"Ugh. Me see-um brothers die; squaws and children murdered in sleep. Medicine man say-um pale face to pay."

"Really, how?"

"Says someday Indian cousin from across-um big waters come. They swarm all over land. They buy up all land white man steal. Move-um white man to heap big-city reservation."

"That's inter-resting."

"Him say someday white man make-um treaty with enemy. Enemy laugh-um when enemy break treaty. Make white man slave."

"He may be right, chief. But right now the white man's after yore land. And he's after gold."

"You mean-um this stuff?" asked the chief as he pulled a large, brown bag off his small pony. He shook some yellow nuggets out into his cupped left hand. "This stuff. Me and Chief Two Feathers have-um plenty."

"Yeah," said Junior as he stood with mouth agape in amazement.

"Stuff worthless. Use to hold-em down treaties me sign with white man. Worthless!"

"It ain't worthless, chief."

"Ugh. Junior right. Do good job hold-um down treaties me sign. Me use-um to hold down skins on tepee and keep squaw from running off. Heap heavy stuff. Me mean treaties worthless."

"Chief, you kin use a poke o' this here stuff to buy about anythang."

"White man no give-um what Chief Long Smile want. Long Smile want land back. Be left alone. Indian want to be free to roam plains. Want-um be like in old days. Have land once more belong to Indians."

"Ya've got a point, chief."

"Me could buy-um gold mine from Whitey Black. Get much more yellow rocks. They go with-um heap big bag me already got."

"I wouldn't do that, chief."

"Ugh. Why-um not?"

"Well, fist of all, the land's yours to start with. If it's aw-ready yours, why buy it back? Another thang. If ya bought it back, the white man would only steal it from ya agin. Best to keep what ya got."

"Ugh, You wise man with-um gift. Chief Two Feathers want-um to give you gift." Chief long Smile called out in a loud, stentorian voice, "Little Doe!" His voice resounded across the vast plains.

From the seared plains grass, a beautiful, young Indian maiden soon appeared. She had plaited, black pigtails, dark eyes, and moved as lithely as a soft, gentle breeze when she slowly wafted across the shortgrass toward them. She stopped behind Chief Long Smile. She shyly stood behind the chief and peeped around his left shoulder through eyes of charcoal that glistened like cut diamonds in full sunlight. She cast her eyes demurely upon Junior. She was one lovely Indian maiden.

"Chief Two Feathers want-um to give gift to white man with gift. You take-um squaw, Little Doe."

"Thanks, chief, but I aw-ready got a squaw. Sort of."

"Yeah, he's wigwamming and he can't handle her," Oscar ejaculated. "He's aw-ready got a kid by somebody else and one o' his a coming. Junior's about hit his limit on squaws."

"Thanks Oscar," Junior said with a resigned frown.

"Then Chief Two Feathers want-um to give squaw to friend of Junior. Friend of Junior almost as good as Junior. You take-um Little Doe," said Chief Long Smile as he looked into Oscar's cringing eyes.

"Gosh, I . . . I don' know," stammered Oscar.

"Come on, Oscar. We can't insult the chief and Two Feathers. They might git mad if we don't take the squaw off his hands. She may be better than anythang at Bell's or Annie's. Heck, she could even be another Shy Ann."

"She-um no Cheyenne!" said the chief in a fit of anger and deep frustration. "She-um from same tribe as Chief Two Feathers. She Comanche!"

"Sorry, chief, He'll take her," said Junior to ease the chief's ruffled feelings.

"Squaw go-um to friend of Junior. Make good wife. Now," said Chief Long Smile with a licentious smile, "Chief Two Feathers want-um white squaw."

"What?" asked Junior and Oscar simultaneously in complete surprise.

"Ugh. Him give-um white man Indian squaw. Now, white man give-um Chief Two Feathers white squaw. That make-um us even."

"I'm afraid ya don't understan the white man's ways, chief. White squaws got to be woo and pamper. Why, my uncle spent a thousand dollars courting and wooing Aunt Flossie."

"Yeah," Oscar said, "and he still didn't git nothing."

"Him got-um yellow rocks," he said as he angrily persisted. "Him ought to have-um white squaw."

"Ya don't understan, chief," explained Oscar. "White squaws ain't use to roughing it like yore squaws. They won't go on buffalo hunts, tan hides, or gather nuts. Why, they're used to being pamper and having thangs hand to them. They spent half o' their time in front of a mirror primping; the other half o' the time they're bossing a man around. Most o' the time ya can't even shut them up. A white squaw ain't no picnic."

"Ugh. White man's burden."

"Tell ya what, chief," Junior said with a sudden inspiration. "I thank we kin work something out. Now, Two Feathers got to be careful, but I thank we kin pull it off. I'm going to write him a note, and he must go after dark. White men git the willies when they see an Indian. The name o' the place is Bell's. It's in Los Villas. Have him to tell Miss Bell that I sent him. He won't need all that gold. A nugget or two will do."

"Yeah," said Oscar as he cut into Junior's speil. "Don't do like me and Junior, blow hit all in one night on jist one white squaw."

"He will have to git a bath," Junior continued. "I'll give him some soap to bathe with. This way he kin have a white squaw and not have to haul her around. That would make him miserable. Ain't nothing worse than dragging a white squaw around and listening to her fuss, cry, bitch, and moan. That's why we got saloons. That's so white men kin git away from them. White squaws are hell to control. Ain't that right, Oscar?"

"Yeah, a white squaw kin shore make a man miserable aw right. Let one in yore tepee and she'll take it over. With a white squaw, Two Feathers would never go on the warpath agin. A white squaw would use all o' his war paint fer make-up."

"Me thank-um wise man white man and friend, Oscar," said the chief as he watched Junior scribble a brief note.

"Chief," asked Oscar as Junior scribbled, "I've wonder. How in the world do ya Indians ride them horses so fast with no saddles? I mean, there ain't no protection at all down here. They's a lot o' bouncing. Looks like it would kill you fellers."

"Ugh. That-um easy. Have-um things to take bounce," he said as he pulled a roly-poly louse from beneath the scanty deerskin covering his loins. As he held it out between his forefinger and thumb for them to see, both Oscar and Junior lurched back.

"Yikes," shouted Oscar.

"Ya will have to tell Two Feathers to git rid o' them before he goes into Bell's," said Junior. "Them white squaws are squeamy about little, unimportant thangs like that, chief. I'll send some o' my lye soap and some larkspur with ya. He kin use the soap to wash with. That ought to git rid o' them thangs fer Chief Two Feathers."

"If him get-um rid of louse, how him ride-um horse?"

"White man's about fix you fellers from riding horses," Oscar quipped.

"Oh, me almost forget. Chief Two Feathers send-um pages for Junior to read. Him been working to give-um Indian own scripture. Him take-um Junior's word to make-um own verses for *Indian Bible*."

"Verses for *Indian Bible*?" Junior asked.

"You say white man's Bible no apply to-um Indian," replied the chief as he reached Junior a manuscript. "Indian write own Bible. Here, you take-em look."

"Gosh, I don't know chief," said Junior as he took the manuscript with reluctance. He opened the tawny scroll, rolled it out, and read aloud the printed words on the parchment.

Against a cold sky the Great Spirit blew his breath against the stars, sun, and moon to make the earth.

The Great Spirit took the earth in his hands and blew the plains, mountains, and a dark sea.

With a great breath the Great Spirit blew with great force against the giant mountains of stone to make trees, grass and animals.

All races of man were made with another strong wind from the breath of the Great Spirit.

Upon seeing there were too many in one place, the Great Spirit scattered man to all parts of great earth.

A tired Great Sprit finished his great work and sat upon a high sacred mountain where he went to sleep never to wake.

All people who lived under great mountain where Great Spirit lay, lived in harmony with grass, trees, bees, woods, and all the animals, especially the great buffalo.

Many moons passed and the red man created by the Great Spirit lived in harmony with all things in the mighty land.

White man escaped from a far corner of the earth where Great Spirit placed him and entered the land of the red man.

And these white men with long knives and fire sticks and self importance made all creatures bend to them.

So, the white savages made muddy rivers, dug their claws deep in the earth, burned trees as waste, and dirtied the sun that walks the sky.

One day he rested and bragged of the good work he had done and called it progress.

These white men ignored the Great Spirit and went forth to boast to all other men that they should be like him.

And, as the white man puffed out his chest, the red man perished by fire sticks, sickness, and starvation on reservations.

Sacred treaties between white man and red man were like dry sticks broken to steal sacred Indian land.

One last great chief went to where Great Spirit sleep on mountain to wake him. . . .

"Hey, this here is great stuff chief. Don't ya thank so, Oscar?"

"Yeah, heck. I might be tempt to read something like that myself."

"This ought to make a nice road map for yore people to follow," said Junior. "This is great stuff. Chief Two Feather's tribe ought to be proud. Who he'ped Two Feathers write these here verses?"

"Ugh. French fur trader who take-um squaw."

"That figures," Oscar said with assurance.

"Figures what, Oscar?"

"The settlers can't write like that. They're too busy fighting Indians and killing buffalo to learn to put their ideas on paper. They go loco when they thank about gold. Yeah, writing is the last thing they want to do."

"Yeah. Maybe Little Doe kin bring out yore talent, Oscar. Tell ya what, chief. This world would be a purty scary place without a God. The Great Spirit is okay, but he went to sleep on ya. Don't ya thank so, Oscar?"

"Why, yeah," said Oscar. "It's like He done all that hard work. Then when He got done, He got a government job and went to sleep. Tell Two Feathers to make a god. He needs to go into more detail and explain it more. He covers from the time o' creation to now in jist one chapter."

"You say no God would let-um Indian perish," said Long Smile with a scowl.

"I know, chief," Junior replied, "but it's a little hard to have the Great Spirit jist die off. See if Two Feathers kin put Him behind the moon to let Him sleep. At least there will be hope that He'll wake up."

"Yeah," Oscar added, "or git Him drunk and have Him stagger around somewhere down in Mexico."

"And ya'll need to write some more. Two Feathers needs to come up with a couple more thousand chapters to make a complete book." Junior said as he muttered mundanely.

Junior handed the parchment back to chief Long Smile. Chief Long Smile rode away with the knowledge that he had been in the presence of a wise, white man.

Junior, with Oscar and Little Doe riding double, traveled in a northeast direction toward Lil's log cabin. It wasn't long before all the participants of the productive powwow on the plains were engulfed in darkness.

They neared Lil's ranch at midnight. Fifteen rods from her cabin, Junior turned to face Oscar and said, "They's a man at the well."

"Heck, all I see is that crazy, white goat."

Sure enough, when Junior turned to look again, the man was gone. All he saw was Ringer chasing an object that swiftly galloped through the shadows of the star-lit night and away from the quaint cabin. "Could a swore they was a man at the well," he said as he shook his head.

They found nothing upon close inspection in the darkness. There was not a thread of physical evidence to prove that what Junior had seen was correct.

This is what happened. A man with a birthmark that darkened a greater portion of the left side of his face was standing at the well. When he bent over to drop an oaken water bucket back into the shallow water, Ringer charged this unsuspecting man from behind and butted him so hard that he fell into the shallow well. Ringer then chased a galloping shadow, which was the man's saddled horse. The horse was still bridled and saddled and had two saddlebags bearing the initials P.P. when it was found on the sprawling plains two days later by some fur trappers bound for the Colorado Rockies.

After they completed their fruitless inspection at the well, Junior banged on the wooden door of Lil's cabin.

Lil greeted the trio and prepared a place on the dirt floor for the two guests. Junior looked into a full bucket of water by the wood stove and saw his facial reflection. "How do we know that we're looking at life and not its reflection in a mirror? Is all we see an illusion?" he muttered aloud.

"If we had a couple of swigs o' something, it wouldn't matter," Oscar replied.

It was a bleak winter that the four spent at Lil's ranch in the Oklahoma Territory. It could be called a Pilgrim winter because the white inhabitants were dependent upon the generosity of Little Doe's Indian tribe. Many times throughout the bitter, harsh winter, they saw Indians on horseback making tracks in the snow to Lil's cabin door. Little Doe's tribe kept Lil's pantry stocked with grain and smoked game of all kinds that included, deer, rabbit, and horsemeat. Mr. Black sent Lil child support payments as promised, but Junior managed to get his hands on that money to buy whiskey and other alcoholic beverages at the Prairie Mariner, a distant Oklahoma Territorial trading post. Also, he bartered many of the supplies given to them by the Indians for whiskey and beer.

Two Feathers's tribe believed they were getting a good value from Junior. He critiqued more than twenty chapters for the planned *Indian Bible*. Little Doe was sick much of the time during the winter, and the chief sent potent herbal potions concocted by the tribal medicine man, Smoking Pine. Lil's gestation with Junior's child must have provided her with immunity from the many ailments that Little Doe suffered. Lil made generous use of an abundant snowfall that she melted to provide the household with clean drinking water. Later, the well water became so rank that she availed herself of the flowing spring water that was a half mile away on the western side of her log cabin. Junior and Oscar didn't get sick because they never touched the stuff—water.

In March there was no more contact with the Indians. With no tribal contact, the flow of chapters for the planned *Indian Bible* also stopped. They missed the visits by the Indians; Little Doe missed them the most.

Oscar led Little Doe from the storm cellar in early April. It was a living quarters strewn with a blizzard of empty whiskey bottles scattered about like small, randomly placed tombstones. In the storm cellar, the glass lips of every empty alcohol beverage container whispered the word "decadence." Oscar stood on the wooden ladder's lowest rung and threw open the wooden cover above their heads that let a rushing wind sweep into their stale abode. Once outside the cellar, their bones basked in the sun's warmth that was heralding a new spring.

Oscar wanted to teach Little Doe how to till the soil. He rigged a harness for her to pull a bull-foot plow through the tough grassy sod atop the deep, fertile Oklahoma soil. His intention was for her to pull the plow to make a furrow to start the first row of a garden spot. He could teach Little Doe to pull a plow that would be useful when she and Lil planted a small garden. Gardening would be left to the womenfolk while he and Junior engaged in more manly pursuits. Manly pursuits like drinking whiskey and carousing all night. Gardening would be difficult, backbreaking work, but he had every confidence that the young women could produce a bountiful variety of foodstuffs in the garden. Oscar reasoned that a gainful, outdoor activity would be healthy for the women.

Junior saw what Oscar was planning. For a private talk, he went to the area away from the cabin where Oscar planned for the women to grow a new garden. He took his cousin aside and whispered, "Look, Oscar, let's be humane here. You know how tough this here virgin plains grass is to pull a plow through. Little Doe ain't up to what ya got in mind. Let's rig up some harness fer Ringer. Lil knows how to handle him. We kin learn the girls to use him to pull a plow."

Oscar agreed with Junior's idea.

Junior looked forward to the first week in May. He planned to make a trip to Los Villas in West Texas in hopes of finding his brother Josh. Furthermore, he was intent on collecting his thousand dollars from Mr. Black, and his winning gambling bet from lawyer Jackson. On the day they were preparing to make the journey, Oscar climbed the storm cellar ladder and sidled over to Lil's cabin. On tiptoes he peeped through a side window with lightly colored, partial curtains and into the one-room domicile that Lil kept as neat as a pin. A pre-marital spat was in progress.

"What do you mean going off and leaving me?" she asked. "You know this water from the well stinks. It foams worse than that bad, green beer you get plastered with. I'm tired of carrying water from that little spring way out yonder. We've got to dig a new well. We've got to plant a garden. We need all kinds of hand tools to make a go of it. I don't know why I ever consented to come out here to the middle of nowhere in the first place. You've squandered every cent I've got. I can't get you to—"

"Oh, darn it, woman," he shouted. He picked up a chair and smashed it across the washstand, breaking the chair, washstand, and a hand-painted water pitcher and bowl. With his worn, leather, left boot, he kicked the small dining table over and broke several gray dishes. As the one week old baby girl, Cora Jane, in the corner began to cry, a scared little, dark-haired boy, James Joshua, curled himself into a little round ball in the opposite corner. He peeped through his tiny fingers at the two combatants. Junior pulled some clean clothes from the iron nails on the rough log wall, threw them into the dirt floor and stomped them. After he kicked over their small, cast-iron stove, he stalked over to the parrot's cage hanging from the ceiling and hastily jerked away the dark, cotton cloth cover.

"*Squawk, squawk*, Junior's got a gift, Junior's got a gift, *Squawk, squawk*," went the parrot.

Junior spit into the cage near the parrot's left talon. With one-eye closed, the multi-colored parrot cocked his head to one side and looked askance at Junior. Junior hesitated a few seconds before he reached for and grabbed the metallic cage. He slammed it against a far wall near a small window where it bounced back and landed in the center of the cabin floor near the overturned cast-iron stove.

When the cage came to a rolling stop, the dazed parrot looked up through glassy eyes at Junior, and said, "*Squawk, squawk*, Shorty's a cuckold, Shorty's a cuckold, *squawk, squawk*, Whitey's a crook, Whitey's a crook, *squawk, squawk*, Lil's pregnant, Lil's pregnant, s*quawk, squawk*."

Junior moved his glare from a squawking Gabby to his terrified family. He spit into the floor and stalked from the cabin.

Oscar rushed to join Junior outside the cabin. Junior bent over and picked up a small, smooth round stone. He was ninety paces away when he hurled the arching stone through a lone side window. It shattered a clear glass pane but fortunately no one inside was injured from the impromptu stone toss. Oscar picked up a rock and slung it in the same direction where it hit a pine log to the left of the shattered window and bounced harmlessly back into green sprouting, grassy yard.

"Gawd, Junior," he exclaimed, "this here's fun ain't it? There ain't nothing in the world like wigwamming is there?"

Junior had a snarl on his face when he looked down at his short sidekick.

Once they were on the trail, Junior said, "Boy, I'd swap both of these here horses fer a shot o' whiskey."

"Yeah," Oscar replied, "ya've aw-ready swap Wheeler fer a jug three months ago."

"Made a real swap, too."

Later that day they stopped to rest their tired horses by a clear spring. They sat in the parched grass with tender green sprouts shooting from the soil beneath. Their horses were grazing nearby. Oscar reached inside the front pocket of his Levi's, and said, "By the way, Junior, right here's a poem I want ya to read." He handed it to him.

Junior read the poem aloud.

One Lonely Indian

She dreads a white man's calaboose
Hewn from oak wood to hurt, abuse.
The fight of her tribe is now gone,
Far from the stars, she walks alone.
Why does this endless blizzard roar?
Gods have forgotten her for sure.
Tear drops don't stop, each day's the same.
With empty heart she lives in vain.
A song she's wafted on the wind,
Though broken like a bird's pinion;
Alone, alone she roams the canyon,
This minion is one lonely Indian.

"This here is great stuff, Oscar. Who wrote this fer ya? Some Frenchman been visiting Little Doe while me and you's been out a carousing? I know you couldn't o' wrote it. Ya got jist enough school housing to be dangerous."

"I didn't say I wrote it, Junior. We come in from a drinking spree last night at the Prairie Mariner. We got home, and I fell down that storm cellar ladder. When I got to my feet, there was this old, dark hag of a woman that look like a prune. Well, her and Little Doe was setting at the table, and this here old squaw had a pencil in her hand, writing. She was mumbling to Little Doe when I turn my back to take a drank. When I turn back around, she was gone. I mean, she vanish jist like she wasn't there and hadn't been there. Little Doe reach me this here poem. She told me this old squaw that had been sitting there—Saka Jaw . . . or something like that—said fer me to hand it to ya. Ya would know what to do with it. I guess she thanks yore smart."

"Bet it's the same one I seen in a stagecoach in Los Villas. She thanks I've got a gift."

"The only gift ya'll ever git, Junior, is the pox."

"Thanks, Oscar. Let me look at that poem agin," he said, reaching for the paper. "Gosh, Oscar, I don't know. It seems a little stiff to set to music. We might stretch the words out a little to make it flow with a melody. I know. When we find Josh, he kin run it in his newspaper."

They stopped three miles from Los Villas. Junior wanted to survey what appeared to be a dwarf pyramid on the vast, grassy horizon. They continued to approach the tan pyramid, and it appeared, at least to Junior, to be a large, brown, square tarpaulin tent with rectangular dots surrounding it. "Looks like a big tent and wagons," said Junior.

"Yore gift agin," Oscar replied with a chuckle.

"Oscar, you sound jist like Gabby."

They rode closer and Oscar realized that Junior was right. A huge tent became more visible and the rectangular dots became stationary wagons, hacks, and buckboards. They approached nearer and nearer until a low rumble in their ears became melodic voices singing hymns. They were within twenty-five paces of the tent when they spotted a well-dressed man in a sable, wool suit standing by a wide opening. He stood there as if he were guarding those singing inside. Junior stared into the sad eyes of the middle-aged man, and softly whispered, "Oscar, right here's a chance to git some whiskey."

Inside the tent, the music stopped. A loud, stentorian voice began to orate in an orotund tone of voice. Oscar replied, "Ain't no way. They're about the Lord's business."

They tied their horses at a makeshift hitching rail. They approached the man at the tent opening and peered inside. Temporary wooden bench seating accommodated a large crowd that watched a dark-eyed, forty-two-year-old preacher who was wearing a black, worsted wool suit, white shirt, and a wide, black necktie. As he continued into his bombastic oration from a raised platform at the front of the large tent, his rapt audience seemed mesmerized by the words rolling off his cloying unceasing tongue. Time after time, he propounded to his listeners the healing power of the Holy Spirit. He seemed to be on a sacred mission.

They observed the ongoing activity in the sweltering tent for a few minutes. As they stood there, the man beside them gave a tacit nod to coax them to retreat toward the waiting wagons. By a scotched, brown, covered-wagon drawn by a sleek pair of black workhorses tied to a stake, he said, "You boys want to make some money? We could use you."

"What do ya mean?" asked Oscar.

"Brother Smith is about to begin healing folks. He needs some volunteers to be healed."

"Why, they ain't nothing wrong with us," Junior said to let him know that he and Oscar were physically healthy.

"Now, Junior," Oscar said as he nudged him gently in the ribs with his elbow, "I don't want to sound out o' turn, but pa aw-ways said you was a little slow. He said he notice a big change in you years ago. It was right after you eat that chocolate coated candy. He said it was soak with kerosene."

"Yeah, Oscar, but I mean I'm as strong as a bear."

"What we need is for somebody to be lame. Somebody lame will permit Brother Smith to heal him."

"I'm afraid ya'll have to git somebody else," replied Junior as he spit near the man's left boot. "Heck, we kin both walk purty good. See, here. Watch me take some long easy strides."

"What I'm saying is that we need to show these folks God's healing power. We can show it by using a vessel that is already healed. We can show it better with one that's healed than with one that's broken."

"What's he saying, Oscar?"

"He's saying that they need somebody to fake being cripple. That's so they kin fleece them clods in there under the tent."

"We're prepared to pay twenty-five dollars. That's for one of you boys to throw a set of crutches away when Brother Smith lays a healing hand on you. It won't take but a few minutes. After that, you can be on your way."

"I don't know," Junior said.

"And," the man added with a sinister gleam in his disquiet eyes, "we're also prepared to give him two pints of the best whiskey in North Texas."

"Where's yore crutches?" Junior asked as he reached to shake the man's hand.

"Need a blind man?" Oscar inquired.

"We've already got one of them lined up," replied the man perfunctorily as he was trying to get the feeling back in his right hand. "Now, don't move, young man, until I get your crutches."

From the wooden bed of his sleek, tarpaulin covered wagon, the preacher's assistant reached beneath a long, narrow bench and withdrew a worn pair of dark, wooden crutches. He handed them to Junior. "Here's your ticket," said the man.

"Could ya use another cripple?" Oscar asked.

"No," replied the man. "You're too short. With your short legs, folks in there might not realize that you were crippled."

Junior used the crutches to swing himself up to the tent opening. He rested on his crutches as he firmly felt the tent flap opening with his fidgety fingers.

Oscar and the faith healer's assistant stood beside him at the wide opening.

Junior didn't have long to wait.

A kneeling man was facing away from the mesmerized audience as Reverend Smith stood before them with an outstretched right arm. A Bible was under his left arm as he closed his eyes and raised his head upward toward the steamy tent top. As the wiry wrinkles on his forehead accented the streaming perspiration on his wide, compelling face, he began to invoke the name of Jesus to heal the consenting man. At last the man stood, looked about in wild wonderment toward the gasping crowd, and shouted in loud exultation, "I kin see! Praise God, I kin see! Glory hallelujah!"

Junior was next to experience a healing touch. Brother Smith's nod and his assistant's nudge were his signal to hobble forward on his wooden crutches. "A man on crutches," shouted the preacher to the gathered throng. He stood with a serious demeanor as he placed both hands on a kneeling Junior. To the crowd, he said, "Oh, Holy Spirit with the power to cast out devils, to speak in tongues, and make the lame walk; heal this man! Heal him! Heal! Heal! Heal!"

After an extended encomium, Junior, using the crutches, stood erect. With rapture-like awe, he stood there for several suspenseful seconds before reacting. "Hallelujah!" he shouted.

He turned to face the crowd while the attendant at the tent opening held two bottles of whiskey high in the air above his head and began to wave them around in wild animation. Saliva flowed instantly toward his thirsty lips, and, in his extreme excitement, he slung the crutches high into the air with one going to his left and one going to his right. On the left, a flying crutch barely missed two shouting believers. On the right, the other flying crutch similarly spared the mesmerized believers. It struck the hot, flimsy tarpaulin tent twenty-three feet above the nearest believer and knocked a wide hole in the top. The crutch cleared the tent and sailed safely into the greening, outside grass. Junior played to the capacity throng as he began to hop in a circle, shout God's praises, and finished by skipping toward the rear tent opening. Oscar, Brother Smith's assistant, and Junior departed the tent for the faith-healing messenger's wagon. It was time to settle up.

As the crowd shouted praises, Junior asked, "How did I do?"

"Good, good," replied the preacher's assistant with a lack of enthusiasm. "Listen, we're a little short on ready cash. It takes a lot of money to do the Lord's work. Besides, we're going to have to repair that damaged tent where your crutch went through. Here's a ten dollar gold piece. That's all we can spare."

"To heck with the extra gold pieces; what about that whiskey ya promise?" he demanded as Oscar looked on.

"You boys know strong drink is against God's plan of salvation. The body is a temple for the Holy Spirit. Strong drink is an abomination to the body and will destroy the soul. It'll send a man straight to Hell. You don't want to spend eternity in Hell, do you?" he asked while breaking into a wide frown that was reinforced by sweaty iron-like rebars across his brow. He seemed to be immovable.

Junior was disappointed. He turned to Oscar and said, "Oscar, look in the back of the preacher's wagon. They might be another set o' crutches in there. I'm feeling a weakness in my knees. Need to hobble back in there fer a full refill o' healing. If they ain't a set back there, they ought to be a crutch out there in the grass summers. Heck, one crutch ought to be enough to do the trick."

"Oh, wait, wait," said the man hastily. "I believe the Lord's about to make an exception." He hastily searched for and found two bottles of whiskey inside his deep jacket pockets. He handed each a bottle.

Chapter 14
Last Days in Los Villas

"I come to git my thousand dollars, Whitey," Junior said to a seated Mr. James Black in his office in the Avalanche Saloon. Mr. Roy Loftis was standing at the left side and in front of Mr. Black's desk.

"What do you mean?" he asked as he looked up from his desk.

"Why, that thousand dollars I was to git fer bringing Lightning back from Colorado."

"I gave it to Word Twister," he replied. A brief wrinkle on his forehead revealed his surprise. "I gave it to him so long ago that I had just about forgotten about it."

"How come ya give it to him?"

"He said that he won it in a bet with you. Seems that you wagered that—which one was it—yes, Spokane Spike. You bet that he would be dead within a certain length of time."

"How did he figure that?"

"It seems that it was nearing 5:00 p.m. You bet him that Spike would be dead within the hour. You had about fifteen minutes before the hour was up, or something like that, to finish him off. Even without that consideration, he figures that he still won due to all the delays. Spike didn't' die until after 6:00 p.m.; that made it over an hour. I've got the certificate of death if you want proof," he said as he cast his eyes down to his top desk drawer. "Furthermore, Shortchange was a witness to your wager. As you know, Shortchange carries a lot of weight in this town."

"O—, oh," Junior moaned as he held his head with the palms of both hands.

"Perhaps, I should have paid you off first. But, as you can see, Word Twister, the lawyer that he is, made a convincing argument. Besides, you weren't around. Word Twister could have made a case that you didn't finish off Spike. You didn't fire your six-shooter; a stampede got him. I paid Mr. Ames right after the incident."

Junior turned to Mr. Loftis who had his right arm in a sling. His left hand was wrapped with white bandages. Junior asked, "What happen to ya this time, Lightning?"

"Tried to turn a herd o' stampeding cattle," he replied.

Mr. Loftis could have added some details to complete the injury report. The particular herd of cattle he was attempting to turn belonged to a feisty rancher in West Texas. This ornery rancher was attempting to prevent his grazing cattle from being rustled by a band of masked outlaws that Mr. Loftis was leading.

A downcast Junior left Mr. Black's office to join a waiting Oscar.

Mr. Black and Mr. Loftis continued their discussion. "I can't understand what happened to Philadelphia Phil?" said Mr. Black as he watched Mr. Loftis who was once again pacing the floor and puffing a big brown stogie. "He was supposed to be here last fall. And Frisco Frank; what a disappointment he was! He's in town fifteen minutes, and he rides off with Tumbleweed and a St. somebody from Wedgewood. Well, if this last one doesn't work out, I guess I'll have to cut back on my operations. It doesn't seem as if anything has gone right since we robbed that gold train at Eagle's Pass. At least, I've been able to build a new hotel for the newspaper convention that's going on right now. I'm hoping Los Villas will become a tourist attraction. After that showdown between Spike and that hillbilly, we've had lots of interest.

"Now, I can't be seen over there at the new hotel right now. I don't want my fingerprints on this. So, have Ivory to meet Charlotte Sean over at the hotel and tell him what I want. He should arrive there any time now. He's to get a thousand now and the rest when he finishes off the sheriff. Here's a bag with the advance money. I want to lay low until this job is done. I don't want the Texas Rangers to find out I had a hand in this. I can't afford to have them snooping around. They could spoil everything."

"At least we got the gold from under the sheriff's nose," said Mr. Loftis. "Too bad that Racketguy man that bought yore salted mine hit it big. He got all that fancy machinery in there and really struck a big vein. He hit pay dirt big time. Who would a thought it?"

"I'm trying to forget about that, Lightning. Hate you got torn up."

"Which time?"

"That cattle stampede in West Texas. You know, the one we planned for days. We figured it from every angle, right down to the last detail. Then there was a cloud burst and that ranch owner and his ranch hands showed up. What's left of my gang got tore up pretty bad."

"We got jist a few scratches and got away. I ain't hurt too bad."

"You're pretty resilient."

"Heck, boss, that's the first time anybody ever told me that I was smart."

Junior met Oscar at the saloon hitching post. Oscar was observing a heavyset, round-faced, fifty-year-old man who was dressed in an ill-fitting suit with baggy pants.

The man was standing on a backstep of a red, covered wagon with Miracle Cure Medicine Tonic written in large, black letters across the side. "Step right up, folks," he said in a mellifluous voice accented by a slight nasal twang. "Red Chief Healing Tonic will cure what ails you. This is the miracle healing tonic of the century. It'll grow hair on a baldhead, take off warts, cure consumption, dandruff, or anything else that ails you. Did you know that the army uses this very remedy before battles? It's from an old Indian recipe and your satisfaction is guaranteed or your money back. This is your last chance to restore your lost youth. Yes, folks, this here tonic is only one dollar a bottle. Who'll be the first, folks. Step right up," he said to the dense, gathered crowd.

"Where are ye going, Oscar. Ya know he's a fake."

"Well, Junior, I ain't found no truth since I left Jewel Hill. This may be my last chance to find it. Sometimes I thank these fellers that preach religion and sell cure-all tonics have something. They provide entertainment fer people who can't wait to be hoodwinked."

"By the way, Oscar, did Whitey pay ya fer he'ping to find Lightning?"

"He shore did. He paid me right after we got back. In fact, Weasel handed me the money the evening after you left Los Villas that morning. I told Weasel I would leave town as soon as I left Bell's."

"Ya didn't tell me, doggone it. So that's what went with yore money?"

"Well, Junior, it's like this. I went over to Bell's and a funny thang happen in there."

"I know, Oscar. Which one o' Bell's girl's roll ya, or was it a team effort? Bell has lined up some real doozies. No wonder she put Virginia House out o' business. They left you penniless, didn't they?"

"Heck, Junior. I don't ast you about what goes with yore money."

"Guess yore right, Oscar."

They soon left the large crowd at the mountebank's medicine wagon. Sheriff Brooks accosted Junior who was on his way to The Prairie Chicken Crier. They approached Sheriff Brooks who was leaning against a four-inch square post that supported a porch awning at the little adobe jail. "Ain't seen you boys around in a while. Don't tell me you're here fer the reporters' convention. Where you boys been?" he asked.

"Been a living over in the Oklahoma Territory. Come back to git a line on my brother Josh."

"Josh Justus, the reporter?"

"Why, yeah. He's my brother."

"I'll be darned. And ole Josh is yore brother? He won't be sticking his face back around here no more," said the sheriff as he laughed. "Not since he took out o' here on Big Harry."

"Big Harry must have been some kind o' horse?"

"Horse, northing. Big Harry was one big, mean, ornery bull. Ole Josh was strapped to him and turned loose on the plains. Why, that devil nearly killed poor Josh. Say, Junior, I've heard a lot about you being with them Indians," said the sheriff as they watched Chief Two Feathers slide through an open window at Bell's, "I'd like fer you to tell me something: I've got a fourteen-year-old grandson I want to teach to wrangle. How could I git him started?"

Junior wasn't paying attention to Sheriff Brooks's question. He was observing a large blue-uniformed army officer entering Bell's. A shiny, black briefcase was in his hand. He had been shadowing Chief Two Feathers.

"Why, git him elect to the Texas legislature," interjected Oscar with a laugh. "He'll learn how to wrangle."

"Shoot, I want him to wrangle, not be a durned crook."

"Hey," Junior asked, "won't that bluecoat kill that Indian?"

"Heck no," replied the sheriff, "These army boys don't like killing defenseless Indians no more than nobody else. Captain Sanders is pretty dang smart. He's in there to git another treaty signed. It's a whole lot easier to git them signed in there than out on the plains. Heck, it's a lot o' work chasing them Indians all over the West jist to git a treaty signed. This way it don't take but five minutes."

Unobserved by the trio was a man who tied his horse outside the Avalanche Saloon. This clean-shaven, tall stranger was wearing two pearl-handled pistols strapped at either side of his slender waist. He approached Mr. Jacobs at the entrance just outside the swinging doors. "Where can I find Whitey Black and the Los Villas sheriff," asked the fancy-dressed stranger.

Mr. Jacobs sensed some fun with this tenderfoot. "Why," the sheriff's in his office at the back o' this here saloon. Whitey Black is that ugly, big fellow with them two young fellers over there in front o' the Jail."

"Why ain't the sheriff over at the jail?"

"He hardly ever goes over there. That big feller, Whitey Black, in front o' the jail is his deputy, and he keeps the peace. The sheriff has lots o' business on the side. He don't go over there to the jail unless he's really needed. He says things run smoother that way. Now, when you go in this here saloon, you'll usually find the sheriff sitting behind the desk in his office. His office is behind the door to the left of the bar and to the right o' the stairs." He looked over the swing doors, and continued, "See that big door yonder. You can't miss it; it's the only big door in there. They're real protective o' him in there, so I wouldn't ask no questions from nobody. Don't look fer no badge because he don't wear one. They may be a tall feller in there with him. He's a sidekick. Don't pay no attention to him. He'll be the feller standing up and smoking a big cigar. If it was me, I'd jist march right on in there," said Mr. Jacobs, satisfied that he had set afoot a practical joke.

Soon after the stranger entered the saloon, a rider dismounted at the jail. "What brings you back this way? asked sheriff Brooks in a friendly tone of voice. "Ain't you Texas Rangers got nothing to do?"

"Ole Shorty sent me," said Mr. Lance McCoy. "He wanted a ranger presence here fer the newspaper meeting. He's afraid somebody might try to plug some o' these reporters. You know how they like to exaggerate and stretch the truth. He also got a line that that lousy Charlotte Sean might be headed this way. Boy, he's a dandy."

"Say," asked Junior, "ever find out who stold that gold from the jail?"

"Yeah, we're pretty sure we know. It's jist that we can't quite prove it. The one we think done it is buddies with Governor Shorty Asher. Be hard to convict him. Besides, he's given money to the orphans and widows o' the train heist at Eagle's Pass. He's also built a brand spanking new hotel here that ought to help with tourists. Since he's done so much good with the money, the folks back east ain't pressing for it. Now, this is just a hunch between me and us four standing here. I think he went to the right schools back east, married the right woman, and made the right friends. Don't think they'll let anybody lay a finger on him. These big shots take care o' their own," Mr. McCoy replied. He turned to face Sheriff Brooks, tacitly nodded, and they slipped inside the jail.

Junior and Oscar strolled toward the newspaper office. Editor Wilson informed Junior that he had received information that Josh was in town and was a reporter for the Plains Star in Wichita, Kansas. Junior was satisfied that at last he had a line on his brother's whereabouts. As they entered the street from the newspaper office, he said, "Oscar, I need to talk to Chief Two Feathers."

"Yeah, he's probably still at Bell's," said Oscar. "So, ya finally got a line on Josh."

"Yeah, Josh was handy with the women. If he hadn't been, I wouldn't be out looking fer him."

They heard two pistol shots from the saloon. Shortly a calm, tall, neatly dressed man emerged. He wore smooth Levi's, a clean, tight-fitting, gray cotton shirt, and a black Stetson hat. He calmly strolled across the street in the direction of the sheriff's office.

Upon hearing the shots from the saloon, Sheriff Brooks and the Texas Ranger hastened to investigate. They met the stranger in the middle of the street. "I want my four thousand," demanded the stranger.

"Four thousand what?" asked the sheriff.

"I just erased a pest for ya," growled the man in a soft, Southern drawl.

"What are you talking about?" asked sheriff Brooks.

"Don't play games with Charlotte Sean, Whitey Black," said the man as he fidgeted nervously with the pearl-handles of his six-shooters. "I jist got rid of that pest of a sheriff for you. Now, I want the rest o' my money."

Sheriff Brooks stood there a long second with mouth agape. Suddenly, as if a light clicked on brightly in his brain, he replied, "Oh, I'll have to git the money from the safe. Come on into the office."

Once inside the jail, Sheriff Brooks and Ranger McCoy got the drop on Charlotte Sean and arrested him. "We're locking you in a cell until we find out what this here's all about," said the sheriff.

In the saloon the mood was glum. Morty had two Avalanche patrons to carry Whitey Black's limp body through the swinging doors and down the street to his mortician's office. A noisy saloon patron yelled, "What's the matter with you idiots? Ain't nobody never seen a killing before? Let's have something to drink and some music before I git mad. Heck, ya don't want me to shoot the lights out or make somebody dance to the music o' my six-shooter, do ya? Is that what ya want?"

Ivory resumed playing for Miss Rush to sing. She did not seem to be overwrought by Mr. Black's sudden demise. Activity in the saloon soon returned to normal as drinks were poured while cards were dealt. Most of the patrons seemed to forget Whitey Black's sudden bucket-kicking experience with the exception of Mr. Jacobs. He sat alone brooding on an end barstool while staring at his empty whiskey shot glass. He sat there in disbelief that his practical joke took such a nasty, unforeseeable turn. For him, Fate had given his practical joke an ugly twist.

Over Miss Rush's singing, Mr. Rowe said to a friend sitting at his table. "Looks like that hillbilly and his friend are back in town."

"Which one is he . . . the hillbilly I mean?" asked a new patron.

"He's the slim, dumb looking one with a hawk's beak fer a nose. His name is Junior. The little, dumpy, short, blonde-haired feller's his sidekick. You would think that little fellow is Junior's shadow."

"Oh, yeah," said another patron, "I remember Junior from the cattle drive to Arizona. Heck, he walked into Hotel Americana in Tucson, Arizona, and asked for a room. The hotel clerk said, 'That'll be twelve dollars, please.' The hillbilly said, 'Got a deed?' 'A deed?' asked the surprised clerk. 'Yeah,' the hillbilly replied, 'if I'm going to buy the place, I might as well git a deed fer it.'" They all laughed.

"Was that the same day he walked by a big, fat woman in the lobby?" said another cowboy. "He looked her over twice and then went outside. He picked up two big lumps o' coal from the hotel's coal bin and come back inside. He held out a lump in the palm of each hand in front of her face, and said, 'Lady, would you set on these?'

"The confused woman asked, 'Sit on them; why? Why do you want me to sit on them?'

"'Well, I've heard enough pressure on coal will make diamonds. A women with a rear end as big as yours ought to make a killing.'

"I tell you, that woman got hopping mad. I thought she'd have a hemorrhage right there in that hotel lobby. 'If I had a gun,' she said, 'I'd blow your stupid brains out.'

"You know what that hillbilly said? He said, 'Why heck, lady, don't git mad at me. I was a going to split half of them diamonds with ya, fifty-fifty.'"

Junior and Oscar darted into the saloon through the swinging doors. Laughter was ebbing from a Junior Justus joke. Miss Rush began to sing "Camptown Races" as they ordered drinks at the bar. They began to gulp their drink when Junior looked in the direction of a downcast Mr. Jacobs. "Hey," asked Junior directing his question to him, "where's Tumbleweed?"

"Oh, haven't you heard?" Mr. Rowe replied from a nearby table. "There was a St. Peter fellow in here a couple o' months ago, and they got to be real close friends. About a month later, some fancy dressed dude named Frisco Frank come riding through these here parts. These three merry men just faded into the sunset in the direction o' California. They all left here riding on the same horse." Patrons roared with laughter so loud that it stopped Miss Rush from singing and Mr. Jones from playing the piano. Mr. Jones and Miss Rush decided to take a short break.

"They's a man out in the street," said Leroy Forbes who came rushing through the swinging doors from the outside.

"He's coming in fer Junior Justus. Goes by the name o' Mad Mex, Sr."

Junior noticed Mr. Forbes bandaged hand. "What happen to yore hand, Slick?"

"Heck, didn't you hear?" asked Mr. Rowe. "He slugged a wooden Injun the night you left town. Ole Doc Witt patched him up and has since reset the bones twice. That hand is now a running sore. It beats anything you ever seen. Ole Doc says it looks like it ain't gonna heal."

"Guess that'll teach him not to mess with them Indians," jested Oscar.

"Who is this here Mad Mex, Sr.," asked Junior.

"Mad Mex, Sr." said Mr. Rowe. "Why, he's the richest hombre in all o' Mexico." His pronouncement got Miss Rush's immediate attention. If there was a connection to money, she could read mute lips with perfect understanding. "Mad Mex, Sr's real name is Pedro Gonzalez Rodrigo Estevez, Sr." Mr. Rowe continued. "He was a leader in a recent revolution in Mexico. He earned, which is being polite, enough gold to become the richest and largest landowner in all o' Northern Mexico. He's noted fer being one mean, tough hombre. You don't mess with Mad Mex, Sr. He's meaner than a rattlesnake. He'd as soon shoot you as look at ya."

Mad Mex, Sr. barged through the swinging doors. As he moved through the whiskey scented, smoke-filled saloon, patrons began to scurry in all directions to protect themselves from his wrath. Tables were overturned, chairs were scooted and scraped at random across the bleak floor by some fearful patrons while others either scurried through the swinging doors or dove outside through open windows. With a thud, Mr. Myers took his customary refuge facedown in the well-worn floor behind the bar. In fact, the spot where he dropped was so well worn that it had the indelible imprint of a man's body—his body. That imprint formed a perfect outline of Mr. Myers.

Halfway across the saloon floor, the swarthy man shouted, "Senor Mad Mex, Sr. ees looking for Senor Junior."

Junior pivoted from his barstool drinking position to face away from the bar. "I'm Senor Junior, Senor Sr.," he replied as his eyes came to rest on the big man with the commanding voice.

Oscar tugged Junior's left arm and asked, "Ain't he a darkie?"

"Na," Junior replied casually, "ya kin tell he ain't a darkie; darkies don't have long, ugly scars across the sides o' their faces."

"Senor Junior keel Senor's Jr. Now, Senor Sr. must keel Senor Junior. Senor Sr.'s Junior deed not geet justice."

"Hold on Senor Mad Mex, Sr.," said Miss Rush as she hurried to intervene. She stepped between the two gunfighters. "It's not really Senor Junior's fault that Senor Mad Mex, Sr.'s Senor Jr. was killed. Whitey Black's to blame. He sent for your son to kill Sheriff Longarm."

"She's right Senor Sr.," squeaked barkeeper Myers's tremulous, hidden voice from the floor behind the bar. "Senor Junior never drew on Senor's Junior. I'd swear to it, Senor Sr. Yore other two sons kilt each other when Senor Junior ducked the lead they spit. You see, Senor Junior did not kill any o' Senor Sr.'s sons. It all began with Whitey Black. It's all his fault."

"Amazing," said Mad Mex, Sr., "how much a man can see with hees eyes facing down een the floor. I can't even see the face that belongs to the voice."

"Oh, please don't shoot that poor, dumb hillbilly," Miss Rush pleaded while holding Mad Mex's gunslinging arm. "A man who's as handsome and smart as you doesn't need to waste bullets. Not on the likes of an hombre as dumb and stupid as this one. A bullet could bounce off his thick skull and kill you." she said as she looked at Junior as though he were frying a polecat for lunch. "Oh, please reconsider," she begged as she draped herself around his huge neck.

"She's right," shouted the sheriff as he came barging into the saloon through the swinging doors. "There's been enough bloodshed in here fer one day. Whitey got what was coming to him. He jist got blowed away by a bullet that had my name wrote on it. Weasel told me everything."

"Senor Sheriff and senorita tell the truth. Senor Mad Mex, Sr. geet no pleasure een keeling a stupid hombre," he said as he looked at Junior with contempt.

"Now that's straight thanking," ejaculated Oscar.

"Thanks Oscar," Junior said as he looked askance at his friend. He turned from Oscar just in time to see his Mexican nemesis strolling arm in arm with Miss Rush. They departed through the swinging doors and out into the street.

"Well," said sheriff Brooks, "I'm a son of a gun. Looks like Senor Mad Mex, Sr. wound up with Whitey's girl."

"And he thought I was stupid," said Junior. He picked up his drink to go in search of a quiet table. He turned a table upright, uprighted a random overturned chair and sat down.

"I'm a little confuse about what happen here," said Oscar to the barkeeper who was now standing erect behind the bar.

"Oh," said Mr. Myers, "I think I can explain it rather easily. You see," he continued as he bent forward to place his right elbow atop the bar counter, "Senor Mad Mex, Sr. had a son named Senor Jr. who came in here to gunfight Senor Junior. Well, Senor Senior's Jr. saw Senor Junior shoot himself in the foot. Senor Sr.'s Senor Jr. died laughing at Senor Junior. So, here's Senor Sr. looking for Senor Junior to even the score for Senor Sr.'s Senor Jr. So, from the looks o' things, neither Senor Sr. nor Senor's Jr. got Justus."

"Thanks," said a confused Oscar who took his drink and slipped across the saloon to sit with his cousin.

"Oscar, I need to go and talk to Chief Two Feathers," said Junior as Oscar approached his table. "Want to go over to Bell's?"

"Yeah, I need a break. This here whiskey will glue a man to a barstool."

Junior pecked on a side window at Bell's. Chief Two Feathers spotted Junior and raised the window halfway. "How goes it, Chief?"

"Ugh, me like-um white squaw." A giggle came from beneath the white bed-sheets.

"What was that army man a doing here?"

"Him here to get-um treaty signed. Me sign."

"Gosh chief, ya made it too easy fer him. You need to show a little spunk when you deal with the government boys. If you don't, they'll think they can run over ya. Of course, they'll get you one way or another, I guess."

"Me no care. Me find white squaw. White man take-um land, anyway. Besides, me no longer chief."

"No longer chief?"

"Running Bull horn Chief Two Feathers out as chief. Him now chief of tribe and call-um Chief Two Feathers buffalo chip. Him say Chief Two Feathers spend too much time at Bell's. Neglect tribe. Give-um food to Junior and Little Doe and let tribe starve. Chief Running Bull want Little Doe back. Say Little Doe him squaw and go find her."

"So, that's why ya fellers quit coming to Lil's cabin. But ya jist sign a treaty. Shouldn't that o' been Chief Running Bull?"

"Ugh. No matter; white man take-um land, anyway. Besides, me like white squaw. White squaw no starve." There was another soft titter from beneath the sheets.

Junior and Oscar returned to the saloon. "Well Oscar," said Junior, "looks like ya got a reason to git drunk. Chief Running Bull is probably riding off with Little Doe right now. A good squaw is hard to find. Yes sir, Little Doe was the right squaw fer ya."

"Junior, she would probably rather be with her tribe. She was sick all the time, anyhow."

A hush fell over the saloon patrons. Ivory stopped playing the piano, and it became as quiet as a musty Egyptian tomb. "Well, I'll be darned," bellowed a bemused barkeeper Myers, "look who's here. If it ain't what's left o' ole Josh the reporter. Rode Big Harry, lately?" he inquired in a tone of voice that demanded laughter.

"Witnessed any saloon shootouts, lately?" replied the young, slender, dark-haired man that Mr. Myers addressed. "I guess you like them better when you're lying facedown flat on the floor behind the bar. You spend half your time back there lying on the floor, don't you, Guts?"

"Well, ole Josh is back," said Mr. Rowe. "He's running around town with all the rest o' them lying reporters. They come here to see who could write the biggest lie that people will believe. Bet he's come back to tell us who that lady store-owner was. She's the one that everybody put a brand on. You can tell ole Red," he said, evoking the patrons' laughter.

"There's a gunfighter coming in behind me, Red. You may want to turn over a table or jump out a window," snapped Josh in a voice that took no prisoners.

"There's my brother Dickens, Oscar. Have to go up and see him when I finish this here drank," he said and then spit into the floor.

"Heck, that won't take but a minute Junior, the way you put whiskey away." Oscar replied.

"How about finding this bull rider a good stiff shot of whiskey, Guts?" said Josh. "You need to keep busy between gunfights. Where's that willowy saloon singer that Whitey was wigwamming with?"

"Oh, he got rid o' her," replied Mr. Myers. "Sent her to Oklahoma with a dumb hillbilly to git her off his hands. He got him a fancy new one that could spend the money. Heck, she could spend it faster than he could steal it."

"A man would have to be awfully dumb to go to Oklahoma to live," said Josh Justus.

"Ole Whitey could spot a sucker a gold mine away," said Mr. Myers. "He even got the ole boy to take his kid off his hands. Who knows, she might o' been carrying Whitey's kid when he sent her to Oklahoma."

"Whitey knew how to spot a sucker," mused Mr. Josh Justus with a sigh. "What happened to that foreman that Whitey had? He was always catching stray bullets. You know, I think he had a magnet in him that attracted lead. He's the one with a wife that took charm school lessons from a ten foot rattlesnake."

"Well, some man from back east come into town today and killed Whitey," said Mr. Myers. "He put another slug into Lightning."

"I heard about Whitey getting it. And Lightning got another slug. He got shot up five different times while I was with the Crier. He was too slow to dodge bullets. Had more scars from bullets than a West Virginia strip mine. Was he badly hurt, today?"

"Doc Witt says he's gonna pull through."

"Yeah, ole Lightning is pretty resilient."

"He ain't neither," Mr. Rowe informed him from his end barstool. "He's dumber than a wooden Injun. Anybody that gets shot up as much as he does needs a new line o' work. He insisted on being Whitey Black's cob."

"Yeah, Lightning collects hot lead." Mr. Jacobs added with sarcasm in his voice.

"What's wrong with you, Washtub?" asked Josh Justus. "You're dragging your nasty beard through your beer. You're usually leading these crude cowhands, raunchy ranchers, and mangey miners in a rip-roaring, rollicking frolic."

"Hey, watch what you call us," said Mr. Rowe who immediately took offense. "We'll put a pair o' tongs on yore buckteeth.

Not only that, we'll pull out that hornet stinging tongue and muzzle yore mush-mouth. Then we'll let ya have another helping o' Big Harry."

"Heck, Red, don't take me so seriously," Josh said in an attempt to calm the big man with closed fists coming toward him. "You need to learn not to be so sensitive. That's the problem with you overly jolted, cow jockeys. You behave as if your inept pea-brains were mixed with spiced buffalo burger and fried for a Mexican diner."

"Why, you little, trouble-making Injun fig, I'll show you!" Mr. Rowe said. He took a sweeping, round house, right hand swing at Josh's ball chin.

Josh ducked the wild swing of the larger man. Mr. Rowe lost his balance and fell into the floor between an overturned table and a randomly overturned empty chair. Junior finished his drink at his table and ambled up to the pair as Mr. Rowe clumsily stumbled to his feet. "Hold it, boys. This here's my brother, Josh," said Junior.

"Junior!" he exclaimed. "You're the last person in the world I'd expect to see. Fancy meeting you here like this!"

"May be the last if he don't put a lid on that loose-lip," said Mr. Rowe as he returned to his seat on the barstool. Mr. Rowe continued by saying, "How about this? Ole Josh gits rode out o' town on mean Big Harry, and his brother comes riding in here tied on a stupid camel. They're the brothers of exotic rides."

"Where are you, now?" asked Josh.

"I'm a living in Oklahoma Tertitory."

"Well, that's great. What are you doing over there?"

"Dranking liquor and wigwamming with Lil," Oscar replied for his cousin. "He's got a little girl o' his own and a boy that belongs to somebody else. They say the kid belongs to Whitey. Guess the kid jist lost a daddy."

"The little boy belonged to Whitey," Mr. Myers added.

"That's great, Junior. You've made me an uncle. We'll have to celebrate. And it's great to see Cousin Oscar, too. How's things going, Oscar? Still taking care of Junior? I know you fellows were inseparable after that time you got drunk behind the barn. I believe you got drunk on blackberry wine."

"Yeah, we're like a couple o' peas in a pod."

"That's great, Oscar. Oh, where's Weasel and what's he doing these days?"

"He got elected to a cushy courthouse job. He retired from helping Whitey," said Mr. Jacobs. "It looks like he got out from under Whitey's thumb just in time. Looks like Weasel is the smart one."

"Yeah, he's a rat's rat," Mr. Rowe added. "I seen him listening at Lightning's window. That was a day before all o' Whitey's boys got tore up at Eagle's Pass. I'm about certain he told them blue boys about Whitey's plans. Can't prove a thing, though."

"And I'm an uncle. Well, we've got to celebrate. What you say we go somewhere and do something exciting."

"We know jist the place, don't we, Junior?" said Oscar.

They left the saloon and strolled out into the street. "Oscar," said Junior, "Dickens went east to git a line on them James boys. Them big newspapers kin send reporters to all kinds o' places. They wanted a story on the James boys."

"Jesse and Frank went east?" asked Oscar.

"Heck no," Junior replied proudly. This was another James gang. Which one was it, Dickens?"

"Henry and William, Junior."

"Yeah, Henry and William," Junior said. "They're the Eastern James gang. Shoot, that eastern James gang is a lot slicker than this western James gang. You never read nothing in the papers about them eastern James's a robbing banks. They know how to rob real quiet like."

"Say, Junior," asked Josh, "how did you come to ride in here on a camel?"

"It's like this, Josh," Junior began. "I was down in Paducah and I was looking fer ya. I got to swigging in this here big, fancy saloon. The first thang I knowed, I drunk more whiskey than I could pay fer. Well, the owner didn't take kindly to me not having no money. So, he had this here camel that the boys in the saloon teased him about. I thank he wanted to git rid of it because they all made jokes about it so. Anyways, him and some o' the boys in the saloon like to kilt me tying me up there. They fired some shots that scared that pore old camel plum out of his wits. Why, the whole world was whirling with me up there on ole galloping Wheeler. That's how I come to Los Villas."

"Say, Josh. Ya kin go back home now," said Oscar.

"How so?" asked Josh.

"Tell him, Junior."

"Well, Josh, it's like this. The postmaster's daughter, Phyllis Flo, wasn't carrying yore kid. She admit it wasn't yours jist after ya left. Heck, she done up and tied the knot with Chester Harkins's oldest boy, Jethro. They're living in a sharecropper's cabin over in Kennel Cove."

"Well, I'll be, Junior. And I can go home without being burned from behind by buckshot. I'm sure glad that you and Oscar found me."

"Yeah, they was a while there we thought ya was ruin," said Junior. "Glad thangs turn out good fer ye."

Patrons in the saloon were treated to another tale about Junior. Mr. Rowe said, "And after that hillbilly got drunk in Tucson, he went out to Boot Hill. Know what he done? He straddled a heart-shaped tombstone and begins kicking its sides and jumping up and down. Well, somebody reported him to the sheriff. The sheriff comes out to the graveyard, and he says, 'What are you doing a straddle o' that tombstone, cowboy?'

"And the hillbilly says, 'Tombstone? Well, durn, somebody done stold my horse!'"

Saloon laughter abated as the three strolled down the street. They were casting long shadows from a setting West Texas sun. As they were getting nearer Bell's, Oscar said, "Look at that there line. Reporters are line up two deep all the way down the sidewalk and around the corner of the building. Ain't no way we're gitting in there tonight, fellers. Guess we'll have to do something else. Junior, tell Josh about Shy Ann."

"Cheyenne?" Josh said. After a pause, he continued, "Hey, why don't we all go back to Jewel Hill?"

"I'm afraid I've drift too far from the farm," said Junior. "There jist ain't nothing like a living in the West. Each day out here is like living in an American dream. Nights are like being in Heaven."

"Yeah, followed each morning by a hang-over from Hell," Oscar added.

"What say, we swing by and see my new, little niece," said Josh. "It's not everyday that I become an uncle. I know that mama would be proud of her Junior becoming a father. Shoot, I bet she would make over that little boy too. I reckon you're raising the little boy too, aren't you, Junior."

"Yeah," replied Junior. "His name is James Joshua."

"What's my little niece's name?"

"Cora Jane," replied Junior.

"Thank we ought to swing by Annie's place first and see Shy Ann, It ain't too far out o' the way." said Oscar.

"Cheyenne?"